Schooled
in
Murder

By Mark Richard Zubro

The Tom and Scott Mysteries

A Simple Suburban Murder
Why Isn't Becky Twitchell Dead?
The Only Good Priest
The Principal Cause of Death
An Echo of Death
Rust on the Razor
Are You Nuts?
One Dead Drag Queen
Here Comes the Corpse
File Under Dead
Everyone's Dead But Us

The Paul Turner Mysteries

Sorry Now?
Political Poison
Another Dead Teenager
The Truth Can Get You Killed
Drop Dead
Sex and Murder.com
Dead Egotistical Morons
Nerds Who Kill

Schooled
in
Murder

Mark Richard Zubro

St. Martin's Minotaur
New York

SCHOOLED IN MURDER. Copyright © 2008 by Mark Richard Zubro. All rights reserved. Printed in the United States of America. For information, address St. Martin's Press, 175 Fifth Avenue, New York, N.Y. 10010.

www.minotaurbooks.com

Library of Congress Cataloging-in-Publication Data

Zubro, Mark Richard.
    Schooled in murder : a Tom and Scott mystery / Mark Richard Zubro. — 1st St. Martin's Minotaur ed.
        p.   cm.
    ISBN-13: 978-0-312-34346-0
    ISBN-10: 0-312-34346-9
    1. Mason, Tom (Fictitious character)—Fiction. 2. Carpenter, Scott (Fictitious character)—Fiction. 3. High school teachers—Fiction. 4. Baseball players—Fiction. 5. Chicago (Ill.)—Fiction. 6. Gay men—Fiction. I. Title.
    PS3576.U225S33 2008
    813'.54—dc22

                                                          2008013403

First Edition: July 2008

10   9   8   7   6   5   4   3   2   1

I wish to thank Barb D'Amato and Jeanne Dams for all their help and support.

Schooled
in
Murder

. 1 .

The screaming didn't start until fifteen minutes after the torture stopped. It was a typical faculty meeting, or at least, typical for this faculty. Bored to tears or furiously battling, the assembled members of the Grover Cleveland High School English department rivaled, in irrationality and intractability, the disputes among the most virulent warring religious factions on the planet.

The initial torture consisted of the mind-numbingly boring speech delivered at the onset of every meeting by Mabel Spandrel, the head of the department. She had a soft voice that droned from opening syllable to closing pluperfect subjunctive verb (e.g., The teachers wish the administrator had been eaten by a fire-breathing dragon before she started speaking). I could picture the punctuation in her speeches pleading for release. I, however, was not about to join the cynics in the back who placed bets on and then counted how many times she used the phrase "educational leaders." I would never countenance such disrespect. Besides, I always lost money in the pool. I always came in too low. Well, somebody's got to hold out hope.

Behind Mabel's boring exterior lurked the heart of a python combined with the cunning of a particularly petrified rock. She was dangerous enough as a dolt. Give her a dose of intelligence and there was no telling what ghastly calamities she might perpetrate. She had a business background and had never spent a minute in a classroom until she got here, a surefire guarantee of an attitude of contempt from veteran teachers. Getting business people into schools had been a big trend for several years. And if kids were widgets, it might have made sense.

After communication-challenged Mabel nearly droned us to death, Francine Peebles always made a plea for civility and decorum. Francine headed the "can't we all get along" faction on the faculty. Frankly, come the revolution, I'd vote for her to lose her head first, and I'm passionately against the death penalty and not all that fond of revolutions unless they're really done right. Francine's peace bloc was a vocal splinter group that managed to irritate everybody equally.

Being someone unwilling to scream publicly at my colleagues, I was often placed in Francine's group. The danger with seeming to be neutral was that both sides rushed to you with their latest lunatic plans, half-baked schemes, and harebrained proposals. This was always done in strictest confidence with whispers and glances around. I expected someone to suggest we meet at the third pillar from the left outside of Pierre's. At the very least, you'd think they'd offer to buy me a cup of coffee late at night at the nearest Starbucks. No luck on any of that yet.

I compounded this nearly lethal mistake of not publicly disagreeing with them at the top of my lungs by listening to them. Patiently. My lack of opposition caused the less discerning to assume I was on their side. The lack of discernment about themselves, their colleagues, and the importance of their issues had reached epidemic proportions.

The two major factions divided the department almost evenly between the suckups and the non-suckups. I hate suckups. It makes no sense to sell your dignity and self-respect at any time. It was even more ludicrous to sell them for the few silly privileges that could be accorded to someone sucking up at Grover Cleveland High School. Whatever it was the suckups so desperately desired, I neither needed nor wanted.

Within fifteen minutes of Spandrel's finish and Peebles's plea, acrimony erupted.

I glanced out the windows. Rain poured down. A few desperate leaves clung to the trees. Late afternoon October gloom was rapidly rushing toward evening.

Over forty of us jammed into the Learning Center for the monthly battle. The pro- and anti-suckup warfare, plus the usual academic infighting, had been exacerbated in recent years by the wild ambition of younger teachers and the mad, although usually inept, machinations of Mabel Spandrel. I loved the passion of these new college graduates and their allies. I hated their blind adherence to the latest education trends. I also admired their eagerness to try out new things in the classroom. As for Mabel, even torture, as envisioned by right-wing Republicans, might not be enough punishment for all the inept and outright stupid things she'd done.

Then again, many of the non-suckups were the "old guard." Too many of them adhered fervently to the dictum, "I've done it this way since dirt, and you can't make me change." A whole bunch of folks in this faction needed swift kicks in their butts. I understood, all too well, the arguments for their position. A lot of them, however, were close-minded dinosaurs who refused to admit that maybe what they were doing in their classrooms wasn't the most effective approach.

Although my sympathies lay with the old guard, I was sick to death of all of them.

Once in a while a brave soul would dare to suggest that both sides of the new-versus-old-techniques factions were talking about the same thing except that now some boob in college academia had given a random educational process or approach a new name. This, of course, was heresy. Far more important to impose your trendy or traditional educational philosophy or psychology or methodology or vocabulary on the unwilling. Never mind that study after study showed it was the teachers' relationship with the pupils that was the key to success in the classroom, not the methodology employed.

The current buzzwords were "best practice." There were always new buzzwords. "Best practice" meant that in your classroom you always used what the research showed to be the best way to get your children to learn.

This is news?

Another big problem was that what the research said was the most effective methodology kept changing. The upshot was that every few years some idiot reinvented the educational wheel. The bizarre shape of this twisted metaphorical sphere often depended on the political orientation of the researcher. Making other people jump through hoops can be so satisfying for the Nazi wannabes.

Today's fracas was over who was going to go to the latest trend-setting seminar. It was going to be a full week in San Francisco paid for by the school district.

Petty debates about silly privileges among those who educate the children in this world? You better believe it. Then again, if it had been just a Saturday in Kankakee, maybe they wouldn't be hauling out their verbal bazookas.

There were those in the battling factions who counted the number of times who got to go to which conference and calculated how far away from home the trip was. There were those who didn't want to leave their classroom for the slightest bit of time, figuring it was too much of a hassle to come back after a substitute teacher screwed up their lesson plans. Others assumed they were too valuable to the children in their classes for students to do without them as a teacher. A few radicals thought they'd been hired to teach and would prefer to do that rather than trot about the countryside ingesting information that a reasonably intelligent person could pick up in the latest educational or teachers' union journals. I was in this last group.

Today, Carl Pinyon, one of the young rebels, actually produced copies of a chart that showed who had gone to which conferences over the past thirty years. Demands to know how he got the information and from whom escalated into accusations bordering on hysteria.

Boring diatribes alternated with shouts, yells, and banging fists.

I graded papers.

It irritated some on both sides that I usually did this throughout the warfare. Today I pondered for quite some time what to do about Fred Zileski. Poor Fred was a senior. He was a little shaky on capital letters at the beginning of sentences and had yet to be convinced that something, assumedly punctuation, was needed at the end of each set of words he put down. One hesitated to label as sentences the bits of prose that escaped from his pencil. They were, in Fred's own unique way, his attempts to express himself. He was a big kid, a football player, kind of quiet usually. I'd been trying for over a month to figure out any practice, much less a "best practice," that would convince Fred to give capitalization and punctuation a try. No luck yet. I figured if we got past those first two hurdles, we'd work on making sure a verb had something to do with his sentences. I'd already surrendered the spelling battle. All computers came with spell checks these days.

Complicating Fred's problems was his parents' continued hostility seven years after their divorce had become final. His mother was currently president of our school board. Because of her, Fred had been placed in honors classes for more than half of his elementary schooling. She'd become president of the board to ensure his being in such programs. To say Fred hadn't gotten the help he needed is grossly unfair to understatements. As far as I could tell, in any school district, the criteria for being in the honors program were aligned to one basic standard. The cutoff line was wherever it was necessary for school board members' kids to get into the program. A travesty? Yep. And it happens far more often than rational people would imagine. And Fred was paying the price. Kids are always the ones who pay the price when adults' egos get skewed.

When I looked up from straining to read Fred's writing, Jourdan Chase was on his feet. He was bellowing at someone I couldn't see. "You're the one who doesn't have respect for his colleagues. You're the one who's been sucking up so fast since you've been here that a vacuum's been created on the third floor. We can barely remain upright for the gale of wind blowing through as you rush about trying to undercut and backstab the rest of us." Jourdan had been with the department since the advent of the printing press. Most of the time he was an annoying dope. Except when he took on the suckups in the department. At those moments a lot of us would have voted for him for sainthood.

In moments the object of his attack stood up. Gracie Eberson pointed her finger at Jourdan and screamed back, "You're the one keeping this department from moving forward. You're the one who says no to everything before the explanations are even finished. I watch you shaking your head 'no' at any new idea." In her early twenties, Eberson affected billowy granny dresses on her sixties-hippie frame.

Her hair hung in cascading auburn ringlets down to her waist. She wore rhinestone-studded pink-rimmed glasses. She often attempted to drape herself in a veil of Earth Mother serenity, very much absent from this afternoon's response. The other problem with her usual persona was that her voice normally sounded like something between a shrill mouse squeak and a bandsaw about to break.

They both stood as they traded accusations. This was a bit different. Usually everybody conducted their assaults while firmly planted on their butts. Jourdan and Gracie were on opposite sides of the room. Their voices continued on high rant. Others began trying to shout over them. A few tried to get them to calm down. Others sat back in horror. A few in the back snickered. Gracie smacked her rolled-up grade book on the top of a computer monitor. Jourdan banged his fist on the countertop of the circulation desk. Moments later, it crashed into shards and splinters. Then Gracie swung her arm around and dislodged the monitor, which lurched six inches to her left. A second later, it plunged to the floor. The loud banging and smashing called a halt to all other noise. Then Jourdan stormed out the exit nearest him, and Gracie the one closest to her. Each slammed the respective doors through which they stormed.

Only a demented and bored English teacher would refer to them as storm doors. I confess to neither.

An utterly satisfying silence ensued for three seconds. Then the remaining combatants started again.

My friend, Meg Swarthmore, the aged and beloved librarian, would be pissed about the destruction. She always left immediately after school on faculty-meeting days. Today I'd urged her to stay and watch the fun. She'd peered at me over her reading glasses and said, "Perhaps, Tom Mason, you and I have a different definition of fun." She told me once that, sickeningly amusing as she thought it might be to keep score and see the budding of burgeoning gossip, she preferred to miss the pervasive hostility. I'd fill her in over our usual Friday-morning breakfast tomorrow.

I toughed it out at the meeting for as long as I could. After another half an hour, I left my stack of papers and eased out the back. Slowly, no need to rush. The battling educators and ungraded papers would be waiting for me when I got back.

I sauntered into the departmental office and ran off a test. Figuring a few more side trips wouldn't hurt, I stopped in the washroom. Then I made a parent call I'd been putting off all day. I used my cell phone and called from the foyer near one of the school's side doors. It was quiet, and I could watch the rain as the sky darkened. The call was to Mrs. Faherty, another board member. Her kid, Spike, was in my classes and came for after-school tutoring, as did Fred Zileski. Mrs. Faherty had only recently been appointed to the board to fill a vacancy. I'd never heard of her saying a word at a board meeting. She had a delightfully realistic view of her juvenile delinquent. She and her husband attended every conference with her kid, and they had for years. The kid was passionate about his motorcycle and little else. The machine was one of the few holds she had over him. I called her once a week to update her on Spike's progress. This week he'd completed an entire essay. Unlike Fred, Spike was quite bright, something that Spike did not want teachers to be aware of.

After I hung up, I realized I'd been gone nearly half an hour. I decided to forego a stop in the departmental storeroom on the third floor near my classroom. I did need masking tape and copy paper, but even I didn't have the nerve to be gone this long. Such an extended absence as mine would cause comment.

I eased back to the library to find only two people present, two custodians cleaning up the mess Jourdan and Gracie had made. The meeting had ended five minutes after I'd left. I'd missed the end. I decided not to weep.

I picked up my papers, then climbed back to the third floor and headed for the storeroom. It was a former teachers' office. Those had long since gone the way of good intentions. Any number of nooks, crannies, hallways, classrooms, and offices had been closed in recent years for the numerous patches, temporary fixes, or reconstructions the building needed. Five school referendums in a row had failed to pass in our district. The community had said no to taxes. The result was their kids attended a school that had been falling apart when they tried to pass the first referendum twenty years ago. Now the rapidly deteriorating building gave decrepit a bad name.

One minor example of what needed to be fixed was the door to the supply room. It could easily have been used to create sound effects for any number of Hollywood horror movies. Purchasing a can of WD-40 might require the passage of a referendum and the replacement of the entire custodial staff.

As I walked into the supply room, I flipped on the light. Two men standing near a broken copier jumped apart. I'd seen enough to know that they'd been attempting to jam their tongues down each others' throats while their hands were on the front of each others' pants.

One was a young member of the English department, Brandon Benson. The other was a youthful gym teacher named Steven Frecking. The choice of venue was odd. Not quite as odd as the fact that Benson was currently married to a woman. Benson was five-feet-seven with black hair cut short. His blue jeans said size twenty-eight on the patch on the back. He wore a white shirt, now half untucked, a blue tie now askew, and a blue blazer half off his left shoulder. Frecking was over six-feet-two with narrow hips and broad shoulders. He had played quarterback for his small Wisconsin college. He wore a pair of gym shorts that were only slightly looser and covered only a bit more than a pair of knit boxer briefs. His baggy T-shirt wasn't long enough to conceal either how far down the shorts now were or how enthused he was about the activity they'd been engaged in as I entered.

I turned to leave and then stopped. In a far corner I saw a designer shower-clog and a foot. I pointed to it. "Who is that?" I asked.

2

They stopped rearranging their clothes and looked behind them. I rushed forward. I figured someone might have passed out. The two of them remained motionless. I shoved several boxes aside.

Gracie Eberson lay on the floor. Someone had crammed one of those oversized chalkboard erasers into her mouth. She wasn't breathing. I yanked the eraser out. No change. I felt for a pulse. Nothing. I pulled out my cell phone.

I felt a hand on my arm. It was Benson. "What's wrong with her?" he asked.

"She's not breathing," I said. "I think she's dead. I'm calling 911." I'd been in the Marines. I'd seen death up close. That didn't make it easier to deal with, but I knew enough not to panic. At the moment, I had a rush of something to do.

Benson tapped my arm. "You can't," he said.

I looked at him, my thumb poised over the keypad.

"Nobody can know we were here," he said.

I said, "This is an emergency." I punched numbers and reported where I was and what the situation was. After I hung up, I called the school's main office rather than hunt for a call button in the nearest classroom. I got the answering machine. It was late. The secretaries must have left for the day.

Still kneeling, I noticed bruising on Gracie's face, mottled with bits of chalk dust and lint. I looked up at the two men. I saw a small patch of wetness on the front of Benson's jeans. Catching my glance, he quickly held a book over his crotch. His face was beet red. Frecking had a gym bag in front of his midsection.

"Ah, you didn't see anything?" Benson asked.

I said, "Was there something to see?"

Frecking said, "I can explain."

I said, "There's nothing to explain. My only suggestion is the old cliché, get a room."

Benson began, "My wife—"

I said, "I don't want to hear it. I'm not interested."

Frecking said, "We're—"

I said, "You don't owe me any explanations. I saw nothing that was any of my business to report to anyone. Yours isn't the first kiss exchanged in this school among faculty members. Once again, I suggest discretion." I pointed at the corpse. "You have a much larger problem."

Benson said, "We didn't see her. We didn't know she was here."

Frecking said, "We didn't turn on the light. It wasn't the first time we've been in here."

More information than I needed. Good to know someone besides the students was up on the trysting places in the school.

I said, "Let's step into the corridor. I'm sure the police will be here any moment." We reassembled outside and several feet down the corridor. It was empty.

"What are you going to do about what you saw?" Benson asked.

"Is there a problem?" I asked.

"We can't tell anyone we were there. There's no logical reason for Steven to be up here. People will wonder what we were doing. You can't say anything."

This was more than a bit much. Lying for trysting lovers, gay or straight or in-between, was not my style. And not when a dead body was involved in the equation.

I held up my hand and asked, "Why would you normally go to this storage room?"

He said, "To get supplies."

"And have you gotten supplies from there in the past?"

"Yes."

"Then you might want to say that."

"What about Steven?" he asked.

"What's wrong with a friend tagging along?"

Benson said, "Won't it sound odd?"

"Not as odd as a dead body in the storage closet."

"How can you be so calm?" Benson asked.

"I'm not dead," I said.

Frecking said, "She had a chalk eraser crammed in her mouth. Like someone was trying to shut her up permanently."

Both of them were pale. Benson said, "I've only seen dead bodies at wakes and funerals of distant relatives. This is spooky."

Benson reached out a hand to the wall. "I think I'm going to be sick." He bent over. Frecking helped him to the nearest washroom. When they were a quarter of the way down the hall, I began to hear distant sirens. Benson was bent over nearly double as they staggered though the washroom door. As it closed, I heard one or both of them puking.

3

Everybody showed up, the helpful and the unhelpful. Amando Graniento, our fourth principal in three years, rushed about like a head with its chicken cut off. In moments less fraught with crisis, he was useful for making grave pronouncements about arcane academic minutiae. He'd been a professor at Governors State University for fifteen years before deigning to take a principalship. I heard the most appalling rumor from someone I trusted who had been on the principal interview/selection committee that had picked Graniento. When asked what he would do with a parent who was out of control, Graniento had said, "I will never say no to a parent." The man was out of his mind. He tended to wear clothes that he thought were trendy. Mostly, he looked like a poster child for hideously clashing colors.

The heart of the interdepartmental conflict had been Spandrel and Graniento's doing. Sure, there were other causes. With the change in the retirement rules for teachers in Illinois, there had been a rash of old teachers leaving and thus an influx of new teachers with a lot of new ideas and no ties to the old guard. But Spandrel and Graniento had thrown gasoline on the fire not just once but time after time. They seemed to thrive on the constant fighting. I always got the impression that the superintendent and head of the school board were cheering them on as well.

The other members of the department, still at school, had been told to wait in the Learning Center. I saw Mabel Spandrel at a distance. She sniffled constantly and wiped her nose. She looked as if tears would flow any second.

Our superintendent, Riva Towne, arrived. She nodded gravely at everyone, huddled with police, and spoke to the other school board members who showed up. At every opportunity she had lectured people that the school district should be run in a more businesslike manner. I knew for a fact she'd been an elementary teacher in Newton, Iowa, for fifteen years before becoming a school administrator. Her experience in the business world was absolutely zero. Victoria Abbot, the assistant superintendent, entered with her. She looked sick and worried.

The River's Edge police, protectors of the suburb in which Grover Cleveland High School existed, mucked about.

I returned to my room. Two local detectives I didn't know questioned me. Frank Rohde, my friend on the department, had been promoted to assistant police chief last year. The other cops I knew on the department dealt mostly with juvenile crimes. Since I often worked with behaviorally disturbed kids, I knew some of the cops. But these two were homicide detectives I didn't know. The older cop was Michah Gault. The other, Earl Vulmea, looked young enough to be one of the kids in my classes.

I described my movements from when I first stepped out of the meeting to when I discovered the corpse. I mentioned Benson and Frecking. I didn't mention what they were doing. Let the cops assume they were looking for supplies. I couldn't imagine anybody committing murder, then passionately making out seconds later and several feet away. Perhaps my imagination is limited, but I couldn't picture it. The cops had showed up before Benson and Frecking had returned from the washroom. I assumed they were being kept in another part of the building along with the other faculty members.

When I finished my statement, Gault, the older cop, shook his head. "You got any witnesses?"

"I assumed most everybody else was still in the English department meeting. I didn't see anyone else. Mrs. Faherty, the woman I talked to on the phone, should remember, and my cell phone provider will have a record of the call, time, duration, and to whom. I have no idea where any custodians, secretaries, and teachers from all the other departments might have been."

Gault said, "You got back to the meeting and only two custodians were there. How come you didn't see the teachers, or they didn't see you when they left the meeting?"

"A lot of people scatter to go home right after a meeting, and I was making a quiet phone call down a hallway where I could watch the rain. It's not the exit to the teachers' parking lot."

"How well did you know Mrs. Eberson?" Gault asked.

"Not that well."

"How'd you get along with her?" Gault was doing all the questioning.

"She was a colleague."

"Talk with her much, go to lunch with her, have an affair?"

"No." The woman rarely looked me in the eye. Faction hatred, homophobia, ignorance, lack of social skills? I never knew. Didn't care much. Never asked.

"She taught next door to you."

"I'd see her in the hall most days."

"She have any enemies?"

Well, this was getting down to it. They'd find out eventually, if they hadn't already.

I said, "The factions in the department fought."

"Were you and her on the same sides?"

"I tried not to take sides."

"Personal problems between you two?"

"No."

"Why not?"

"Why would there be?"

"What did you fight about?"

"In the department, the fights were about everything."

"What's everything?"

"Who was in charge. Who wasn't in charge. Who wanted to be in charge. Who was qualified to be in charge. Who got to put out memos. Who was putting out memos. Who was taking notes at meetings. Who wasn't taking notes. Who was supposed to be taking notes. Who was going on trips. Who was sucking up. Who wasn't sucking up. Who was being helpful to whom. Who would be a traveling teacher. Who would have their own classroom. Old guard versus new. Dumb versus smart. New, rigidly enforced methodology and curriculum against old guard. If it breathed, it was worth fighting over."

Earl Vulmea, the young cop, spoke up. "You guys are teachers? I thought teachers were supposed to be role models."

"You been a cop long?" I asked him.

"I just made detective."

"Teachers are human," I said.

"Who'd she fight with today?" Gault asked.

"We had a faculty meeting. The factions fought. They always do."

"Anybody in particular?"

I told him about the faculty meeting.

"You didn't speak up?" Gault asked.

"Didn't see the need."

"You a coward?" Vulmea asked.

"Just being a role model."

The cops stood up. Gault said, "Don't leave." They walked out.

I called my lover, Scott Carpenter. To my announcement of finding a dead body, he said, "Again." Using the tone Rocky the Squirrel used when Bullwinkle J. Moose had done something ineptly stupid for the umpteenth time.

I said, "It wasn't my fault."

"What did I tell you about finding more dead bodies?"

"Something about lack of chocolate for an extended period of time." I sighed. "I've got dead bodies plopping in my path, and you're going for humor."

"Are you okay?" he asked.

I filled him in on the horrors I was in the middle of.

"You want me there?" he asked when I finished.

"Let me see what happens."

"You want me to call our lawyer?"

"Might not be a bad idea."

"You sure you're okay?" he asked.

"So far."

Scott asked, "They were making out in the storeroom? Isn't that kind of 1950s behavior? What if kids had walked in?"

"Maybe they could have gotten extra credit for their sex education classes?"

"And Benson is married?"

"Yep, to a female woman of the opposite sex."

"How well do you know those two guys?"

"Benson is in the department, so I sort of know him. Frecking I'm aware of from being on a cross-curricular committee with him." During the meetings Frecking had never said a word and spent his time surreptitiously reading a sports equipment catalogue he'd hidden under the table.

"Be careful," Scott said. "Don't trust anybody. This is murder."

I told him I'd be more than careful.

▲ 4 ▲

I diddled and dithered and wondered what the hell was going on. I graded a few papers. One of my *Lord of the Rings* posters was starting to come loose from the wall. I retaped it.

I poked my head outside my door. Various members of the rival factions had clustered at opposite ends of the hallway. I made my way to the teachers' lounge for some coffee. I'd have preferred to go home. It was near seven. I was hungry. Not hungry enough to snarf down the stale chips and past-its-sell-by-date candy the machines in the lounge disgorged. Someone had started a new pot of coffee. I washed a cup and poured. I took a seat at a table near the back.

Morgan Adair entered a moment after I sat down and joined me. He was in his early thirties and a friend. He was one of the youngest members of the non-suckup faction. The factions didn't break down strictly along age lines, although the suckups did tend to be younger.

Morgan said, "This is awful. I heard you found the body. Are you okay?"

"It's not something I'm looking forward to having happen again."

He leaned close and said in a breathless whisper, "I've got to tell you this as long as no one else is here. I know what happened to Gracie is awful, but I haven't had a chance to talk to you in the past couple days."

I raised an eyebrow.

"I met a guy."

"Congratulations," I said. I tried to work up an "I care" look. I must have been successful, because I didn't detect a dampening in his headlong gush about his new love. I was tired and out of sorts. Hot new boyfriends and dead bodies were not a good mix. Morgan had been trying to find Mr. Right since he got out of college. The long series of tales of his dating woes could fill a season at the Lyric Opera. Morgan was tall with dirty-blond, short, spiked hair.

He burbled into my ear. "And he teaches right here at Grover Cleveland. He is a hunk."

"Oh, really?"

"He's a stud. I'm not supposed to tell anyone. He's very closeted, but I know I can tell you."

I got an awful feeling.

"Steven Frecking. We met in Chicago at a bar last Friday night. We were both surprised to find out we taught in the same school. I sort of recognized him. He's sweet and funny. We've been out twice since then."

The arrival of two more of our colleagues spared me the choice of whether or not to tell him he was dating a philandering boob.

Luci Gamboni and Jourdan Chase entered and joined Morgan and me around the table. Luci Gamboni said, "You really found her with an eraser crammed in her mouth?"

"Yep," I said.

Gamboni held her hand in front of her face. She had straight black hair that hung down to her ample bosom.

Jourdan Chase said, "It's not funny."

Gamboni said, "It is, in a sort of a Chuckles the Clown kind of way. I mean, I've been hoping someone would shut that cow up since the day she was hired. You know what Gracie said to me the day she was hired? She said, 'Why do you have the honors classes?' She claimed they should be spread out among all the teachers. Me! I've been here practically since they built the place. I waited my turn for the best classes. She just wanted to step right in and hog the whole show. And as for going places for conferences. Well!"

Jourdan said, "Those statistics Pinyon had didn't look right to me. I don't remember going to a conference in the early eighties."

Luci said, "Even if we have been to conferences before doesn't mean we should or shouldn't go again. They're all like Gracie. She couldn't wait her turn. Stupid cow. And she said older teachers should have to give up their classrooms! And travel! On carts! So young people could have rooms. I don't work thirty years in a place to get a low-class assignment. That's against the union rules, isn't it?"

After all these years of not coming to my senses, I was still our building's union rep. I said, "They need to show cause to make a change in working conditions." Being made to schlepp all your materials from class to class using a cart was considered the lowest-class assignment.

Luci said, "These new teachers have no concept of what it's been like. The fights we had to get this far. What it took for me, for us, to get what we have." Luci was the commando grandmother in our department.

"Selfish," Jourdan said. "They only want what's good for them, not for the group."

"And if we dare to criticize them, we're accused of not being team players," Gamboni said. "Team players? We were working in teams in this department when most of them were still in diapers. Team players? And a few of us are barely ten years older than they are, but they think we're all ancient."

Morgan asked, "Did you touch the body?"

"I checked for a pulse."

Morgan shuddered. "I couldn't do that."

Gamboni said, "We're turning into the Cabot Cove of the educational world."

Jourdan said, "That could be a good or bad thing depending on who dies."

Gamboni said, "Oh dear."

Morgan said, "You've had some experience with this kind of thing, Tom. What do you think?"

I said, "Whatever's happened in my past doesn't give me any special insight now. I know the police don't like it when amateurs try to interfere."

"Who would want to kill her?" Morgan asked.

"All of us," Luci said. "Look at that fight today. Jourdan, what did the police say to you?"

"They asked a million questions. They wanted to know all about even the most minor set-to. Well, what could I say? We do fight. There were a million witnesses to today's battle, not to mention all the other fights we've all had. I'm not the only one who's had public fights with these people, but I'm the only one who had somebody murdered right after. I think I'm in trouble."

Brook Burdock entered the room and hurried over to the table. Brook was the kind of guy who was always just a few minutes late for everything. He was a few pounds overweight and a couple years past forty. He struck me as a bit too bluff and friendly, seeming to be a bundle of energy that was always ready to burst forth. Brook worked out once every two weeks and called himself in shape. His wife dressed him in trendy male fashions from Ralph Lauren that never fit quite right. He sat down and said, "The kiss-asses are dying. Dead.

Dead. Dead. I am going to do a dance of joy." He drummed his fingers on the tabletop.

Luci gasped. "That's awful," she said.

Brook thumped his hands on the table, a drummer giving himself a cue. "There is news. You are not going to believe this."

"What?" Luci asked.

"It is the latest hot rumor. They arrested Mabel Spandrel for the murder."

A round of astonishment swept the group.

Morgan said, "I knew it. I knew it. Those two were having an affair."

Jourdan leaned forward in that hot-gossip-tell-me-more posture. He asked, "They were lesbians?"

"I've seen them go out drinking together constantly," Morgan said.

Brook said, "I was told they met secretly at bars on the near north side of Chicago, but I assumed that was to plot and plan. I'm not so sure it's proof they were having an affair."

Luci asked, "You have proof of an affair?"

"I don't have videotape, no," Morgan admitted. "But I know Gracie drives to Mabel's house, and then they go off together."

Jourdan said, "Gracie's been sucking up like mad to her since she was hired. She's been her spy on the rest of us. You've seen her taking notes at every single meeting."

I thought maybe she was just efficient and conscientious. I asked Brook, "Did someone say why they think Mabel killed Gracie?"

"Nobody saw Mabel after the meeting."

"That's it?" I asked.

"That's what I heard," Brook said. "I haven't been this happy in ages. I am not going to be a hypocrite. I hate those ass-kissers. I have always hated those ass-kissers. I hope

24

some more of them bite the dust, and I hope it's painful, and they suffer for a very long time."

Luci said, "She's dead. It's sad."

Morgan said, "You were trying to avoid a Chuckles the Clown moment a few minutes ago."

"Well, that was bizarre, but this is gloating."

"You can be a hypocrite if you like," Brook said, "but I've heard you talk about them in public and private. You hated them as much as I."

"That may be so," Luci said, "But now she's dead."

"I know that," Brook said. "I hated her when she was alive. Sometimes the evil do die young."

Not often enough, I thought. I said, "It was murder. Those who fought with them are going to be suspects."

"I didn't kill her," Brook said. "I've got rock-solid alibis for every second from after that meeting to now. Nope. She's dead. I'm glad. They've tried to undercut the rest of us. They've stabbed us in the back. They run to Spandrel or Graniento to tattle on the rest of us. They are awful colleagues. This time the suckup died young. I, for one, am celebrating."

Jourdan said, "I'm worried about being a suspect. I have no witness, no alibi. After I left the meeting, I went to my classroom to cool off. I shouldn't have said those things. I should have kept my big mouth shut. I always regret it after those fights, but I can't help myself."

Morgan said, "You're standing up for us. We appreciate it."

Jourdan said, "Maybe others should be speaking up. Did anybody else hear the rumor that Mabel Spandrel is planning to resign as head of the department? If that's true, there'll be more bodies than just this one. Who would replace her? Gracie was the assistant head of the department. Would she have just moved up? There are teachers a lot more senior than Gracie who deserve that job. And now that she's dead and if Mabel quits, would we have to replace both of them?"

Morgan said, "More important right now is, who killed Gracie? It could be someone from outside, although that doesn't make a lot of sense. They'd have to hunt through the school, wait for the meeting to get over, and know she'd be in that storeroom."

Brook said, "It could have been someone from outside who was very patient and very determined and very desperate."

Morgan said, "Yeah, but for that kind of person to succeed, there are a lot of things that would have to go right. They'd have no ID, no idea what other people's schedule was. I think it's got to be somebody in the school."

Everybody nodded agreement.

Luci said, "It's not likely a kid. Would any of them still have been in the building?"

I said, "A few athletes might have been in the gym, but that's a long way to go undetected or risk being seen."

Jourdan said, "So it's got to be one of the adults, faculty or administrators or custodians or secretaries."

Morgan said, "It wasn't done with a conventional weapon, so they can't blame the metal detectors for not working."

I wondered if the killer held Gracie down or knocked her out first and then crammed in the eraser. The boxes hadn't been disturbed, so I didn't think there'd been much of a struggle—although the storeroom is a mess most of the time, so it would have been hard to tell. The bruising I'd seen on her face might have meant the killer had held her down.

Brook said, "Maybe they'll think it's Francine. Maybe she finally got fed up with nobody listening to her peace overtures and turned to violence."

Luci said, "Remember that peace party she tried to have over the holidays last year? I heard she made this huge spread and decorated until she nearly died and nobody went."

"It was sad," I said.

"Did you go?" Brook asked.

"I was out of the country."

Brook persisted. "Would you have gone?"

"No," I admitted. I didn't go to a lot of faculty parties. This was where I worked. This wasn't normally where I socialized.

Morgan said, "I've never been able to figure out how anybody knew she went to all that trouble if nobody went to the party."

Brook said, "It can't be nobody went. Someone must have gone, but I don't know who."

Jourdan said, "They're going to think one of our faction killed her."

Luci said, "They can't think we did it. None of us are like that."

"Who would be more logical?" I asked.

"But killing her wouldn't gain anything," Morgan said. "She was assistant head of the department, so her position would be vacant, but would somebody kill for such an unimportant position?"

"I can't imagine it," Luci said.

"It must have gained somebody something," I said, "otherwise she wouldn't be dead."

Brook said, "Spandrel would have only picked another suckup. Maybe they're finally turning on each other. They have no morals. They're worse than Nazis. They'd turn on each other in a heartbeat."

"You have evidence of this?" I asked. "They seem to pretty much stick together."

So did the non-suckup faction, for that matter, but I adjusted my comments to my audience.

Jourdan said, "Not a one of them has ever broken ranks."

Brook asked, "Do I have evidence they have no morals, or that they'd turn on each other? Once you've stabbed someone in the back, what's another one or two? What more logical step than to commit murder?"

"Maybe she crossed one of them," Morgan said. "Maybe she was a traitor to them."

"Again," I said, "do we have any proof of that?"

No one did.

Jourdan said, "None of us would have done it. I mean, come on. Murder? Over this stuff?"

Brook used the old cliché, "Wars have been fought for less."

"What's going to happen tomorrow?" Luci asked. "It's that stupid institute day. Maybe they'll cancel it because of the death."

Brook said, "These asshole administrators are never going to call off school."

"What about Monday?" she asked. "I hope this is over by Monday. I'm not going to have to give up my planning period, am I? I have work to do." This work during her planning time consisted mostly of making personal phone calls and surfing the Web, planning her next vacation, then erasing the evidence of her Internet searches. It would be like Luci to obsess about the part of an issue that affected her. Destruction of half the planet? Was it going to bother her schedule? If not, then it wasn't a problem.

"Grief counselors," Brook Burdock said. "The school is going to be lousy with them. I've never seen such hypocritical nonsense in my life."

Morgan said, "At least the lazy-ass social workers will have something to do."

All public schools in Illinois now had, by law, crisis teams. Each teacher had to have a copy of the district's "crisis plan" that had to be attached visibly to some part of their classroom. I don't know one teacher who has read it or one teacher for whom it has made a difference. Certainly the administrators all feel more important because it gives them something to do and makes them feel like they're protecting kids. They can shuffle paper instead of actually talking to teenagers. The stark reality is that insane things do happen, and sometimes they can't be prevented. And that's sad, but you cannot live your life because you fear the sky is falling.

I come down on the side of taking all necessary precautions, but madness and useless panic resulting in nonsensical paperwork and pointless rules are not my style.

The referred-to social workers at Grover Cleveland High School were a stunning collection of younger men and women who desperately wanted to be in private practice. I don't remember one child in whose life they actually made a difference. Of course, they didn't have to report to me, but teachers usually hear.

Jourdan said, "And the kids will be weeping. They loved Gracie Eberson. She never gave homework. Never."

Some of the young teachers believed in the philosophy that kids won't do homework so why bother to assign it? I thought anyone who held that philosophy was a lazy-ass fool who didn't belong in the classroom. Yeah, it's a battle to get them to do homework. What did these young teachers think they were going to do when they got in the classroom? And those silly studies claiming homework is harmful? Yeah, it's too burdensome for some parents to say things like, "Do your homework" to a teenager. That might require enforcing a rule, turning off a television, hanging up a phone, not texting a friend, postponing an Internet chat. Those parents want to be their kid's friend, and they don't want to be the bad guy. They don't want to be the one to say no. Letting teenagers run the asylum was not an option, at least not yet, not in my classroom.

Luci said, "She was the most popular English teacher among the kids. She and her ilk cultivated them as friends."

Morgan said, "The ones I can't stand will be the students who didn't know her and who are weeping. Trust me, there will be tons of those. Remember when that junior died in a drunk-driving accident? His teachers barely knew him, and before the accident he didn't have friends. No one sat with him in the cafeteria at lunchtime, but the weeping went on for weeks. It was sad that the kid was dead and that he'd been lonely, but they were taking advantage."

Brook shuddered. "Teenagers clustered together in the halls and washrooms feeding on each others' melodramatic nonsense."

"Did Gracie have kids of her own?" I asked. "A husband?"

Luci said, "She married her childhood sweetheart right out of high school. They've got four boys, six, four, two, and the one she had in August. I've seen pictures. Cute kids."

"It's going to be awful for them," I said.

Luci said, "I met the husband once. He seemed nice enough. An electrical engineer who couldn't get a job out of college. He opened a coffeehouse. How does a family recover from this?"

Time and pain, I thought. What else was there when faced with a relatively young person's unexpected death? As the Deborah Kerr character says in the movie of Tennessee Williams's play *Night of the Iguana*, sometimes you just have to endure.

Jourdan said, "I hope Mabel did it. Even if she didn't, she's been arrested, and she'll be humiliated. That's what I want. To see her humiliated. She is an asshole and a moron and evil incarnate and a Nazi."

"We'll get you a thesaurus in a minute," Morgan said.

The door to the faculty room crashed open.

5

Ludwig Schaven rumbled in huffing and puffing. He was three hundred pounds at least, by far the most heavyset man in the department. His jet-black hair was slicked back from his forehead. He'd played tackle on his high school football team. After his third concussion, the doctor told him to stop playing before he did permanent brain damage. There were those of us who thought the damage had already been done. His friends called him Looie. The less kind in the opposing faction tended to call him Looie the Loon.

Carl Pinyon, he of the travel chart at the meeting, and Basil Milovec, another leader of the suckups, followed in Looie's wake. Milovec was in his late twenties, black hair in a jumble of natural ringlets the envy of women in both factions. Most days of the week, he wore tight black jeans that emphasized what a stud he thought he was. He was thin and scrawny with a scruffy goatee which he let students tease him about relentlessly. He was a taciturn young man given to reciting Wordsworth in the faculty lounge at lunchtime. He believed that teaching teenagers poetry was the way to save their souls. Probably better than drugs, but I wasn't sure by how much.

They marched up to us. "I heard you people," Looie screamed, then banged his fist on the table. "I heard you people. You were saying terrible things about Mabel and Gracie."

Morgan said, "How long have you been standing out there?"

"Long enough," Looie said.

"They're all true," Brook said.

Did anybody really think this was a good time for a fight? Obliviousness in the face of tragedy was more than simply a presidential failing.

Listening outside other people's doors was a tactic some of the more immature members of both factions had adopted. It was depressing. Many of us wound up talking in whispers in the middle of rooms. I would never admit to deliberately leaning over to a colleague and whispering a string of nonsense words when I thought one of the suckups was trying to listen.

Jourdan barked. "Lower your voice. Be a professional."

Mistake.

Schaven went nuts. He roared at full volume. "We're the ones who are professional. We're the ones who are trying to make this school better. You're the ones who are trying to destroy children."

Jourdan said, "And sucking up is the way to be professional? Spying on the rest of us is the way to be professional? Sucking up and spying help children how?"

"We've never spied on anyone. None of us would do that."

Luci said, "I walked in on Gracie Eberson going through my files. I saw her. She didn't notice me at my classroom door. She was going through everything. She made some lame excuse and left. When I checked the computer, I found it had been tampered with. Not hard to figure she was up to something."

Milovec spoke for the first time, "Exactly what good would that do?"

Luci said, "Precisely. She wouldn't need to use my computer to get on the Internet. Why bother? There was no point in hunting in my stuff. She couldn't have been looking for curriculum materials. All she had to do was ask. There was nothing in those files."

"So what's the problem?" Milovec asked.

"Snooping on other people's computers, hunting through other people's files and desks is okay with you?" Jourdan asked.

Schaven banged his fist on the table. "You have to stop talking about Gracie and Mabel."

Jourdan said, "We still have constitutional rights. You Nazis aren't in charge yet. Who are you going to report us to? Gracie's dead and Mabel's been arrested."

Milovec said, "Mabel was not arrested. They're just taking some time to ask a few more questions."

"Yeah, right," Brook said.

Schaven said, "There are laws about slander."

I had heard more than enough. I stood up and said, "I'll see you all later."

This brought proceedings to a halt.

Carl Pinyon said, "We'd like to talk to you."

"All three of you?" I asked.

"It's a union issue," Pinyon said.

I agreed to speak with them.

The others began to stand up and clear their places. While I was washing my cup at the sink, Jourdan sidled up next to me and said, "Can I talk to you?"

I was going to have to give out numbers like at the deli counter. I told him I'd see him after I talked to the suckups.

6

Once out in the hall, Schaven said, "Let's talk in Milovec's classroom, it's closest."

It was also directly across the hall from the storeroom, which now had crime scene tape over the doorway. I was suspicious about their motives, but I was willing to listen to them.

The four of us huddled up near Milovec's desk.

The key with a lot of faculty is they often tell their union representative a lot of things, sort of like their father confessor. For example, Milovec two years ago had been worried about what would happen if the administration found out he was having an affair with one of the Spanish teachers who, at the time, had been married to another guy. I didn't see a problem, but he was worried. Over time I became his confidant about his little conquests with female members of the faculty. So often straight guys have absolutely no one else they can talk to. He did confess to using school e-mail accounts to send the Spanish teacher letters. At the time, I strongly suggested he not use the school accounts. My current understanding was that Milovec was engaged. His confiding in me had stopped, presumably so had his affairs. I didn't ask. Wasn't my business.

Schaven said, "You're sitting in the lounge with the obstructionist old guard. They are all negative assholes. I always knew you were on their side."

Schaven too had once confided in me. His problem was that when the school hired him he hadn't disclosed a past history of fighting cancer. He'd come to me, and I had reassured him that in this day and age, they weren't supposed to ask for medical histories. He'd been cancer-free now for three years.

I wasn't about to put up with crap from these guys, not because I knew stuff supposedly no one else knew, but because I was not going to put up with madness from either side.

I said, "I will sit with whom I wish when I wish. What you may choose to interpret about that is not my problem. What did you want to talk about with me? It's late."

"You're the union guy," Schaven said. "You have to be impartial."

"To whom is that news?" I asked.

Milovec said, "You're our union guy, you've got to help. Gracie's dead. You've got to do something."

I said, "There's nothing about a murder investigation in the union contract."

"Look," Milovec said, "we need to know what is going on. Gracie was a good friend. It's awful she's dead. They've been questioning everybody. We need union representation."

"Did you kill her?"

He seemed taken aback by the question.

"Of course not. No."

I turned to Schaven. "Did you?"

"Don't be absurd. Certainly not."

I gazed at Pinyon.

"I didn't do it," he said.

"Then you three have nothing to worry about."

Milovec said, "They're trampling on our rights."

"Which rights?"

"First Amendment rights."

I sighed. Another moron misinterpreting the First Amendment. I asked, "What does the First Amendment say?"

"It says we have rights," Milovec said.

"You need to read it again and realize that it has nothing in there about police activity, who they can and cannot talk to, and who they can or cannot arrest. You may be thinking of the Fourth or Fifth Amendment, but you have no First Amendment rights here."

Pinyon said, "The union has to hire us a lawyer."

"Not in this case," I said.

Pinyon said, "I knew there was no reason to join the union. I knew you couldn't protect us."

Years ago this kind of statement had been followed by a threat to quit the union. Then we negotiated a "fair share" clause in the contract. That meant that you didn't have to be in the union, but since you got the benefit of the services you had to pay dues. Anti-union people hated it. I found it wonderful. I always thought I'm-going-to-quit-if-I-don't-get-my-way stopped when you were about ten.

I said, "Are you saying you need protection here? Because if you are, my advice is to shut your mouth, get your cell phone out, and start calling attorneys."

Pinyon said, "I didn't kill her, but they can't keep us here."

I said, "I'm sure they're questioning everybody."

Schaven said, "It has to be one of the goddamn old guard who killed her."

"Why's that?" I asked.

"Who else had motivation?" Milovec asked.

I said, "I wouldn't know, and that's not union business."

"But it's part of what's happened to us," Schaven said. "Those people are going to divulge all the fights in the department. It's going to look awful."

Pinyon said, "You know people in the other faction. You talk to them. Maybe you could find something out."

"I talk to both factions."

Schaven said, "But this is murder. Think how this reflects on all of us."

"As far as I can tell," I said, "it doesn't. How would it? There's a killer. It reflects on him or her."

"But a killer? How could we have been working all this time with a killer and not know?"

I said, "Most of us are capable of crimes of passion. It's just that we have enough blocks to stop ourselves before we go through with it. Were Mabel and Gracie having an affair?"

Schaven said, "Yes."

Milovec said, "No."

Pinyon shrugged.

I sat down on a nearby desk. I raised an eyebrow. I said, "Any one of you care to explain?"

They all started to talk at once. Glares all around. Fighting in the ranks of the suckups. A good thing? I hoped so.

When their squabbling ran down, I asked, "Do the police know there are varying views on their relationship?"

"I didn't tell them," Milovec said.

Schaven said, "They're going to find out. It's not as if it was much of a secret."

I said, "I'd never heard about it."

Pinyon said, "I'd heard a rumor."

I said, "Who would know if they were having an affair? Isn't Mabel Spandrel married?"

"Her husband is always somewhere at some convention. He writes lurid science-fiction novels that he's trying to get someone to buy. He goes to these conventions to try and get an agent or an editor or something. He's never around."

"It couldn't have been either husband," Milovec said. "They would have had to get into the building. Even our security guards have that minimal level of competence."

I said, "They could easily get in the faculty entrance."

Schaven said, "It's not a motive for murder. Maybe if Gracie's husband found out, but he's never home. He runs that coffeehouse."

Milovec said, "Why would any of us care if they were having an affair?"

"Somebody jealous?" Pinyon asked.

I asked, "Who do you think killed her?"

Schaven said, "Brook? Jourdan? You heard what they were saying."

"As did you. Don't you get tired of listening at doors? Don't you find it childish?"

Schaven said, "I find things out. I learn about plots against the administration."

"What are they going to do," I asked, "overthrow them, put tanks in the parking lot, machine gun emplacements at the top of stairways?"

"You know how schools can be," Schaven said. "If the teachers are against you, it can be awfully tough for an administrator. I wanted the department to run well. I wanted everybody to get along. Some of us were working on that. Others were trying to thwart us at every turn. Mabel was lucky that she had some people behind her."

I said, "But Mabel's not dead; Gracie is. If someone is angry about the way things are going, why not kill Mabel? Gracie's death won't have an effect on the administration. Although I suppose it would on a personal note, if they were having an affair, but school policy wouldn't change."

Schaven said, "It would if Mabel was unfairly accused of murder."

Pinyon said, "Maybe it was a conspiracy hatched by the old guard. They'd kill Gracie and try to pin it on Mabel."

"Do you really think that many people could keep that kind of thing quiet?"

Pinyon said, "Well, maybe one of them thought it up and carried it out. He wouldn't have to tell the others, but the conspiracy and death could have the same effect. They're trying to ruin what we're doing."

I said, "I've seen lots of paranoia on both sides. Some of it might be justified, some not." I pointed at Pinyon. "Where did you get that information you had today on who'd been where?"

"I don't have to reveal my sources." His face was red from the roots of his spiked blond hair to the scruffy bits of hair that clung to his chin.

I said, "No, you don't have to reveal your sources, but you're the ones who came to me. The fight started at the meeting. The focus was what you knew. I'm sure the police will be interested."

Pinyon said, "I haven't talked to them yet. Do you think I should be worried? Maybe I should get a lawyer."

"Did you do something illegal to get those records?"

"I didn't."

"Meaning somebody else did."

"I'm not saying."

I said, "The only place all those records would be is in each teacher's personnel file, current and former employees. You don't have access to those files, or you're not supposed to."

"I didn't look in anybody's file."

"Then who did?"

Milovec said, "I'm sure those files had nothing to do with the killing. It was just something to make a point."

I didn't agree, but I didn't think I'd get any information either. I was more suspicious than ever about what these three were up to.

I asked, "Does Mabel have an alibi for the time of the murder?"

Schaven said, "I don't know. But you've got to help us. You've dealt with this kind of thing."

"My experience doesn't give me any insight. Anybody can ask questions, but the police usually don't like it."

Schaven said, "No one on the faculty knows more cops than you do. You always have those behaviorally disturbed kids. You're always meeting with some social worker or therapist or BD teacher or learning disabilities teacher. We've all got to do something. The school's reputation is at stake. If the fighting that was going on gets into the papers, we're going to look like fools. What if the police blab? These kinds of things always get out. I don't want to be mentioned in the papers. People's good names could be ruined in this community. Think of people's names in the paper. Mabel doesn't deserve to come under suspicion."

Milovec said, "I think someone in the old guard did it. I think this is the thing that is going to finally bring them down, and they are going to lose their grip on this department. They think they run the place."

Jourdan and the others earlier hadn't sounded like a group that was running anything.

I said, "If there was something I could do to help prove who killed her, I would do so. I can't make any promises to help any faction or to get any results or even to do anything proactive. If you or any of your friends are questioned, my suggestion is that you tell the truth."

I left. Police personnel still cluttered the halls. I saw the administrators down at one end of the hall talking to Gault and Vulmea. I wondered if Mabel really was under suspicion or even arrested. That rumor and a million others would continue to fly. I wondered what Schaven, Milovec, and Pinyon wanted out of me. I walked down to Jourdan's classroom.

7

"You've got to help me," Jourdan said. "You're the union rep."

"What's happened?" I asked.

"The police were awful. They asked about every single thing I said to Gracie today and any other day. They wanted to know about every fight. I began to tell them. They didn't see how awful those assholes have been. I could tell they thought it was all me. They just wanted to know how involved I was. I couldn't help myself. I kept talking and talking. I should have shut up. I should have asked for a lawyer. Does the union provide lawyers for stuff like this? I can't afford a lawyer. What am I going to do?"

This was actually a large part of a union rep's job, holding their hands in the midst of a crisis over which the union had no jurisdiction or power or influence. As with so many of them, there was history here. Jourdan's secrets were murkier than most. It had been during my first year as the building's union rep some years ago. Jourdan had actually been head of the department at the time. I knew the two versions to the story because the woman involved had come to me as well. Depending on whom you believed, at the departmental Christmas party that year Jourdan had made a drunken pass at her, trying to use his power of evaluation over her to get her to consent. The other version was that she was drunk and trying to seduce him so that she would be given tenure. This version included Jourdan turning her down because he was faithful to his wife. Each had come to me the day after the party. I immediately got in touch with the union president and attorneys. Meanwhile, Jourdan and the woman both called the police. Both called the federal government offices that handle sexual harassment cases. Then the next day, poof, it was over. I got no explanation. Neither came to me and said it was over. It just died. I'd gotten abashed looks from both of them but no explanation. They weren't telling, and I knew better than to ask. I don't go looking for business. The next year Jourdan was no longer head of the department, and the woman no longer taught in the school district. I have no idea which of them was lying. Maybe there was even a third explanation—they were both drunk and said embarrassing things which they were sorry for later, but they didn't know how to apologize or how to back off. Or a fourth explanation—they were both lying sacks of shit, trying to cover their asses.

I said, "Jourdan, you didn't kill her."

"But I don't have an alibi. I think those suckups probably planned all this. I think they'd kill one of their own in some convoluted attempt to destroy the rest of us. Remember when Pinyon was getting those hate notes? It turned out he was writing them himself."

"No one proved that," I pointed out.

"They were typed. They were left in his mailbox. There was never a written signature. No one ever saw anyone else near his mailbox. Of course he wrote them. They were trying to get sympathy for their own side. They wanted to make us look bad."

I said, "I'm not sure they're capable of Byzantine plots on that level."

"I wouldn't put anything past them. They are desperate and sick people. Killing one of their own would be the exact kind of thing their sick minds would come up with."

Good to know each side was accusing the other equally. Sick behavior didn't respect political boundaries.

Jourdan said, "Those people aren't rational. They're so emotionally committed to every single one of their positions, and why? What is the point? And they all back each other up no matter what. They will tell any lie. Where'd they get that information on who'd been where on their travels? Huh? It had to be an administrator. Some administrator is feeding the suckups. I think we should all be very afraid. If Mabel has been arrested, someone will find a lie to get her off. They'll keep themselves free, you watch. Somebody will dream some shit up. They'll lie to convict one of us." He drew a deep breath. "What do I do if they accuse me or try to arrest me? Can the union get me a lawyer?"

I said, "Unfortunately, the union deals only with legal cases connected to the contract between the teachers and the board. Don't say anything more to the police. Wait for representation. If you can't afford one, the courts provide you with a lawyer."

"I think one of my wife's friends is an attorney."

"I'd suggest you call her now and put things in motion."

He said, "This is so awful." He buried his face in his hands and said, "I should never have said anything at today's meeting. Why can't other people do the fighting?"

"They do sometimes," I said. "Today was just a bad day for you." I reassured him as best I could. I wanted to get away and get my own reassurances. I was hungry and I wanted to go home.

8

When I left Jourdan's classroom, I saw Morgan Adair at the top of the stairs at the east end of the building. He was deep in conversation with Steven Frecking, who had his back to me. Frecking still wore the same outfit he'd been in when I caught him with Benson in the storeroom. I saw Morgan touch Frecking's arm. Frecking yanked his arm away as if he'd been burned. As I approached, I heard Morgan say, "Can we get together?"

"No."

"Are you okay?" Morgan asked.

I could hear the first wisps of heartbreak in his voice.

"We can't talk here." Frecking's voice was a savage whisper.

"It's okay. No one can hear us."

I slowed. Obviously Morgan hadn't heard what Frecking had been doing in the storeroom. In fact, other than me, the two involved, and maybe the police, I guess no one did know.

Frecking said, "This is not worth the hassle. I can't do this." I waited for him to admit what he had been doing earlier. Nope. Instead, "You are not worth all this hassle. I gotta go." Frecking turned, spotted me, and rushed toward me. Morgan looked like he'd lost his best friend, which, in a way, he hadn't.

Frecking didn't make eye contact as he stormed past me. He bulled his way toward the exit.

Morgan saw me and hurried over. "He's so closeted. He's so hot. It's sad."

I said, "He just totally dismissed you."

"You heard that?"

"Sorry, yeah."

He hung his head. Had he no pride? Was he that desperate for a relationship? I guess so. Morgan would find out eventually about Frecking being in that room, and he'd find out I knew. So I said, "You know where I found the body?"

"Yeah."

"When I walked in, I saw Steven and Brandon Benson making out."

"They were there?"

"Yes."

"With the body?"

"They didn't know it was there."

"Maybe they were just talking."

"With their hands on each others crotches?"

"Benson is married to a woman."

"I know."

"They wouldn't do that in school. Are you sure?"

"I'm not in the habit of altering reality."

"He wouldn't."

"He was."

"I . . . You're sure?"

I just looked at him.

"I can't believe it. I thought he was the one."

Morgan did tend to have mad crushes on men after one date.

46

I said, "I'm sorry."

"We had wild sex last night. I thought he'd be exhausted. We did it four times."

"More information than I need," I said.

Morgan said, "I can't talk about this now. I'll talk to you later."

I didn't see the cops. I didn't see any administrators. No friends in sight. I trudged to my classroom.

9

Rain still pelted the windows. The drops joined together and formed rivulets down the panes to the puddles of water that always seeped through and onto the ledges inside the windows. I'd been trying to get that fixed for years. No luck there either.

I sat at my desk for a few minutes and fretted. Then I got fed up and decided to go home.

My classroom door opened. It was my lover, Scott Carpenter. He wore faded blue jeans, running shoes, and a sweatshirt. Water sluiced off his umbrella as he shook it and then placed it open on the floor. We hugged and kissed. I explained what had happened since we talked on the phone. I finished, "The cops said to hang around. This isn't good."

Scott said, "I called our attorney, he's on his way." Seconds later the two detectives barged into the room. Gault said, "We'll need a DNA sample from you, Mr. Mason."

"Why?"

"We're investigating."

An obvious and incomplete answer. I said, "I need to speak with my attorney."

Gault got pissed at that. "You refusing to cooperate?"

Scott asked, "Why do you want a DNA sample?"

Gault said to Scott, "Who are you?"

Scott said, "Scott Carpenter."

Vulmea said, "You're the baseball player."

Scott plays professional baseball. He's good. He's famous. He was home in October. The team wasn't that good.

For a few minutes Scott's status as a baseball player focused attention on him rather than corpses, killings, and suspects. I call that the "Notting Hill effect." As in the movie *Notting Hill*, when the Hugh Grant character shows up at his younger sister's birthday party with Julia Roberts, who is playing a stunningly famous actress. The family's reaction is priceless and endearing, and I love the movie. I didn't have time for the detectives' being in awe of a star right then, but they weren't asking me. And for a few moments they'd stopped asking for a DNA sample. They'd get back to it.

The reigning administrative triumvirate in the school district barged in: Amando Graniento, the principal; Riva Towne, the superintendent; Kara Bochka, the president of the school board and mother of Fred Zileski. Bochka had remarried since divorcing Fred Zileski's dad. I knew the custody arrangement was complicated and that the biological parents hated each other. Victoria Abbot, the assistant superintendent who had been around earlier, was not present.

Bochka had a thin hatchet face. She always wore elegant clothes and looked as if she'd come straight from her job as the vice president of a bank in downtown Chicago. I didn't know her personally, but her public persona was forbidding. I'd seen her at school board meetings putting parents, other board members, and administrators in their place with a withering look, a cutting remark, or the banging of her gavel. We'd been on opposite sides at the negotiations table before. I'd watch her attempting to whittle away at our side. Our nickname for her was Kara the Terrible.

Fortunately, our current union president, Teresa Merton, was excellent in combating this harridan. Merton was quiet, calm, and low-key in her responses, which initially gave the impression that she was weak and ineffectual, but by the time she was done, the opposition would be gaping at the depth, breadth, and thoroughness of her assault. I wasn't sure Bochka actually understood all of what Merton said. Bochka struck me as startlingly slow, but when Merton was finished, even Bochka could catch on that she'd been refuted and rebuffed; her arguments demolished and twisted to the point of absurdity.

Bochka said, "What's going on?"

Gault said, "This person is not cooperating with the police."

Bochka said, "Of course he'll cooperate with the police." Gault explained what the police wanted. Bochka turned to me. "Give them DNA samples."

"Are you an attorney?" I asked.

"No."

"Then perhaps your suggestions aren't as helpful as I need right now."

Amando Graniento, the principal, said, "If you have nothing to hide, why would you refuse?"

Ah, the give-up-all-your-rights defense—a great vehicle for bullying by those in power: "If you were innocent, why would you object?" Because it is insulting and demeaning and treating someone as if they were a suspect.

I said, "I think we all need to calm down." I turned to Gault and Vulmea. "You've made a request. You know that if I refuse, you need a court order. I've refused." To the school personnel, I said, "This is a union matter, a police matter, and a personal matter."

Bochka said, "Well, we can't just have people refusing to cooperate with the police."

"Depends on how you look at it," I said. "Although I admit that, whether it's an assertion of basic rights or a refusal to cooperate, the result is the same."

Gault said, "We'd hoped for more from the school district."

Maybe he could bully Bochka, Towne, and Graniento into giving DNA samples.

The cops broke the impasse by saying, "Don't leave. We'll be back."

I said, "Wait a second. Has anyone mentioned to you the hate notes Carl Pinyon received earlier this year?"

Graniento said, "I'm sure that was nothing."

Bochka said, "What hate notes?"

I explained about what he'd received and included the fact that some people suspected he wrote them himself.

The cops took some notes, then stalked out.

Bochka turned to Scott. "Who are you?"

I said, "I'd like to introduce all of you to Scott Carpenter." I performed proper introductions.

Towne, Bochka, and Graniento shook Scott's hand.

"The baseball player," Towne said.

"Oh, yes," Graniento said.

They discussed neither his fame nor his fortune. They weren't fans. It was nearly refreshing.

Towne said, "We need to speak with you, Mr. Mason."

I nodded, said, "Yes?"

Bochka said, "We can't have this kind of scandal at this school."

"Which kind?" I asked. Did she mean the body or the sexual trysts? Did they know about them? If so, Benson and Frecking should be very afraid. Perhaps it would have been helpful if they had felt that fear before they started humping away at school. I wasn't naïve. I knew kids and adults attempted illicit trysts where they could. Adults were supposed to know better.

Bochka said, "A dead body! A teacher. This is awful. The papers are going to drag the school district's reputation through the mud. There are news trucks outside already."

I said, "The concern should be for Gracie's family and for trying to find out who killed her."

"Murder," Bochka said. "That is just not acceptable in this school."

I asked, "There's a school where it would be acceptable?"

"Well, no." She fluttered her hands on her expensive necklace.

Yes, I know, we're all supposed to tremble and quake when we're talking to school board members. I don't. There are a few who are not self-important boobs. When you find those, treasure them. The rare times I've spoken to school board members, I've found them to be just as human as teachers and all the other common folk. Bochka had been on the wrong side of the DNA question. You start something fatuous with me, you better be ready for something snarky in return.

Bochka didn't seem to notice my tone. She said, "Could a student have done this? They play so many violent video games. They think violence is acceptable. It's terrible."

I gave myself bonus points for not guffawing in her face at this stunning display of excessive inanity.

"Did the police arrest Mabel Spandrel?" I asked.

Towne said, "They've taken her down to the station for questioning. They claim they're keeping an open mind. One of them tried to imply that Mrs. Eberson was having an affair with a student."

"What exactly did they say?" I asked.

Towne said, "They say they found evidence of sexual activity in the room where she was discovered."

"Why would that imply a student?"

"Spandrel led them to believe that. She told them Gracie tutored several boys in math. Only boys."

"Did she tutor them in that room?" I asked.

"Well, no," Towne replied.

"Why would tutoring imply sexual activity?"

"Well," Towne said, "it's odd. Suspicious."

What a crock. I asked, "How is it suspicious?"

"It just is," Towne said. "That policeman said they had evidence of sexual activity. Isn't that why they want DNA samples?"

I asked, "Did they say what kind of evidence they found?"

Towne leaned toward me and lowered her voice. "Fresh semen."

"In the room?" I asked. "On her body? Was she sexually assaulted?"

"I don't know," Towne said. "I heard a couple rumors from different sources, and the police hinted. They must suspect something or someone."

Graniento said, "Do you think the police believed Pinyon's notes are part of a murder? Pinyon didn't die. Gracie did."

I said, "It was a threat, and it happened here. I have no idea about the connection."

"We've got to find out something," Bochka said. "We can't be kept in the dark. I don't like that older detective, Gault. He was rude to me. I'm going to report him to his superior."

"How was he rude?" I asked.

"He told me not to interfere in the investigation. I'm president of this school board. I'm responsible to the voters. All I did was try to go into the storeroom to try to see what was going on."

"He was just doing his job," Towne said.

Bochka pointed at me. "Haven't you had experience with this kind of thing before?"

The bodies-plopping-in-my-path reputation had preceded me. I repeated what I'd said to the members of the factions. "I'm sure I don't have much more insight than anyone else. You're already annoyed with the cops. You said they were rude. If they knew someone was trying to investigate, they'd be more than rude."

Bochka said, "You seem to know some of the River's Edge police. Could you ask them?"

I said, "I have no official standing."

"Yes, but you know these people," Towne said.

"The one I know best is not here," I replied.

Graniento said, "This questioning could go on for hours. They're demanding to talk to custodians, secretaries, members of other departments. It's awful. Our reputation will be ruined. The teachers are saying awful things about what's been going on in the English department."

Like the truth, I thought.

Graniento was continuing. "They've got more questions for everyone. Every petty bit of squabbling is going to come out. Every minor tiff and spat. The police are going to know all of this. It's all going to get into the papers."

I said, "Then maybe it will stop. It should have stopped a long time ago."

"What do you mean?" Graniento's voice was low and threatening.

"With your implicit consent, this infighting has escalated tenfold since you've been here. You may or may not have encouraged it, but you did nothing to stop it. You took no action. Other administrators have been around longer, and they've done nothing to stop it. One could lay some of the guilt for this murder on yourselves, if the motive for the killing turns out to have been driven by the interdepartmental war."

Graniento said, "We've done nothing."

I said, "We must have a different definition of nothing."

Among other things, Graniento and Spandrel had rammed a new curriculum and new pedagogy down the throats of the members of the English department. They'd modified and ordered implemented what's called the "work-shop model." It's a methodology that makes some sense. Students learn by doing rather than passively listening to lecture after lecture. However, there is an emphasis on group work often to the exclusion of individual achievement. It also demands a level of attention to individual students that is difficult for some teachers to attain while still controlling a class. Graniento and Spandrel had demanded the model be used but that the kids work silently. They never fully explained how group work was supposed to be done silently or, if it was silent, how it was group work. They'd insisted on teachers' having at least thirty individual contacts with students during each class period, and they'd showed up in people's classrooms with charts and ledgers, keeping track. They'd stopped counting mine after fifty in one class period. Well, that day the kids needed help writing correct openings for essays. What was I supposed to do?

The administrators had soon tired of the onerous duty of being in so many classrooms. Fortunately for the teaching staff, the administrators have tons of paperwork to shuffle.

Towne said, "All schools have problems."

Bochka said, "No one told the school board about any problems."

"Bull," I said. "One rumor I heard is that you met with one of the factions in the department and were openly supporting them."

"That is absolutely not true."

I said, "It was just a rumor." Which I had from an impeccable source.

Graniento said, "I let my department heads have a free rein. They make the choices."

Scott and I sat on the tops of school desks that were next to each other. He watched each of them intently. Occasionally, one of them would glance at him, but none addressed themselves to him. I took great comfort from his presence.

Towne said, "The police seem very impatient."

I said, "Cops often are."

Towne said, "We want to seem cooperative."

Graniento said, "They were talking about fights among the faculty. What they said about today's meeting was a disgrace. Adults shouting at each other? In a school?"

I said, "You encouraged it."

"I beg your pardon," he said.

I said, "At the meeting with the new teachers this year, on the opening day of school, you told them to speak up, to challenge the way things have been done."

"You were there?" Towne said.

I said, "The union building rep talks to the new teachers on the first day every year. We give them contracts and some dos and don'ts. One of them told us what you'd said. The others confirmed it."

"Who told?" Graniento asked.

I said, "I'm not going to tell you."

"That's insubordination," Graniento said.

"No, actually, it's not. I've heard you use that term to attempt to frighten, bully, demean, and silence those who oppose or disagree with you, but insubordination is very clearly delineated in the school code. I suggest you peruse it."

"You encourage rudeness?" Towne asked Graniento.

Graniento said, "I didn't mean for them to be rude at meetings."

I said, "You've encouraged them to come to you. I've gotten rumors all year that they run to you with departmental problems. That you encourage them. That you've been undercutting the heads of one, some, or all of the departments since the day you showed up."

Graniento said, "Mrs. Spandrel and I speak every day. I have no problems with her."

"She'll be glad to hear that," I said. "So will the rest of the heads of the departments."

Graniento said, "I have most certainly not encouraged dissent."

"I'm just telling you the rumors," I said. "You know the truth of them. Who knows how many of them will get into the media?"

Bochka said, "That's one thing we're concerned about, the media."

"And the Internet," Towne added.

Bochka said, "You're the union person in the building. Reporters might call you."

This was getting down to it. Police. Media. Containment. Cover your ass. Control publicity.

I said, "Are you asking me to lie? And nobody's going to be able to control the Internet."

Bochka said, "I'm not stupid. I know I can't control what someone puts on the Internet, but nobody believes what's on the Internet, do they? No, it's the regular media."

"Or the police," Graniento said. "Couldn't you get them to not say things to the media?"

Towne said, "Nobody wants you to lie, but maybe if we all said the same thing."

I said, "I don't have the power to stop what the cops say to the press. I doubt reporters are going to call me. If they do, I will handle them as I always do."

"How's that?" Bochka said.

"With professionalism and respect."

Bochka said, "I guess I may have heard rumors about the English department. That the teachers are out of control."

I said, "How is that a concern of the school board?"

"Everything that happens in this school district is a concern of mine."

"It is and it isn't," I said. "If you're micromanaging the place, it might be. My understanding is that school board members are supposed to take care of the budget and set policy."

Bochka said, "Any parent can be concerned."

I said, "And parents can be out of control."

Towne said, "Mr. Mason, we're serious. There may have been flaws in the system, problems in the school, but we need your help. Can't you call someone?"

"The main person I know is no longer in homicide. The others I know are in the juvenile youth services department, not homicide."

"But they must speak to their friends. Don't you still talk to your friend?"

"What is it that you think he'd tell me?"

"We'd like to get inside information," Towne said. "We're hoping you'll help."

We went around and around on handling cops and finding out what was going on and about not telling reporters what was going on. Reluctantly, I agreed to do what I could. I didn't say precisely what I'd do, or when I'd do it, or how vigorously I'd pursue it, but that I'd give it a shot.

Even odder than their asking me for help was their persistance in asking for it. While I hadn't met the strict definition of insubordination, I'd been fairly direct and honest, something I'm sure they weren't used to from usually cowering teachers. Yet I only got fairly mild sparring in return. I didn't trust these administrators as far as I could throw a curriculum guide, and our curriculum guide was thicker than the yellow pages for New York and Chicago combined.

Teresa Merton, our union president, strode into the room and marched over to where we were standing. Bochka and Towne looked annoyed. Graniento looked superior.

Merton stood about five-foot-two with long blond hair in complex ringlets down to her waist. She might have weighed a hundred pounds if she was wearing heavy winter clothes including a sweater and a parka. Nobody messed with her. Competent and smart as union president, she was also an excellent teacher. She said, "What the hell is going on?"

The administrators hunched a bit closer together. Bochka explained her version of events. When she finished, Merton said, "Nobody's submitting to DNA testing until they talk to their lawyers. You weren't thinking of doing anything to these teachers, taking any action against them?"

"No," Towne said.

"Good. I'd like to speak with Tom alone."

The administrators left. I introduced Scott.

She said, "If you want him to stay during our conversation that's fine. Now, what really happened?"

I gave her my version of events, including a description of what Benson and Frecking were doing when I walked in.

"You haven't told that to the administrators and to the cops? All you said was they were in there?"

"Right."

"Okay, but be careful about being too cute. Don't lie to the cops is my saintly advice."

"I figure it's their incident to tell about."

"Maybe. They could get their asses fired for that."

"Should I talk to them?"

She repeated one of the great union dictums. "Don't go looking for business." The problem with hearing a rumor or assuming someone needed help and going to them first was that then the next person could say, "Why didn't you come to me when you heard the rumor? It's your fault I'm in trouble, because you didn't come to me." They've got to come to you.

"And if they do come to me?"

"Send them to me. It's going to be a mess. Those administrators coming to you for help is kind of a compliment."

"It's odd."

"You do know people in the police department, and administrators like to stick their nose into everything. Although, it's funny that both factions in the department came to you. What do they expect you to do, wave a magic wand? Walk on water? Murder is not a union issue."

"They'll claim we didn't help."

"Don't they always?"

Unless you could alter reality to meet some people's distortions, they would never be satisfied with what you did as union official. Mostly they had some movie-version notion of unions breaking legs and forcing evil enemies to obey. People watch too many movies. Being unable to alter reality, I was at times at a loss. Explaining reality to them was another problem.

I said, "You know, in the past when I've suggested they talk to you, they say they're afraid of you."

"Good. They should be. The farther away the stupider ones stay, the better. I hate those suckups, and I'm not even in the same department as you." She taught physics and calculus to seniors and juniors.

"What if the media calls?" I asked.

"You've handled them as much as I have. I have complete faith in you."

I appreciated the vote of support.

She said, "I'm going to see if any of my other charges need to be protected from errant administrators."

I thanked her for her help. She left.

Todd Bristol, my attorney, entered the room. He was tall and waspishly thin. He shut his umbrella with a snap. He took off his Burberry overcoat and folded it carefully over a student's desk. I had only ever seen him in his courtroom attire. His charcoal trousers were held up by black suspenders stretched over a white shirt. He wore a perfectly knotted tie and glasses with thin gold rims.

I told him everything. He said, "Keep your mouth shut. No DNA sample."

I said, "I want to go home."

Todd said, "Let's find the cops."

The hallways were deserted. It was quiet. The old school smells, chalk and human sweat, permeated the atmosphere. I glanced out a window. Rain continued to pour. The part of the faculty parking lot I could see was nearly empty. I wished Frank Rohde, my friend on the River's Edge police force, were still in homicide.

▴ 10 ▴

Scott, Todd Bristol, and I found the cops in a room on the first floor. They had firm, set looks on their faces. I introduced my attorney. Gault's frown deepened. Vulmea looked pissed.

Gault held a small notebook in his right hand and tapped it on his left wrist. He said, "We've got a little problem."

My attorney said nothing, so I kept my mouth shut. That's why they created lawyers: so that someone knows what to say when the police come calling.

Gault rested his butt on a student's desk. I saw a mustard stain in the middle of the wrinkles and creases of his dress pants. Scott would never have let me get out the door with such a sartorial faux pas. Gault said, "You claim Brandon Benson and Steven Frecking were with you when you found the body."

My attorney said, "That's what my client told you."

"Yes, he did. Unfortunately, the two gentleman in question deny they were there."

Scott moved closer to me and put his hand on my shoulder. My attorney kept his eyes on the cops.

I began, "I—"

My attorney said, "Be silent."

I clamped my mouth shut. I was mystified and furious. Those two assholes—who I'd been thinking of checking on, to see if they needed any help—had turned on me. As far as I was concerned, those two shits could fry. I was eager to tell what they'd really been doing and whose DNA the cops should check for, but my attorney had said, "Be silent."

My attorney said, "Tom has told you what he knows."

Gault said, "And now we have it contradicted by two people."

My attorney said, "Why would he add those two to such a scene at such a moment?"

"To divert suspicion from himself," Vulmea said.

My attorney asked, "How would making two people up who could easily deny it divert any suspicion or make any sense? It might make sense if he made up one person, but not two."

"Killers do crazy things," Gault said, "illogical things, irrational things. They've just committed murder. They're out of control."

"Does my client look out of control to you? Has he looked out of control?"

"Maybe he's a psychopath who's plotting and planning every second. Maybe he'll kill again."

My attorney said, "You can't have it both ways. If he's plotting and planning, then he's not out of control. If he's not out of control, then he planned the murder carefully and my question remains, why would he add two people to the scene who were not there? Your question should be, why did they lie?"

Gault said, "Maybe you're right, but we've got two guys' word against one."

"Did you talk to them together?" my attorney asked.

Gault said, "I know my job."

"Did their stories match?"

"Yeah."

"Where did they claim they were?" my attorney asked.

"In Mr. Benson's room discussing a kid's grade. Some athlete who was failing."

My attorney said, "Tom, it's okay to tell the police the reason they are lying."

I hated to rat out my fellow teachers, but this wasn't some gang or mafia vendetta where the code of silence might be breached and death follow dishonor. That crap mostly exists in the minds of teenage boys when they are attempting to cover their own butts for bullying and doing minor illegal drug offenses. Or in wild imaginations of mindless school administrators when they've done something stupid. However, my statement would also out both men, which, on general principles, I opposed. Outing the innocent was wrong. Outing the guilty, however, struck me as a way, in this instance, to get even. Not only were they trying to make me into a liar, but worse, a murder suspect. And my lawyer had given me the go-ahead. What's not to like? I said, "They were making out."

"They're gay?" Vulmea asked.

"I have no idea. What I saw was each of them with their hands on the front of the pants of the other. Their clothes were awry. They were kissing."

"In school?" Vulmea asked.

My attorney ignored the obviousness of the response to this question and said, "So, you'll have to talk to them again. Anything else?"

Gault said, "This is bullshit."

My attorney said, "I couldn't have put it better."

I said, "The superintendent told us a rumor that you'd found fresh evidence of sexual activity."

Vulmea said, "We're not commenting on that."

Gault said, "We got a call from Frank Rohde. He said he wouldn't be able to get here tonight. He said to trust you. Must be nice to have friends high up on the force."

The cops picked up their coats and notebooks and left.

"Those fuckers," I said.

My attorney said, "Are you referring to the police or to your colleagues?"

"Both," I said.

Scott said, "They really think they can tell that kind of lie and get away with it?"

My attorney said, "It takes a special kind of stupid to make up that kind of lie. It's late." We returned to my classroom where he unfolded his coat with meticulous precision, put it on, and picked up his umbrella. He added, "Don't talk to the cops without me present."

We left.

11

The rain fell in sheets. I dashed to the car. The parking lot was as dark and gloomy as usual. One quarter of the overhead lights gave weak illumination to the bleak scene. Some were out as a result of student vandalism. Most didn't work because the custodians did not put a high priority on replacing burned-out lights in the parking lot. The media trucks and their bright lights were out in front of the school. The teachers' parking lot was in back. We weren't permitted to park out front.

Scott would drive his own car back home. Inside mine I set the XM radio to the folk music station. I put the SUV in reverse to pull out. The car wouldn't move. I shoved it in drive and pulled forward to the bumper block then tried backing out. No luck. I didn't want to just try and run something over. There shouldn't have been an obstruction.

I turned off the car and got out.

I didn't remember running over a dead body as I pulled in that morning. That's the kind of thing I notice. But that's what was blocking the rear wheels of my car now.

12

I recognized the corpse. It was Peter Higden, one of the greatest suckups in modern history. He was a fifth-year teacher. You'd see him in the department office in the mornings, bringing in doughnuts. He'd be in the main office before and after school, smiling and using his charm on the secretaries. He was bluff, friendly, and a Nazi. Few dared say anything to him about his prejudice because he was also African American. I heard him make an anti-Semitic remark once. I was appalled that the other six people listening to him said not a word. I did. I told him that it was an unacceptable and rude comment. He did apologize, and he stopped making any kind of slurs around me. Others told me he still made all kinds of slurs about any number of groups. I often asked why they didn't speak up. They claimed they were afraid.

It must have been frightening to sit down on a bus and not move in Montgomery, Alabama, in the mid-1950s. Speaking up about a slur in a school in 2007? Courage? Can they say *adult*? Cowards needed to die as badly as the suckups. That's what the bullies want: silence in the face of their unpardonable behavior. And when their behavior gets thrown back at them, they act all stunned and innocent. The world had changed since the 1950s. Obviously not enough.

Higden's bushy, throwback-to-the-seventies hair was caught under my left rear tire. His jacket was slightly awry. Rain flowed into his lifeless eyes and beaded down his cheeks. I felt for the pulse in his neck. Nothing. He was dead.

Two deaths in less than eight hours.

I leaned against the side of the car. I don't remember if I felt the rain pelting down on me. I shook my head and bent over. Death in unexpected places was always a shock. For a few moments I thought I might be ill. Marine training or not, all this was not easy to take.

I saw Scott pulling around. He drove up to see what the delay was. He peered out his windows at me. His windshield wipers swished back and forth. I opened the passenger door of his Porsche and climbed in.

He said, "What's wrong?"

"Peter Higden is dead."

He looked out the windows. "Who is he? Somebody on the radio?"

"No. One of the teachers."

"Where?"

"About three feet from here. Just this side of the back wheels of my car."

"Did you hit him?"

"I haven't moved from my parking space. I tried to go backwards. He was wedged behind the rear wheels. I couldn't move the car." I shuddered. "At least I didn't try and use the four-wheel drive to climb over him."

Scott said, "Nor did he plop in your path."

"Close enough."

He touched my arm and asked, "Are you okay?"

"I've been better."

He pressed the OnStar system button. In a few seconds a

voice came through the radio speakers. He told them to send the police. They didn't need to ask where we were. The satellite system would pinpoint our location.

Scott took out his cell phone and dialed our attorney. Todd had gotten to the interstate but promised to come back immediately.

Scott turned off the windshield wipers and then the engine. He left the headlights on so the police would be able to spot us more easily. The rain thudded on the roof. I pulled my jacket tighter around me. It was a warm, furry one I'd purchased when we were in Provincetown last summer.

"Cold?" he asked.

I nodded. He turned the engine back on and turned up the heater.

"Did you know him?" Scott asked.

"A leader of the suckups. I didn't know him all that well."

"I think I remember you talking about him. The African American Nazi?"

"Yep." I sighed. "It's going to be a long night."

"He was a leader?" Scott asked.

"He went out drinking with the gang every Friday night. That was their criterion for letting you into the group's secrets."

Scott said, "Did they have a secret handshake?"

"Only if it involved fewer than two steps."

"You used to go out with the staff, didn't you? I remember stories of mild escapades."

"Years ago. Not with these people, and *mild* is the operative word. We were young. We went out. We were enjoying the world. We weren't trying to shove our crap down everyone else's throats."

"Which does seem to be the operative problem tonight," he said.

"It was, until this guy decided to nap under my tires."

Twirling red and blue lights interrupted our morbid repartee.

It was the same two detectives. Gault said, "You again."

"I found another one," I said.

Half an hour later, I was being interviewed. We stood under umbrellas in the pouring rain. Scott always kept an extra one in the car. He made sure we had one in both cars, along with a first-aid kit, flares, the OnStar system, and every other crisis-management equipment devised for auto travel. He used to keep a full gas can in the back of his car. I had put my foot down about that, but the likelihood was that he stopped only because carrying extra gas had been ruled hazardous.

Cars' headlights, more rotating Mars lights, and cop floodlights illumined the scene.

"You know this guy?" Gault asked.

"Yep."

"Colleague."

"Yep."

"This guy know the other corpse?" Gault asked.

"We were in the same department."

"They friends or enemies?"

"They were on the same side in the fights."

"They get along?"

"As far as I know."

"You fight with him?"

"Never directly."

"What does that mean?"

"We had differing views on some issues, but we never disagreed in public. I never had a private discussion of educational philosophy with him." I added the bit about the anti-Semitic remark.

Scott asked, "How did he die?"

Gault said, "We're waiting for the medical examiner."

"Did he die here?" I asked.

Gault said, "When we can tell you something, we'll let you know. For now, stick around."

My attorney said, "No."

Gault glared at him.

I said, "I'm tired. I'm hungry. I didn't kill him. I'm going home. Unless you're going to charge me, I'm not staying. You have my address. My car hasn't moved. Scott will drive me home."

My attorney nodded.

Then Vulmea asked, "Mr. Carpenter, may I have your autograph? For my kids."

They always added "for my kids." I sighed. Scott is unfailingly polite. The cop held out a scrap of paper. Scott signed.

⊾ 13 ⊿

At home I changed into jeans, thick white socks, and a heavy sweatshirt. I checked our messages while Scott began putting dinner together. I had a call from Meg Swarthmore. She wanted to know if I was all right and if I needed to cancel our usual Friday-morning breakfast. The message said that no call from me meant that breakfast was on. I didn't call.

For dinner Scott warmed some spinach-cheddar soup he'd made the other day. I unpacked fixings for sandwiches. Two kinds of Genoa salami, plus ham, roast beef, prosciutto, sharp cheddar cheese, hot olive salad, sliced tomatoes, toasted bread, olive oil, a dash of vinegar. We started with soup.

Scott said, "I'm worried about you."

"Thanks."

"This is more stress than any teacher needs."

I said, "It's not the kids, it's the adults that drive me nuts. Murder. This is insane."

Scott said, "Aside from the corpses, the part I don't get is crowd after crowd rushing to you for help. Certainly, I'd pick you as the one to go to, and frankly they're right, but it doesn't make sense. Did I get this right? The suckups and the old guard came for help, and the administration wants some kind of intervention."

I said, "Maybe they could all just die. It would make my life easier." The soup was great reheated. He'd been downloading recipes from the Food Network and trying them. Over the years he'd become a reasonably decent cook.

Scott said, "The administration put up with a lot of verbal abuse from you."

"I guess I was kind of rude."

"Kind of?"

"Okay, I was honest to a fault."

He sighed. "The real question is, *why* did they put up with it?"

"They want something. They're in on it? One of them is in on it and has the others duped? Some odd combination is going on there. I'm most pissed about Benson and Frecking. Those two assholes are going to pay."

"What are you going to do?"

"Talk to them."

"That doesn't sound lethal."

"How the hell do people just lie like that?"

"They did. They aren't the first ones. They won't be the last. They're desperate."

"I thought that closeted stuff was on its way out."

"Less so than we thought, I guess. Although the lies in this case might have more to do with that Benson guy being married. Two-timing, gay or straight, does have a way of making a guy reticent."

"Yeah, well, their butts are going to be in a sling."

"Will they be fired?"

"I'm not sure how the cops are going to handle it. I don't know if they'll tell the administrators. I don't think the making out had anything to do with the murder. The cops aren't required to tell the administrators anything about their investigation. It might depend on how well the administrators know the cops."

"They didn't seem to. They came to you for help."

"I don't know." I bit into the sandwich, thick with condiments. I dipped one end into a small bowl of hot olive salad to absorb some of the oil, took another bite, then grabbed a spoon to pick up some of the olives. Comfort food.

After I finished chewing, I said, "What I don't get is why Peter Higden is dead. That makes no sense. Of course, the first murder already made no sense."

"And what was he doing under your car?"

"Not much."

"That is a very old joke."

"And not a very good one."

More chewing and almost a smile. Another swallow, more soup, some spicy olives. I said, "Two suckups die. The most logical suspicion has to rest on the old guard."

"Did you see Jourdan again after you two talked?"

"No. The cops will have to be around again in the morning. By the time we left almost everybody was gone, and it was late. They can't very well roust everybody out of bed in the middle of the night."

"Gault and Vulmea?" Scott said. "I wouldn't put it past them. They seemed to be willing to push efficiency to the point of tediousness."

"We'll have cops swarming around the school tomorrow. At least it's a teachers' institute day so there won't be any kids."

"Who benefits from those two dying?" Scott asked.

"I'm not sure anybody does. The old guard cannot be assured of nonsuckups being hired. In fact, it would be the other way around. A younger teacher might be appointed to fill Eberson's position, but murder for such a nothing job? I can't see how anyone would benefit. Certainly, it's not someone who's obvious."

Scott said, "If it was, there wouldn't be a mystery."

"Don't be snarky. It's obvious to the killer. Not to us."

"One killer?" Scott asked.

"Got to be," I said. "Two dead bodies and it happens to be coincidental? The first one is obviously murder. You don't cram an eraser down somebody's throat accidentally."

"It had to be somebody strong," Scott said.

"Presumably. Or at least someone who surprised her. Before she realized what was happening, it was too late."

"Or he hit her first, then crammed it in."

"Or she, let's not discriminate. Lots of women in the department. The second one could have been explained as an accident up to the point where the body was under my car."

"Maybe it was a hit and run," he said. "It could have been thrown from where it was hit and landed there."

"More likely someone was trying to frame me and dragged it there. Then Benson and Frecking lying. That strikes me as at least partly a frame-up." I shrugged. "I'm not sure what this all means."

"The police didn't say who they believed, you or those two guys."

"I was lucky Frank Rohde called and that our lawyer showed up."

"What are you going to do tomorrow?"

"I'm going to talk to Benson and Frecking. If I believed in beating the shit out of lying fucking assholes, they'd be at the top of my list."

"A not unreasonable thought, but I wouldn't recommend it. Nor would our attorney."

"I suppose not."

14

It was the middle of the night. I tossed and turned. Scott was asleep on his stomach. He had his arms under his pillow. It takes a lot to keep Scott from getting a good night's sleep. I slipped out of bed and headed into the living room. I took a book from a bookcase and a blanket out of the cupboard. I sat on the couch and snuggled in with the blanket close around me. The wind was up. Rain rattled against the windows. I'd picked an Agatha Christie mystery I hadn't read yet. I love her books, and dear Agatha is a mystery master, but she also puts me to sleep. There is such comfort in her surety and expertise. I read for a while. The house was quiet.

I thought about turning the heat up, but the flannel blanket was warm, and I was finally feeling drowsy. My eyes would start to close, then Peter Higden's face would rush into my imagination, and I would start back awake.

.15.

I awoke the next morning exhausted. A miserable night's sleep, finding both bodies, being involved in an investigation, and anger at Benson and Frecking's betrayal combined to enhance my apprehension and fear. Betrayal by friends, enemies, can be devastating and in this case endangered me and entangled me much deeper in a murder case.

Scott was up early. He had meetings that morning in Chicago with his agent and some advertising people. While I showered, shaved, and dressed, he hovered around me in his underwear. I knew he was trying to distract me for a little while. A video of him in his snug boxer briefs would prompt viewers to rush to a store to buy whatever brand he was wearing.

Okay, it was distracting, just not for long enough.

Scott drove me to breakfast. Meg would drive me to school. I wasn't sure when I'd get my car back. As Scott kissed me good-bye, he said, "If you need anything, call. And keep our lawyer's cell phone number handy. Don't be afraid to just chuck it all and come home. If you need me to, I'll cancel my meetings. I'm not sure I shouldn't anyway. I'll be back in time for lunch. I'll stop at school."

I thanked him and assured him I was all right—that I was meeting Meg for breakfast, so I'd be starting the day with a trusted ally. I told him I loved him, and he drove off.

The weather had cleared and the first cold snap of the fall was settling in.

For years Meg Swarthmore, the librarian at Grover Cleveland, and I had met on Friday mornings for breakfast. On institute days especially it was essential to fortify ourselves with gallons of caffeine and a decent breakfast in hopes of being able to keep alert, active, and awake during the day. The institutes could be more leadenly boring than the speeches by Mabel Spandrel at our departmental faculty meetings, although the institutes tended to have far less acrimony.

Meg saw me, hurried over, and gave me a quick hug. "You look awful." Direct and to the point, as always, one of the many things I liked about her.

I said, "I've been better." She wasn't much over five feet tall and was plump in a grandmotherly way. She was the ultimate clearing house for all school gossip. If there were secrets to be known, Meg, if not knowing all, would know a great deal.

The manager seated us in our usual corner. Meg used a cane these days. A year ago, she'd broken her right hip falling from a ladder in the library at school. She used the cane on occasion when her hip pained her. Mostly she used it to rap the tops of the desks of kids who were talking above a whisper in the library.

The waitress, familiar with us from our years of Friday breakfasts, asked if we'd heard about what happened at the school. I deflected her with noncommittal answers. She clucked in dismay at the state of education today and the incidence of violence among volatile teenagers.

When she left, Meg asked, "Did you really almost run over Peter Higden?"

I said, "Almost. He was on the ground behind my car. He was already dead."

"How did he die?" Meg asked. Her voice was a whisper. "I received phone calls last night, each rumor more ludicrous than the last."

"However they killed him, after they did it, they put his body behind my car."

"To implicate you in some way."

"I was lucky. If I'd run over him, there would have been evidence. As it stands, though, the simplest forensic investigation will show there isn't any residue of his death under my car."

Meg said, "A logical deduction to make based on where the body wound up is that we've got a stupid killer who is trying to implicate you."

I said, "Or he wasn't killed by being run over. I didn't see any blood. He must have been murdered somewhere else, them moved. They could have killed him somewhere else in the parking lot and planted him near my tires. I don't know where he parks his car."

"Lots of possibilities."

I said, "And if I'd just bulled ahead with my car and run over him, it would complicate my situation. I'm not sure how accurate they can be in determining when he died if it's a matter of minutes, but I'd sure like to know what the police estimate is."

"Thank god you stopped. And all this, after your having been the one to find Gracie—I'm surprised you have the wherewithal to go in today."

"To not come in might suggest that there was something I had to feel guilty about. Plus I want to have a little talk with Brandon Benson and Steven Frecking."

"What happened?"

I told her the story from the beginning. Our food arrived in the middle of my tale, a fruit medley and plain toast for her and an omelet with tomatoes and feta cheese for me.

When I was done with my story, she said, "You were lucky with the police. Hell, after all that, I might have thought about arresting you."

I said, "They were officious, tough, typical. I've got to remember to thank Frank Rohde for putting in a good word for me. The oddest thing, besides the murders, was the different groups that came to ask me for help. Both the suckups and the old guard want union protection, and the administrators think I can get them inside information."

"Frank Rohde is a friend of yours. They're kind of right."

"As if I'd help them."

Meg said, "With two of the suckups dead, it's got to look like the old guard did it. Or at least they need to be questioned."

"Jourdan was pretty nervous," I said

Meg said, "I think the suckups did it. I think they'd devour their own. It would be a convoluted conspiracy, but that's the best kind of conspiracy, a convoluted one."

"But why do all that?" I asked.

"They're nuts? Because they can? Those people have never made sense to me. I think they are capable of any lie, any distortion, using any insane self-justification."

"Proving there's some vast conspiracy is another issue."

Meg said, "Look at those threatening notes Pinyon got. I heard the same rumor you did, that he wrote them himself. I never noticed the administration paying particular attention to them or doing much to investigate at the time."

"Maybe they did but didn't tell you."

Meg said, "They don't consult me quite as often as I'd like. With the rise of the suckups, I've been getting less gossip."

I said, "Maybe word is out that you're not a back-stabbing Nazi."

"Shows they got that right. Maybe they're only ninety-nine percent stupid instead of one hundred percent."

I said, "I'm not sure that's much of a difference."

Meg said, "Something that doesn't make a lot of sense to me is that Graniento, our idiot principal, has encouraged dissidents to come to him, yet it's the suckups and Mabel Spandrel who are in the driver's seat in the English department. They wouldn't have to go to Graniento; Spandrel is already on their side."

"I'm not sure of the politics of the whole thing. Spandrel and Graniento could be working together, but to do what? They're already in charge. Nuts as they are and as revolting as they may be, I don't think they'd lead a rebellion against themselves. Even they aren't that dumb."

Meg said, "Maybe they want to be superintendent and assistant superintendent. Although I'm not sure what the hell for. It doesn't make a lot of sense. However, I don't think those two are the most dangerous. If I was going to pick an administrator who I think was capable of killing someone, I'd pick Bochka."

"Technically she's a school board member, not an administrator."

"Usually you're not quite so punctilious," Meg said.

"Sorry, I'm a little shook up this morning."

"Understandable," Meg said. "You're forgiven. My money's on Bochka, the overdressed Nazi bitch, not that I want to prejudice you against her."

"We're not supposed to call them Nazis."

"So says the right wing who want to control us and the language we use. Those people are what they are, and Nazi describes it perfectly. Especially Bochka. That woman's got murder in her beady little eyes. Anyone who wears that many designer outfits can't be right in the head. Or who can afford that many."

I noted Meg's understated jeans and sweater.

"Bochka's a killer?"

"She's got my vote," Meg said.

"What would she have to gain?" I asked.

"Maybe at those conventions school board members go to they have competitions. Who can make the most teachers miserable, who can be most autocratic, who can be the most penurious . . ."

"Penurious?"

"I can be a walking dictionary just as much as you. I bet they get points for which one is the biggest asshole. It's like this big competition."

I said, "And if you murder a teacher you get bonus points?"

"Think about it," Meg said. "Competition would explain a lot about their loony behavior. Remember when they wanted to build a new junior high but call it a middle school? Not a one of the board members understood the difference between the two concepts or what it would take to build one or the other. Of course, the good old voters shot that one down, as usual, so the board got nothing for all its trouble. Who in their right mind wants to be on a school board? Or why would anyone with an ounce of sense want to be a school administrator?"

"I've known some good ones," I said.

"Whose fault is that?" Meg asked. She shook her head. "I'm being too harsh, sorry. Being a school administrator is a thankless job. Everybody hates you: kids, teachers, the union, parents, your bosses. You get pressure from everyone and satisfaction from none."

"A few of the administrators, some board members, too, have been kind people who would listen and really want to help. Not many." I shrugged. "Maybe it's something simpler. Maybe they want to fire all the old-guard teachers."

"It could be part of some huge sinister plot to do that, but they could accomplish the same thing by doing their paperwork. It's not that hard to fire a tenured teacher, despite what the right-wing assholes would have everyone believe about how powerful unions are. How would resorting to murder help any of that?"

I said, "Depends on who gets accused of murder and who they kill. Still, murder just doesn't seem a logical response. They already think it's easier to make a teacher miserable and get him or her to quit than to do their administrative jobs. You know the drill. Look what they've tried to do to Jourdan in the past year."

Jourdan had been under pressure to change the way he'd been teaching. He lectured to the kids and put them to sleep. Same lectures. Same stories. No projects. No group work. No changes. Nothing that connected to their lives or anyone else's. The kids in his classes did the same thing day after day: desperately try to stay awake. He needed to change. As usual, the lazy-ass administrators wanted to accomplish this by bullying, commanding, and/or breaking the contract. All they would have needed to do was file some paperwork, do a bit of homework and follow-up, and make recommendations that have logic behind them, mixed with cajoling and authority. Some dare call this leadership.

I said, "Spandrel's been in there with her evaluation forms numerous times. I've had to talk to him and her. The meetings with the two of them are pretty nasty. But if Jourdan was angry enough, why kill Gracie Eberson? It would be much more effective to go after Spandrel. She's the one who wanted him to change."

"The whole situation isn't making sense," Meg said. "And speaking of not making sense—"

"And we were."

"I've heard of dissension in their ranks. They wrangle and fight among themselves, but then they go out drinking and partying and then everybody's best friends again. My problem with them conspiring among themselves to do each other in is that they'd almost certainly have had to plan what they were doing. I don't think they could organize any better than a first grader. They are not the brightest bunch."

"They may be stupid, but they're running things."

Meg said, "Remember when they tried to organize a strike before negotiations even began last time? I've seldom heard of anything stupider. Gracie and Peter were at the heart of that. Remember that huge meeting they called?"

"And they were the only ones who showed up to the meeting. Even the other suckups weren't willing to go along with that. But their lack of success at organizing didn't stop Gracie and Peter."

Meg said, "I heard they had buttons and fliers and banners and picket signs printed up and all set to go before the beginning of school, nearly a year ahead of time. Actually spent real money on it."

"What I never understood about all of that," I said, "was that if the suckups are total buddies with the administrators and the president of the school board—"

"And they seem to be."

"—then why would any of them be part of organizing a strike which assumedly the school board and the administration would be against?"

"Maybe all of them wanted a strike."

"But why? What does it gain any of them?"

Meg shook her head. "You're right. It doesn't make sense." She sighed. "I don't get the administrators."

"Does anybody? One thing I don't understand is why no one on the board stands up to Bochka. She's queen bee of that board, sure, but this isn't an absolute dictatorship, yet. Although I've seen them at meetings. They all seem to be best friends. Nobody dissents."

Meg said, "I told you I heard that Bochka was supporting the suckups, invited them to her home for a holiday party?"

"She denied supporting them."

"Well, she'd have to, but my source is unimpeachable."

I seldom asked Meg for her sources. That could be delicate, and she was a good friend. She'd never steered me wrong.

"Can your source get more information about them?"

"I will try." She shook her head. "How you maintain that neutrality between the two factions, I'll never know."

"Yeah, I hate the suckups and their stupidity, but I haven't noticed the old guard making a great case for themselves."

"They need a leader. Someone with sense and experience. You'd be my candidate."

"I've got enough balancing rival factions in my life. Navigating the maze of politics in the gay community would keep an army of lab rats busy into eternity and beyond. With halfway decent leadership in the English department this wouldn't be happening."

"But it is. I did pick up some hot gossip in all the flurry of calls last night. It seems our administrators and more than one school board member are under investigation for fixing test scores and inflating graduation rates."

This was hot new nonsensical educational crap brought about by the same people who thought killing other people's children based on colossal lies was acceptable behavior. The ostensible reason for No Child Left Behind was to help children. The real goal was to destroy the educational system and ruin or dilute the power of the teachers' unions. The mindless drones behind it wanted mobs of ticky-tacky drones to succeed them. What better way to do this but to institute endless testing that doesn't test kids' ability to think but their ability to memorize random bits of useless knowledge? Basic knowledge is important. Being able to be articulate and accurate about what you are thinking about is even more important. If you didn't produce enough drones, some administrators resorted to cheating. Grover Cleveland High School was on the dreaded "watch list." I had this vision of the watch list police coming to get administrators, taking them away in handcuffs to prisons where they would have no rights of habeas corpus.

I asked, "Is there proof?"

"Supposedly inspectors have been in. Notice Graniento and Spandrel have been around even less lately? Word is they're attending meetings to cover up the problem, and/or do paperwork on the problem."

"Who exactly is in on this?"

"I heard mentioned Graniento, Bochka, Towne, and Spandrel."

"They could lose their jobs and their careers."

"Yep. I'll try to get more for you."

I said, "Speaking of gossip, are Mabel and Gracie lesbians?"

"It's an odd question. Gracie always struck me as relentlessly heterosexual. She's got pictures of her husband and kids all over her desk in her classroom. He is a hunk. I'm sure the success of his coffeeshop has a whole lot to do with him being out front and smiling from the minute they open."

"You've been?"

"It's pretty much on my way to work. I like coffee. I'm curious and nosy. I like to check things out. He was worth checking out. If I wasn't a few paychecks short of retirement, I'd think about having an affair with him. I'd also have to be fifty years younger."

"What about Mabel?"

"Her I'm not so sure. You know she's married?"

"I guess I knew that. I'm not sure I ever cared before."

"Her husband writes those science fiction novels, but for his day job, he's some kind of fitness trainer. Supposedly he's a partner in that big fitness club they just built on Route 30 in Frankfort."

"Is he a stud, too?"

"I've never seen him. I think Mabel has kids, but they're older. She never struck me as lesbian."

"How about Gracie having an affair with a kid?"

"Nah. Gracie doesn't strike me as the type." Meg said, "That she only tutored boys isn't odd. You only get the kids who sign up."

"And supposedly Spandrel is the one who did the implying."

"Meaning she's turning on her friend?"

"That type would," I said. "They have no morals and no sense of loyalty or decency."

"You got that right," Meg said, "but it just doesn't make sense about her doing it with a kid. I mean, if she had several hundred males in there it might seem odd, or, I guess, having just one would be most suspicious, but it's a program run by the school. Kids just sign up. They don't know which teacher they're going to get. If she threw out all the girls and only kept one or two boys at a time, that might be something else. The evidence of the sexual activity in that storeroom most likely came from the two darlings you discovered."

"My guess is kids use the place, too. Hell, maybe other teachers do. Maybe everybody's been humping away in there and once again, I'm the only one missing the action."

"Well," Meg said, "I wasn't supposed to tell you, but . . ."

That elicited my first smile of a grim morning. I said, "I can't believe Benson and Frecking were so stupid as to deny even being in there."

"They must have left you and immediately started

planning their version. It wasn't a tough lie to tell. We were in this place instead of that place, and we were just talking. Doesn't take much."

I said, "I've seen some pretty stupid stuff in my years as union rep, but that's right up there with the stupidest."

"Did you really think the police believed them?"

"I couldn't tell. Benson and Frecking's story hung together. They weren't in the hall when the police first arrived. They could have easily gotten to Benson's classroom without being observed. It's right across from the washroom they were using."

"Why not use the classroom for their tryst?"

I said, "Too easy for a student to walk in on them, like I did in the storeroom. A bathroom is a more traditional venue for gay men, or at least a cliché, but their choice to have sex anywhere in school is dumb. I suppose which venue they chose was subject to chance and their belief in how safe they were. That stupid storeroom door does creak. I'm just still really angry that they tried to dump it all on me. They told an out-and-out lie. I'm flabbergasted."

"What are you going to do?"

"I've got to find out who committed the murders. The cops were not nice."

"What can you do?"

"Talk to people, I guess. I have strict instructions from my attorney not to say a word more to the police without him being present."

"Sensible advice. I'll snoop around a bit. There's got to be gossip. I could even indulge in the time-honored custom of sneaking around and listening in corridors."

"You wouldn't?"

"To catch a killer? Yeah. To find out what these people are up to? Yeah. Because I think these people are a danger to you? Yeah."

"I'm certainly under suspicion."

"Somebody's lying and that's got to stop, but there's at least one killer on the loose and that's more dangerous. We've got to find out who it is before they strike again."

I said, "Even if it's just another suckup that dies?"

I got a grim smile from her. "I wish it were that simple. You hate to think of the killer branching out to someone we like. And I'll talk to Victoria Abbot, the assistant superintendent. I knew her mother, who was also a teacher. Maybe I can find out what she knows. Or at least get her to talk to you."

16

The did-they-arrest-Mabel-Spandrel question was answered when I walked in the school door and saw her surrounded by a bevy of suckups including Milovec, Pinyon, and Looie the Loon. All traces were gone of the near-tears from the night before. Their voices murmured and then Spandrel's laughter rang through the corridor. It sounded brittle and forced.

When I walked into the school's main office that morning, Georgette Constantine, the school secretary, gave me a brief hug. "How are you holding up?" she asked. "Is there something I can do for you?" Georgette often presented a befuddled persona to the world. I'd long ago learned that behind the veneer of dim-wittedness was a smart, tough secretary who was an expert at every computer program used in the school district. She saved many a teacher at grading time.

"Thanks. I think I'm okay."

She said, "It must have been awful."

I said, "I still shudder when I think about them."

She said, "I'm sorry. I won't mention it again."

"It's okay. I don't mind friends being concerned." I leaned

over the counter. She moved closer. I said, "I've got to find out more about Peter Higden and Gracie Eberson."

She looked left, then right, then eased herself to the far end of the counter. I followed. Others in the office would be unable to overhear. She placed her elbows on the counter and leaned farther toward me. She said, "He was in this office day and night. That fake cheerfulness of his? What a pain in the ass. Some days I'd want to just slug him. And he always brought those plain, cheapo, crap doughnuts. Day-old, usually, and never chocolate-filled doughnuts." Frankly, this last was a hanging offense as far as I was concerned. "Unfortunately, besides being an obsequious dolt, he often had some business in here. He always had to talk to an administrator. There was always some kid who was complaining about him or some faculty member who was after him or some parent who was unhappy. Did you know that one of the staff referred to him by using the *n* word?"

I said, "I would have heard if that teacher was fired. He or she should have been fired."

"It was a scandal that no one is supposed to know about. Bochka was in here for hours. Some kind of deal was made."

I said, "Why would Higden make a deal, and what on earth could he get?"

"For someone on the staff being a racist and using the *n* word in front of him, I bet Higden could get a great deal. It's a big bargaining chip. What does he get in return for his silence? What's the biggest thing a fourth-year teacher needs?"

"Tenure?"

She nodded. "So now he had tenure. We all know he was one of the worst teachers around here."

I knew who "we" was. The secretaries in a school know everything, and if they don't, the custodians do and are happy to spread the news.

Teachers in Illinois have four years of probation before

they can be up for tenure. That fourth year was often fraught with tension. Higden had never brought any problems to me.

I said, "But he was one of the suckups. Why wouldn't Mabel Spandrel have given him tenure?"

"Who was it you think used the *n* word?"

This got a genuine gape out of me.

"Spandrel? Really?"

She nodded.

I said, "But Higden was on her side in the fights."

Georgette said, "I just report the facts. No one is supposed to know about the deal. Several people do. If it will help, feel free to use the knowledge, but please don't say who you heard it from."

I didn't question her. She was a good friend and a help. I said, "Of course." And I wouldn't. I always keep faith.

She said, "I couldn't stand Higden. None of us could, and while the administrators loved him, there were problems. No administrator is completely blind. I always assumed that's why he was sucking up so much: to get tenure. Some of them go that route. At the very least, they try to keep a low profile. If I hear anything else about that, I'll let you know."

We leaned back and sipped our coffee. I know she waited every year at about this time for Starbucks to come out with its pumpkin spice latte. We glanced around the office. It was still early enough that the lights weren't on and most of the staff wasn't in. Nevertheless, I leaned toward her again and asked, "Were Mabel Spandrel and Gracie Eberson having an affair?"

"Possible." She thought a few moments. "Not likely. They may have gone drinking to the same places together, but Portia sometimes went drinking with that crowd. She didn't say a thing about it."

Portia was one of the other secretaries. I asked, "Is Portia reliable?"

"As any of us. I'll check with her for sure."

I said, "Do you know anything about administrators fixing grades?"

A look of relief flooded over her face. She said, "Finally."

I gave her a quizzical look.

"You know how those new computer programs are designed to bamboozle people?"

I nodded.

"I studied them. I figured them out." She craned her neck around the office. No one was near us. She said, "No one, absolutely no one, is supposed to know this. The administrators have been at that program for months. They asked me once how to do something, but I chose to be my befuddled self." She fluttered her hand against the gold chain around her neck. "Good thing. They tried to get Portia to show them things, but Portia actually doesn't understand the program." She leaned close enough so she could whisper in my ear. "They wanted her to change grades."

"You're sure?"

"Portia has no reason to make that up. What they don't know is I can detail how and when people get into various programs in the office and even when they try to do it on the Internet from home. I also know where they keep the file of secret passwords."

"Georgette, that's dangerous."

"Not to me." Again she swiveled her head around. "How do you think the state got wind of something fishy going on in this district? These people have got to be brought down and brought down hard."

"Georgette, I've never been more honored to know you."

"Pah," she said, "these people are insane. They can't keep doing what they're doing and not get caught. I caught 'em. I'm proud of it."

"Do they know that?"

"Oh my, no. I'm very careful. No, the board and those administrators have been after the secretaries, trying to cut our benefits, extend our workload. We've had to fight like the teachers have, although some of us haven't been willing to fight. This way is perhaps more satisfying."

"Is the scandal going to be made public?"

"If I have anything to say about it."

"Who exactly does what?"

She looked around. Several of the other secretaries had come in.

I said, "Scott's coming in for lunch with Meg and me. Would you like to join us for lunch?"

She nodded.

A crowd of teachers looking for schedules for the day trooped into the office. Georgette grabbed a stack and began passing them out. When they left, she handed me one. She said, "If you need anything, you know all you have to do is ask."

I smiled at her. "I know. Thanks."

17

As I stepped into the hall, a weeping Francine Peebles rushed up to me. She carried a jumbo box of tissues with her. Trust Francine to move from ineffective peacemaker to hysterical mourner.

"You found the bodies." Her voice was just below a shriek. She grabbed tissues and wiped her face.

Milovec stomped up to me, "They should have called school off. Can't the union do something about that?" Instead of a tapered white shirt and garish tie, he wore a white T-shirt with a pocket and his trademark tight black jeans.

Francine said, "The students, oh my, the students. We should call school off for a week. Will they ever recover?"

From the week off? Gracie's and Peter's death were sad and certainly students may have felt close to them. I didn't see that as a reason for hysteria. I thought all the kids in both teachers' classes should be talked to Monday by a social worker and the principal. Then any students who wished to talk to a counselor should be allowed to do so. But, just like you can't vote against Santa Claus, you can't argue with death-driven unreason. Just ask the Republicans. They're masters at it.

Francine said, "Aren't we in danger? How can they keep the school open if we're in danger? Isn't there a killer on the loose?"

Milovec said, "Can you get them to call off school and not have to make up a day?"

Ah, the I'm-in-deep-mourning-as-long-as-its-convenient faction had been heard from. I said, "I'm sure they'll follow whatever is the protocol in these situations."

Francine said, "I'm frightened. The school district and the union have an obligation to keep us safe. I don't feel safe. We have to be safe. And the children on Monday, will they feel safe? I'm so frightened. What's the union going to do about it?"

To Francine I said, "Can I get you something? Would you like to sit quietly for a while? Do you need to lie down? I'm sure you could go home."

"Would they charge me with a sick day?"

She wasn't that distraught.

"Probably," I said.

"Well, then, I'll stay. I'll be able to comfort some of the other members of the staff. Or should I talk to Teresa Merton? I'll get some people together, and we'll talk to her. She'll make them keep us safe. You are going to do something about this?"

"This what?" I asked.

"None of us feels safe in the school." Once again she repeated her fears, paranoia, and hysteria.

If she repeated them enough times, I might be tempted to find my own supply of overlarge chalkboard erasers. I said, "We aren't the police. We don't have goon squads or a protection racket. This isn't some poorly written movie with a mafia-teamsters plot."

"The union has to do something!"

"You want armed guards to patrol the halls? To accompany all the teachers? You want one guard per teacher?"

"Something has to be done. We're not safe. You should talk to the superintendent."

I said, "You were right earlier. I believe the best person to talk to is Teresa Merton. I know she'll listen to your concern, and she'll know exactly what to do."

"Yes," Francine said. "You're right. What about the wake and the funeral? Are they going to call off school for both of those? If they're during school, are they going to allow us to take time off to go? Or will they pick representatives from among the faculty? I should be one of the representatives. I was close to both to them." This was news to me. Before I could respond to any of this, she was off down the hall in a flight of panic. I knew Teresa would have the right instincts: to put off Francine's request without getting Francine upset. I wasn't sure anything I would say at this moment would mollify Francine. I was leaning toward "Get out of my life" and "Grow up." Not as helpful in delicate situations as one would like.

I motioned Milovec farther down the corridor, away from any other teachers. I said, "About Peter Higden."

"You ran over him."

"No. I found him before I could drive over him. Do you have any idea who might have seen him last?"

"I don't know. Everybody's running around trying to figure that out."

"Did he talk to anybody after the meeting?"

"Not that I know of."

"If you find out anything, let me know. The more I know, the more I might be able to help you guys out."

He looked like he bought this. He left.

Georgette came out into the hall. "Victoria Abbot, our assistant superintendent, has officially told me to say she'd like to talk to you."

Meg had been busy. We stood off to one side of the office. "Is she available now?"

"She just went into a meeting with Bochka, Towne, Graniento, and Spandrel. I don't know what it's about." Georgette smiled. "She got a call from Meg a few minutes ago. Abbot is one of the few people around here who is likely to be on your side."

And the secretaries usually knew everything.

She added, "Did you know Graniento, Towne, and Bochka met until after one this morning?"

"What for?"

"That I don't know. Towne was complaining about the lateness when he came in."

"Were they meeting here?"

"I doubt it."

I said, "Carl Pinyon had tons of information about who went to out-of-district conferences."

"Yes," she whispered. "We've been going nuts the past few minutes trying to figure out how he got it. It will take us a while, but we should be able to figure this out. We secretaries keep a tight rein on things. The more recent data would be in the teachers' building files, but the old stuff is in storage. It would take hours and hours for several people to find all the data. It's strange. We're the only ones who go back there, and none of us have been in weeks. There's no reason to, and I'd know if someone had been back there for hours. I do the time sheets for all the secretaries and clerks. None of them has put in for excessive overtime, and it would take excessive overtime to find that stuff."

"Somebody is desperate," I said.

"Or out of their minds," Georgette said.

I said, "Was there much of an investigation when Pinyon reported getting those threatening notes?"

"Oh my, yes. We were told to keep an eye on the teachers' mailboxes. For a while they were thinking about getting surveillance cameras in the hall. There was no money for it

in the budget. He could have put the notes in there himself."
She shrugged. "Hard to tell."

The police made their presence known; detectives interviewing, uniformed officers patrolling the halls. They had all kinds of people to talk to about the Peter Higden murder. They were set up in a conference room near the main office of the school.

18

I didn't see Benson in the English department office. I wanted to confront the traitor. My first session for the day was supposed to be learning how to be a Web master. One of the teachers had taken a week-long, six-hours-a-day class. She was now going to teach us all she knew in one hour-and-a-half seminar. Maybe that's what she would do. Pity. An hour and a half was ridiculous.

Knots of teachers loitered in the halls. I found Benson lurking in his classroom.

"Go away," he said.

I said, "Fuck you, you lying son of a bitch." I stood in the doorway and decided I wasn't going to move. He was far slighter and shorter than Frecking. I wasn't going to wrestle the twerp, but I wasn't going to let him past me until I got some answers.

He said, "You're a shit for telling on us."

"I told the police you were there."

"You mentioned sex to them."

"After you denied you were there."

"They want a DNA sample."

"You're screwed."

"It's your fault."

"I'm not the closeted married man making out in storage rooms with dead bodies in the back. You lied about me, you shit. It's all going to come out."

"Am I going to lose my job?"

"It's likely."

"Doesn't the union have to help me? You're the union guy. I want someone else besides you as my rep."

"No," I said. "You don't get to choose."

We'd had this fight before in the district. The union decides who the reps will be. You don't get to pick and choose. What happens if the individual picks and chooses is that they usually select a friend who is neither qualified nor likely to know any of the proper procedures or rules of conduct, how to keep notes, or ins and outs of the contract and is as big a fool as himself. It's nearly like when clients say they want to represent themselves at trial, only this time they want their best friend to be their lawyer. That's why they created professionals, to be used and paid for.

He said, "I want someone else."

I said, "Fine, we'll waste our time looking for Teresa Merton. She'll tell you the same thing."

"Well, you've got to help me. Somebody does."

"Has to? For this conversation, you need to focus on the lies you told. In fact, you might want to consider resigning before the administration finds out what you were doing. It'll be easier on you and your record if you do."

"We weren't doing anything that odd. A whole lot of other people have done the same thing."

"Very probably true. Again, you have the getting-caught-in-a-lie issue, a big problem when you already have a dead-body issue."

"Don't you understand? I had no choice in what I said. I couldn't admit what I was doing. My wife would kill me."

Which would add to our corpse count. At the moment, if his wife strangled the stupid shit, I would lead the cheering. As long as I wasn't the one who found the body.

I said, "There are always choices. The union will give you professional representation in contractual matters. My memory might be a little shaky, but I don't think the contract has a permissible fucking-in-storage-rooms clause. I've got questions this morning, and I expect the truth. Maybe the administration won't find out. Maybe because you're in the suckup faction, you'll get away with it. I don't know. Sometimes I get the impression that being in the suckup faction could save you even if you raped a nun at high noon in the cafeteria. You people are a menace."

"Go ahead, be nasty. Do you think it's helping?"

"I'd be happy to threaten you with telling the administration if you don't give me answers to questions."

"Will you help me if I answer them?"

"There's no question that I'm going to help you. Don't start that the-union-rep-refused-to-help-me crap. We can meet with Teresa Merton if you like. She will listen and then turn things over to me. However, I may be convinced to keep silent. That depends on your answers. To be totally honest, as a union building rep, at this moment my advice would be as I said earlier: if I were you, I would find a way to quit. Today."

"I can't. My wife will find out."

I sighed. "You really want to live your life as a closeted gay man?"

"I'm not gay."

I wanted to beat him into insensibility. I also understood. Every gay man understands being in the closet.

I said, "Let's try a few questions."

102

He shrugged.

Better than a flat no.

I asked, "Do you know if Gracie Eberson and Mabel Spandrel were having an affair?"

"I never believed the rumors. They did meet for drinks, but meeting for drinks isn't an indicator of two people having an affair. Sometimes I went out with the crowd. My wife usually came with. Some of the wives and husbands do."

"How about rumors of Gracie having an affair with a student?"

"I never heard of anything."

I asked, "Do you know where Carl Pinyon got his statistics?"

"No idea." I couldn't tell if he was lying.

"Any notions on what those hate notes he got were all about?"

"No."

"How well did you know Peter?"

"Higden was a shit. A total shit. He only cared about himself. I never trusted him. He could be charming. A few of the stupidest parents loved him. All the kids loved him. He was sneaky. He was one of the administration's main spies."

"How did he spy?"

"He'd report anything he heard."

"I thought you all did that."

"Some of us were loyal."

"Loyal to whom?"

"Who was going to give us tenure? The union can't save our asses if they don't give us tenure."

It was useless to pursue a debate on loyalty. I asked, "Was Peter there when you went out drinking?"

"Sometimes. It wasn't always the same people. It kind of varied. I didn't take attendance."

"Did you have an affair with him?"

"No."

"Give him a blow job in the storage room?"

"No. This is getting absurd."

I said, "You got that right. What I don't get is why you people are so desperate to do all these things?"

"What things?"

"Inflict your semi-valid theories and practices on people with their own semi-valid theories. What does it gain you? How do you profit from people fighting? From people hating each other?"

"Hey, I don't do any planning. I'm just trying to do what I think is best for kids. I get caught up in the fights because the other side is so unreasonable." Many members of the old guard were unreasonable. It would be so great if one side was all good and the other was all bad.

"And you thought being part of fights was helpful to this, how?"

"Look," he said. "I know you're angry. I guess I'm stuck with you as union guy, but I don't know any of this shit. Do you really think I should resign?"

"Yes."

He thought a few moments, then shook his head. "I just can't."

I said, "If you change your mind, talk to me. If the administration wants to talk to you, I suggest you find me before you do. My strong recommendation is you not talk to them without a union rep present."

I left.

Georgette ran into me in the hallway near the office. She handed me a note, leaned over, and whispered, "Read that."

19

It was a note from Victoria Abbot, the assistant superintendent. It said to meet her outside the teachers' parking lot entrance immediately. I was already late for my assigned seminar. I passed through the library on my way to our tryst and mentioned it to Meg.

I finished, "I don't know her."

"She tries to fly below everybody's radar. She navigates the politics of this district like a fish in a hurricane."

"Huh?"

"As far under water as possible. If any administrator in this district can be trusted, it would be she. Just don't press your luck."

As I was turning to go, I said, "If I don't come back, I want at least one person to know where I was going."

"You're that suspicious?"

"I'd like to believe I don't need to be."

The assistant superintendent was not among the huddle of teachers and custodians catching a quick smoke outside the building. I walked a few steps into the parking lot. The wind gusted but the rain had cleared. It was a perfect, crisp, clear, autumn morning. I looked over at the line of administrators' cars in their assigned parking spaces, the ones nearest the entrance, a sore spot and cause of vicious fights at the negotiations table. In the driver's side of a black SUV I saw someone gesturing toward me. I walked closer. It was Abbot. I hurried forward.

Her window slid down as I got closer. She peered in each direction and said, "Get in."

I did.

She put the car in gear and pulled out of the parking lot. I glanced at the trees and lawns of suburban quiet and dismissed thoughts of wild kidnappings.

"What's going on?" I asked.

"Meg talked to me. She was a dear friend of my mother's. I'm scared."

"Of what?"

She said, "You need to be very, very careful. I can't say much. I'm sorry." She seemed to peer at each passing car, examining the drivers and passengers.

"Careful about what?"

"Everything you do and say."

"I beg your pardon."

"I can tell you a little, but please, please, don't ask me for more. I'm trying to help. Truly, I am. And please don't tell anyone we talked. Please just listen."

"I'm listening."

"Part of the reason I can't tell you much is that I don't know much. Bochka, Graniento, Towne, and Spandrel are in this up to their eyeballs."

"In what?'

"Everything." At LaGrange Road she turned right and headed south.

"You wouldn't want to be a bit more specific about that?"

"I can't."

"Did they kill Eberson and Higden?"

"I don't think so. No. I'm warning you about keeping yourself safe."

"Are they planning to kill me?"

"They don't have that kind of nerve. I don't think." She pulled into the parking lot of a new Starbucks near the entrance to Interstate 80. She maneuvered the car far away from all the others and let it idle.

"Then what is it?"

Her hands gripped the steering wheel. Her face was white with fear. Her eyes darted around the parking lot. Any car that got close was subject to inspection.

"Are you afraid someone is following us?"

"That we might be seen together."

"Why is that bad?" I asked.

"This whole thing is a mess. Murder! In my school! I've had a terrific career in education. I've loved it. I still love it."

"Are they trying to fire you?"

"They can have the damn job. I'd prefer to go back to being an elementary PE teacher. That was bliss. Little ones running about. That was the good part about being in education. Bochka, Graniento, Towne, and Spandrel are in on something together. They may be trying to fire you."

"For what?"

She said, "This is just terrible."

I was exasperated. "Are you going to tell me what 'this' is?"

"I can't. I just can't. Just be careful. Trust no one. Absolutely no one. Including me. It's a good thing you've got a lawyer. I hear he's good."

I said, "Have they been having secret meetings?"

"I've been to at least one meeting at Bochka's house. You weren't mentioned at that time. I think there may have been other meetings that I was not at. They don't completely trust me."

"What do they discuss at these meetings?"

"The one I was at was about the next textbook adoption. They want to pick the book themselves, without the teachers."

"Don't they realize that will cause another huge fight?"

"Yes."

"Why not use the current system?"

"Because they can't control a faculty committee."

"Were Eberson and Spandrel having an affair?"

She gaped at me. "They were at the meeting with me. They didn't strike me as a couple. They have husbands."

"Was Higden there?"

"Yes. I don't know him well."

"You know anything about the threatening notes Pinyon received?"

"First I heard of them."

I said, "There was a rumor mentioned last night that Spandrel was going to resign as head of the department."

"I've heard no such thing. Can you imagine the fights?"

I could. I said, "Do you have any notion of how Carl Pinyon could have gotten the information about who had gone to out-of-district seminars? He had information going back thirty years."

"Didn't he think people would ask that question? That's kind of bold."

"If he's being protected by Graniento, Spandrel, Bochka, and Towne, he'd have nothing to fear."

"I don't know where he got it."

She put the car back in gear and began to drive back to school.

I said, "Do you want me to scoot down in the seat so I won't be seen?"

"It's not funny. People have died."

I said, "Or I could get out a block or two before we get to school."

"We may have to do that."

"What the hell is going on?"

"Fear. Danger. Everything. Be afraid. Be very afraid."

"Are you threatening me?"

"No. No. No. I'm trying to help." She was near tears. "Just believe me. You need eyes in the back of your head."

Two blocks from school she pulled to the side of the road. I looked at her. She was shaking.

"Why are you doing this?" I asked.

"Because it's the right thing to do. I wish I could do more."

"Are you afraid someone is going to try and kill you?"

"No. Don't be absurd." She looked at me. "They wouldn't."

"Spandrel, Graniento, Towne, and Bochka?"

"Anyone. I think we'd all better be very careful."

"Do you want me to get out here?" I asked. I wasn't sure if I would.

She looked at me. She looked at the road, the sun, the sky, the grass, the houses, and then me again. She said, "This is madness." She drove to her parking spot and let me out.

"Thanks," I said.

She said, "Be careful." As my hand was on the door, she said, "Don't worry about missing the first seminar. I've fixed it. You were meeting with one of the LD teachers about an emergency staffing for a kid."

"Thanks," I said.

I didn't care about the seminar. I hurried to the library. Meg was behind a stack of books she was beginning to catalogue.

I said, "She told me to beware of Graniento, Bochka, Spandrel, and Towne."

"Good advice."

"But she wouldn't tell me to beware of what."

"Everything. You should talk to Ludwig Schaven. I saw him earlier. He was in tears."

"He wasn't last night."

"He was upset this morning and claiming that no one would listen to him. You might be the perfect person for him to unburden himself to."

⌐ 20 ⌐

I didn't see Schaven anywhere. I waited for Carl Pinyon outside the gradebook seminar. When he came out, I said, "Can I
talk to you for a few minutes?"

He looked uncomfortable.

I said, "It might help with what you guys were asking me
about last night."

He nodded.

We slipped into my classroom.

I said, "I'm curious to know where you got your figures
about who went to which seminars going all that far back."

"How will that help you find out information from the
police—and find the killer, for that matter?"

"Maybe someone thought you uncovered something
shady in their going to conferences—fraud in submitting
travel vouchers, illegal or improper or unethical activity of
some kind. Maybe your information was the motive for murder. Cheating on travel vouchers, depending on the amount
of money, could be a serious problem for someone."

"I can't tell you where I got it."

I said, "Maybe Eberson and Higden had knowledge that you had. You're not worried that you could be next?"

And if he wasn't, maybe I could get the idea planted in his head, get it to fester, and thus get more information out of him. It was worth a try.

"No one kills over that kind of stuff, do they?" He sounded uncertain.

I said, "You couldn't have asked all the people involved. Some of them are retired and even if you got in touch with them, they would be suspicious and unlikely to answer. From that long ago, a few could even be dead. I'd have heard if you were asking those kinds of questions of people currently on the staff. The information has to have come from their files. Everybody has to submit paperwork when they take a trip somewhere, and a copy is kept in their permanent file. Either the people with legitimate access did all the work for you, or you went through all those files yourself. That would have taken a lot of work for one person. My guess is it would have taken hours and hours for several of you. No one is allowed into the personnel files except administrators."

"I've done nothing wrong. You should be concentrating on who's been stealing stuff from other teachers. People always accuse the progressives of being spies for the administration. Well, the other faction has been stealing things from our classrooms."

This was not a new accusation either.

I said, "That is not a union issue."

"And who went where on what conference is a union issue?"

"Not really."

"But you're asking about it. If you ask about one, you should ask about the other."

Pinyon was short and stout. The way someone who has stopped working out once he got married would look after about three years of continuing to eat at the rate and in the quantities he did when he exercised.

I said, "Remember, you guys came to me yesterday."

"To find out what happened to Gracie—and now Peter, I guess. That means someone from that ancient faction must have been angry enough to kill."

"They'd be angry at whoever got that information. Maybe you're next. Did Peter and Gracie help you get it?"

"Ah . . . no."

If a teenager had spoken with that hesitation and look away, I would have said he lied.

I switched to a different track of questions. "Did Peter have enemies?"

"No. He was a real friendly guy. He was always ready to go out and party. He was great. Knew all the best places for drink specials. He knew how to throw a party. I don't guess anybody would be really angry with him."

"Maybe he made an anti-Semitic remark in front of someone who didn't like it."

"Hey, he didn't mean those things. He was just trying to be funny."

"Were other people laughing?"

"Sure."

"No one stood up and said, 'Stop that, I find it offensive'?"

"He was just being funny. He made comments about all ethnic groups. Arabs, Jews. Everybody. He's got free-speech rights."

The good old First Amendment defense reared its head. I said, "Because he has First Amendment rights doesn't put him above criticism. It doesn't mean somebody else isn't offended. I assume you also think the offended person has free-speech rights to say they are offended? Did you hear him make those kinds of remarks?"

"I guess. Sure."

"And it didn't offend you?"

"Everybody was laughing. It was a joke. Look, I'm not here to be criticized by you."

I said, "Did he fight with anyone in the young teachers' faction?"

"No. Never."

"Was he always that overbearingly friendly with everyone?"

"Sure."

There had to be people besides Benson and the old guard who found him offensive. If Benson was annoyed, maybe others in his faction were, too.

21

I hustled to the second seminar and arrived on time. It was a group-dynamic seminar presented by someone who lectured the entire time. So much for her belief in group work. At least it wasn't another one of those ninnies with their multi-colored Post-it notes, replacing product with process. Yes, yes, paying attention to process is vital, and you need to do the basics every time, but when process-is-the-product becomes a style of work, nothing ever gets done. At least she didn't pitch the fifty-third revision of our mission statement at us. Mission statement for schoolteachers—let's think about that, it's a tough one: to teach children? You might think that, but that would be wrong. Or at least, that simple statement doesn't involve enough process to justify some ninny's five-thousand-dollar fee for a seminar. I stayed awake throughout. I considered that a triumph. Mostly I stewed and brooded about factions and murder. Not so good.

Tammy Choate, the head of the GLSEN chapter at the school, found me as we were breaking for lunch. GLSEN is the Gay, Lesbian, Straight Education Network and does wonderful work with gay and lesbian teenagers. She and I had traded off duties running the group for a couple of years until she took it over completely. It was a relief for me to have one less responsibility.

She motioned me into an empty classroom. Tammy was an out lesbian, a slender attractive woman in her early forties. During the month before school ended during her first year, a student, who was a spy for the religious right, attended one of the GLSEN meetings. Tammy had mentioned the importance of safe sex. She hadn't asked if anyone was having sex or suggested that they do or do not engage in intimate activity, just that safe sex was important. She'd been warned about talking to kids inappropriately. A few parents had gone nuts. Bochka, the notorious school board president, had led the charge to get her fired. Tammy chose to take a warning letter in her file rather than fight. She was grateful for the job I'd done of stepping in and helping her out. She taught French to freshmen and sophomores.

She said, "You've heard all the rumors about Gracie and Mabel? That they're lesbians."

"Yeah. Do you know if it's true?"

She took a deep breath. "It's true," she said. "I'm afraid it's going to come out, and there's going to be a scandal. And it might reflect on the GLSEN teen group. Or me. I don't know if I can go through a fight."

"How would them being lesbians affect the group or you?"

"Anything that makes us look bad can have a negative effect."

"But the kids aren't involved."

"It can hurt."

"Are you sure the rumor is true?"

"Yes, they used my apartment in the city for their trysts."

Well, there was confirmation in trumps and spades.

"You mean they stayed overnight."

"They couldn't stay overnight. They were both married. A lot of those supposed shopping trips and dinner and drinks at trendy north side bars?"

I nodded.

"Not happening."

"Did you go out with them?"

"A few times. They were fun to go drinking with. Mabel could be hysterically funny."

I tried to put this delicately, "You were never invited to join them?"

"In the bedroom? No. I have a lover. You've met Bernice." I vaguely remembered a heavy-set woman.

I said, "You weren't worried about drinking with the head of the department?"

"She wasn't head of my department."

"How'd this all get started?"

"I was on some stupid cross-curricular committee with them. We'd go to lunch together. We had great times. We started going out in the evening. Sometimes it was just a girls' night out. Sometimes others would join us, most often Peter Higden, sometimes Ludwig Schaven and Basil Milovec, maybe a few others."

"Were Higden, Schaven, and Milovec in on the sexual activity?"

"We all stopped at my place, but Schaven and Milovec were never there without me being there."

"You sure?"

"What do you mean?"

"Maybe they went back when it was only supposed to be Eberson and Spandrel."

"I can't imagine Schaven. He's very involved with his kids. He wouldn't have the time."

"He had time to go drinking."

"That was once in a while."

"You left Higden out of the list of who was there when you weren't."

"Spandrel and Eberson would laugh about him. He said he enjoyed doing it with two women. Should I be telling you this? I'm so worried."

We'd always trusted each other. I said, "It might help catch the killer."

"Oh right. Well, I'm not sure how this would, but Spandrel and Eberson said Higden wasn't as good as something hand-held. That he wasn't very . . ." She lowered her voice. "Big."

"Oh," I said. More information than I needed, but I wasn't going to stop her either.

"And," her voice got even lower, "not just small, but really small, and that he wasn't very good. He got done in minutes—sometimes seconds. The three of us would laugh about it. Is that terrible?"

"I don't think so. For Peter, maybe—not for you. Has Spandrel tried to talk to you at all today?"

"I tried to find her, but she's been in meetings all morning."

"You were buddies with that faction," I said. "What did they say about the old guard in the English department?"

"They never said anything about you. That might have been because they know we've worked together with the gay kids."

I asked, "Did they ever talk about why they were so desperate to impose their views on the rest of us?"

"Not really. Mostly we were out partying and having a good time. They'd make fun of the people in the other faction sometimes."

"Spandrel would make fun of other staff members in front of teachers in the department?"

"I know she isn't supposed to, but she would sometimes." She shook her head and said, "As long as none of this comes down on the kids or me."

"I wouldn't worry," I said.

She ran her hands through her clipped-short hair. "Two friends of mine are dead. It's just so awful." She sniffed and gulped. "And I'm a little scared. What if the deaths had something to do with them being together? Could Spandrel be in danger? Could Spandrel be . . ."

"A killer?"

"She wouldn't. She couldn't."

"She might have been afraid of Eberson or Higden or you telling."

"I never would. They never had. None of us would. Why be afraid now?"

Good questions to which I had no answers.

22

I hurried to the library to find Meg. When I walked in, Scott was sitting behind the circulation desk. I smiled. We hugged briefly. He asked, "You okay?"

I nodded.

Meg strode in. She said, "Let's blow this dump."

On institute days teachers had an hour for lunch.

We picked up Georgette in the office and left. Meg drove. I filled them in on what I'd learned.

When I finished, Meg told us what she found out. "I have a confirmation on the lesbian affair angle as well."

Scott said, "I don't get it. Who cares if they're lesbians?"

I said, "They were both married."

"To guys?" Scott asked.

"Yep."

Scott said, "Maybe the husbands were pissed off."

"One or both," Georgette added.

Meg said, "My sources say neither spouse knew about the infidelity. Medium-reliable on the source."

Meg had a classification system for her sources, from unreliable to medium to very reliable.

We stopped at the Pancake Palace on LaGrange Road.

Georgette asked, "Is somebody saying that one of them would break into the school, or sneak into the school, and kill his wife's lover or his wife?"

"It could happen," Meg said, "although it doesn't strike me as probable."

I said, "Having tawdry affairs is way up there on the gossip meter, but I'm not sure it adds up to murder. Although if either husband knew . . ." I shrugged. "That could change things."

Scott said, "Isn't this all kind of sordid? This school district is like *Peyton Place* on speed."

I said, "You've heard my stories over the years. Obviously murder is out of the ordinary, but tawdry affairs, sure." Plus, I'd been in on union meetings where I heard about adults behaving in ways that most people would find extremely odd.

Meg said, "If Peter Higden was doing three-ways with them, it's a connection. It's sexual. It's got passion. It's just not clear if that is the connection that led to murder."

"Do we tell the cops?" Georgette asked.

Scott said, "Not until we talk to our lawyer. And remember, we don't have the word of any of the individuals involved. We only have secondhand knowledge."

"They used Choate's apartment," I said. "She wasn't part of it."

"Said she wasn't," Scott said. "Trust no one."

"Why would she tell me if she had something to hide?"

Scott said, "I think we need to be completely suspicious."

I nodded, then said, "Pinyon getting that information about teacher travel is suspicious."

Meg said, "The deaths came immediately after that."

Scott said, "Killing turkeys causes winter," the catchphrase he and I used to summon logic police to counter remarks such as "That hurricane hit because you are sinners." Proximity does not mean causation, a concept the religious right and far too many other people find difficult to master.

Meg smiled, "I get the idea, but something caused them, and we can't find anything logical—to us. Something has to be logical to the killer."

Georgette said, "None of the secretaries know who got into the files. It has to be an administrator. I don't suppose the police would take fingerprints in the storage room."

Meg said, "Probably not on what we've got so far."

I asked Georgette, "Who was fixing grades?"

She ticked the points off on her fingers. "Spandrel, the head of the department, changed answers on the kids' standardized tests. Graniento, our beloved principal, fixed grades for athletes and to keep the graduation rates up. I have copies of everything from before they started messing with the computers and each subsequent day."

"How long has this been going on?" I asked.

"It was going on for sure last year, and I think from when they started working here."

"How do you know they did this?" I asked.

"As you know, we keep all the records in the office. Last year, Luci Gamboni came to me. She'd transposed two kids' grades, an honors kid and an LD kid. One was supposed to be an A the other an F. It would have been embarrassing for her to have to explain to Spandrel and Graniento that she'd messed up. She came to me. I'm not supposed to, but on occasion teachers are desperate at the end of grading time. I help. I went in to switch it, but the honors kid's grade was already switched. The LD kid's grade was the same. Someone fixed the one and not the other."

Scott said, "Maybe she just forget and didn't realize she only messed up the one."

"Luci had the original printout. It was clearly wrong for

both of them on it. No, someone had changed the one and not the other. So I began to keep track."

Some of us always printed our grades after we posted them to the computer. It was just a bit of redundancy that could save a ton of time if the computer system went kaflooey.

Scott said, "You mean you made copies of the grades for the whole school? Isn't that a lot of paperwork?"

"You change the font and make the type size smaller, do a merge and compress, you get a lot on a few pages." She smiled. "And I have a flash drive with a very large memory, and a back-up drive with an equally large memory. I have chronological records for the past few years: copies of what the teachers put in, and copies of what came out. I'd spend a weekend after each grading period with my husband at home going over them. It was tedious work but very satisfying. If I can be part of bringing those people down, I will be very happy."

Scott said, "You must hate these administrators."

"Only some of them. Graniento and Spandrel inflict misery on good teachers for no reason. Their decisions are capricious. They make no sense, about our work or the teachers'."

Scott asked, "How do you keep up that befuddled front?"

"They look down on the secretaries. To them we're all women with fewer degrees than they have."

Scott said, "Did you get a chance to talk to Frecking and Benson? They must be frightened out of their minds."

"I only managed to find Benson. He's petrified about his wife finding out."

"He should be," Scott said.

Meg said, "Are they going to tell the cops the truth?"

"I don't know."

Meg said, "I also found out that Peter Higden was going to be disciplined for doing drugs."

I said, "It wasn't on school grounds."

"You knew about this?" Meg asked.

"I always keep faith," I said. "You know that." And I did. Gossip is one thing. Something told to me in confidence as part of my union duties stayed in confidence.

Scott asked, "What happened?"

Meg said, "I heard several versions, each more ludicrous than the last. Supposedly on days the kids aren't here, like institutes and parent conferences, he'd go out at lunch and get high and drink."

"He was never drunk," I said.

"He only did drugs?" Scott asked.

"He never admitted to anything," I said. "I'll say this much in this extremity. Three witnesses saw him. Two parents and a teacher. The teacher turned him in. The parents confirmed it. He was called in. He denied it was him. Absolutely, simply bald-faced lied."

"Are they sure it was him?" Scott asked.

"One of them recognized the license plate of the car he was sitting in."

"And they're sure it was drugs?" Scott asked.

"They said they were close enough to see that it wasn't a cigarette, and they claimed they could smell it. Other teachers said they smelled it on him when he got back to school."

Meg asked, "Did they inspect his classroom and his car?"

"No. It wasn't reported until the following day. They had no physical proof. It wasn't on school grounds. He wasn't caught or arrested by the police."

Meg asked, "Who were the parents and teacher?"

"I don't know."

"I've come up with a few things," Meg said. Our food arrived. I barely touched mine. Meg said, "On Peter Higden, did you know he played cards at lunch most regular days with members of the PE department? It was poker, and they were gambling."

"In school?" Scott asked.

She said, "Tom knows how labyrinthine all those old PE locker rooms and offices are. They've got more storage down there than the rest of the school combined. They play in the athletic director's office."

I asked, "How high were the stakes?"

"Five-dollar ante for each pot. Dollar raises. Limit of four raises."

Scott asked, "How do you get that kind of information?"

"The women in the PE department don't like the men, although a few of them have dated a few of the men. One of the women is not happy. My notion is that she is jealous about being frozen out of the games. She's not planning to turn them in. She doesn't think they know she knows."

Scott said, "Gambling is illegal on school grounds, right?"

"Yep," Meg said.

Scott said, "We aren't talking multimillion-dollar gambling debts, are we?"

"Schoolteachers?" Meg said. "Hundreds for sure. Most likely not thousands. Certainly not millions. At least, not that I was told. Besides the athletic director, there were a couple of other coaches, plus Steven Frecking, and Higden."

Scott said, "Can't they get fired for that?"

"You'd get in trouble, sure," I said. "But unless it was significant amounts of money or a mob-connected, people-getting-hurt thing, I don't see them losing their jobs. Probably a letter in their file and a warning not to do it again."

"But two people are dead," Georgette said. "And it is something illegal. It could be part of a pattern."

Meg said, "Eberson was not in the noon group. It was all male. What else I heard was that supposedly the ones at the table were participating in a scheme to double dip on athletic pay."

I said, "I've heard rumors about that. Nobody actually ever complained or got in trouble."

Meg said, "The word I have is they organized themselves pretty well."

"How does that work?" Scott asked.

I said, "Say there are four football coaches. Maybe three stay on the field and one goes to another job at a gas station or fast-food restaurant. They rotate and still get full pay for coaching but are actually around for only three fourths of the time."

"Nobody notices?" Scott asked.

Meg said, "They cover for each other. They're buddies. They play poker every day. The problem is that they were afraid someone in their group was turning traitor."

"And they didn't know who?" I asked.

"Right," Meg said.

I said, "And Peter was a suckup in our department, so maybe suspicion fell on him. Not enough for a guilty verdict, but a definite he's-buddies-with-the-administration, I-wonder-what-the-son-of-a-bitch-is-up-to kind of way."

Meg said, "Frecking was the youngest member of the group. They were suspicious of him, too. He's bluff and studly and friendly, just like Peter, and he was a real athlete at his college as opposed to most of these overweight pretenders. He played in some minor Bowl game his senior year. He's popular, but he's the one they know the least."

I said, "He's petrified of coming out to them."

Scott said, "For some people, popularity gives them all the more reason to be frightened. They fear losing their status, their reputation."

I asked, "What would it benefit Peter to tell on his buddies about the double dipping or the gambling?"

Meg said, "I don't know. Supposedly the guys had a fight one day this week. It's another medium-confidence source. The games may have stopped."

I said, "Maybe that would explain Peter being dead, although I'm not convinced, but that doesn't account for Gracie Eberson being murdered."

Meg said, "She was definitely not part of the group."

Scott said, "We're sure the two murders are connected?"

I said, "We can't be sure of anything, but you don't have two murders within hours of each other in the same school being a coincidence."

"Wait," Scott said, "was someone going to tell about the card games or the double dipping or both?"

"My source wasn't sure. She was pretty angry."

"Is this normal in a school?" Scott asked. "You guys sound like the teamsters except none of the bodies are missing. Yet."

"Normal?" I asked. "You get petty jealousy everywhere. Workers fight, disagree. Why wasn't somebody angry or at least offended about Higden being openly anti-Semitic?"

Meg said, "Nobody ever called him on it. Nobody mentioned homophobia either. The only other thing I got were accusations in the department about teachers stealing."

"Stealing what?" Scott asked.

"Supplies, teachers' manuals, old tests, just about anything that isn't tied down. Peter claimed the woman who retired and had his room before him had stripped the place clean and left him nothing."

I said, "Ah, that is so not true." The last day Sandra Barkin had come to me. She was in her seventies and hadn't been able to retire at a younger age. She'd stayed home to raise her kids and only started teaching in her forties. Then her husband had died. He'd been a freelance writer and had never made a lot, so his social security was negligible. She'd had to keep working. She was one of the feistiest of the old guard and had battled with those who she considered evil—up front and in their faces. Spandrel had hoped Barkin's retiring would let her run amok. Barkin had come to me that last day to say that she knew they would accuse her of stealing. She made Georgette and me come down to her classroom. She'd showed us every textbook, teacher's manual, test, and all the remaining classroom supplies. Then she'd taken us out her classroom door, locked it behind us, and given the key to Georgette. She'd said, "They'll accuse me. You know the truth."

I told all this to Scott and Meg, and Georgette nodded her confirmation. Then I added, "I heard Peter accusing her. I said what I knew, and Jourdan and Morgan defended her. It was another point of conflict."

Scott said, "It doesn't sound very important."

I said, "I don't know. In a place where everybody is counting up the smallest slight to use in the next battle, you don't know what's going to set anybody off."

Meg promised to keep listening. Georgette went back to the office. After a brief hug, Scott left.

23

I slipped into the back of my afternoon seminar, in which the members of the English department were supposed to learn yet another new grade book program. This one was to be implemented before January first. It was the third new program in four years. The administration kept buying the cheapest one. They never got the service contract or warranty that required the company to come in and train the teachers. The administration got what they paid for. We constantly had to learn new programs from scratch.

The new program was similar to the one I was using, but different enough for the company to charge thousands and thousands of dollars for the upgrade. Some of my colleagues insisted they'd never learn the new program. And it was a mess. I'd been doing my grades electronically for years. I didn't mention that to a lot of people. But they knew. And some were jealous. They needed to get a life. One huge life. Judging themselves by what I was doing in my classroom was nuts.

Luci Gamboni had saved me a seat. She leaned over and whispered, "Are you all right?"

"I've been better," I murmured back.

Spandrel walked up to me and said in a stage whisper, "You're late."

Schaven, Pinyon, and Milovec walked in.

I nodded toward them and said, "As are they."

She frowned and drifted over toward the three even later comers.

The Advanced Grade Acquisition and Distribution Techniques Gradebook software had enough bells and whistles to cause a hard drive to have a seizure. It would allow parents to go online and see every grade their student got during the quarter by assignment. Some teachers were furious about that. They didn't want parents to be able to see their grade books. I always gave parents a printout listing their kids' assignments and grades. Silly me, wanting to give parents and kids precise, up-to-date information about what the child was learning in my classroom.

Spandrel mostly hovered near the suckups. They chatted and laughed during much of the presentation. The leader of the seminar walked past them several times and glared. It didn't help.

About half an hour into it, Luci leaned over and said, "Is this right?"

I looked at a page filled with grades, student names, averages, point count. She tapped her finger near the bottom left of the screen. "I was practicing with last year's grades. I made a copy so the original wouldn't be messed up. Look at that."

"I'm not sure what I'm supposed to be looking at."

She pointed at the very bottom row. "That's Fred Zileski's final grade from last quarter last June. I know I gave him an F. He's the first kid that's flunked one of my classes in three years. They've got to work to flunk my class. Bochka the bitch, our idiot school board president, tried to get me to change the grade. She got Graniento and Spandrel on my case. I refused. Somebody changed the grade."

"Maybe the kids did it. They can hack into anything."

"But this new program will be the first one to open grades to the Internet. Last year's grades were only on the school network."

"Kids can break into that."

"Not into mine. I double protected it with a secret code. You taught me that. I did the same thing you do on your computer so the kids can't sabotage it. No one knew the passwords and codes. No one except Spandrel. She had to have it to get into the program for when they printed out the grades. She had to be the one who changed the grades."

I said, "That's against the contract."

We'd had that problem in the district before. Administrators wanting to increase graduation rates to look good on national statistics routinely went in and changed grades. The state of Illinois took extraordinary measures to keep the yearly statewide tests secret and sacrosanct prior to testing. That hadn't stopped cheating. And Luci had certainly heard the rumor that Spandrel was feeding the suckups information so that the scores of the kids in their classes would be higher than those of the old guard. Another problem was that PE teachers were notorious for conniving to get grades for athletes changed. And with the No Child Left Behind bullshit, the problem of the accuracy of records was endemic.

Luci said, "I know Spandrel did it. No one else could have done it. I'm going to confront that bitch right now."

"No," I said.

"No? I'm going to fight this. This is an outrage."

I said, "Yes, we're going to fight this, I just don't think this is the exact right moment for it."

She looked uncertain. She leaned close. "What is going on?"

Graniento and Spandrel were drifting in our direction. I said, "Let's discuss it with Teresa Merton on Monday. You aren't the first one to complain, but you may be among the first to be able to prove it. Print out what you've got there."

Graniento and Spandrel were upon us. Luci tapped my computer screen. "Are you sure that's what I need to do next?"

I was at a command page and moved my mouse to explain the next step in the new program.

◣ 24 ◢

I wanted to talk to Ludwig Schaven. I found him sitting in his chair behind his teacher's desk. He barely glanced at me as I walked in.

"Did the police tell you anything?" he asked.

"No," I answered.

He had posters of great literary figures in history on his walls. Each had a pithy saying by the author under the portrait.

When I got to the front desk, I said, "You've lost two friends. I'm sorry."

He looked at me. "Not very many people around here seem to be sad. They're running around worrying about themselves. We should be thinking about Gracie and Peter." He sighed.

He stared out the window for a few more moments, then said, "What is wrong with these people?"

"Which people?"

"Gracie and Peter are dead. They walk around as if somehow it was the fault of two dead people that their living, breathing, lucky asses were inconvenienced."

I said, "That's kind of sad."

"And people are still willing to fight. I'm ashamed of how I acted in the teachers' lounge yesterday evening. Shouting at moments like that. I was just so upset. Gracie was a good friend."

"It's hard when friends die, especially when they're young."

"It's so sad."

"We're you close to Peter?"

"I didn't go out drinking with them much. If you weren't part of the drinking group you weren't on the outs with them, but you weren't one of the in-crowd either."

I said, "I heard Peter was part of a group that gambled on school grounds at lunchtime."

"Peter gambled a lot everywhere. I heard he had several bookies in Chicago."

"Was he in debt?"

"He used to brag about owing a dime or making a dime. I never knew if that was a hundred dollars or a thousand. Could that have been the cause of his murder? Although that wouldn't explain Gracie's."

"If he owed a vicious bookie a ton of money or was late on payments, Peter could have been in trouble."

"Have you found out anything that might be a clue to either murder?"

"I've got lots of wild rumors. Most of which I don't believe. One, and we discussed it yesterday, is that Mabel and Gracie were having an affair."

Schaven said, "They never confessed to one to me. Do you know they took a cruise together last summer?"

"I thought they were married."

"They are. It was one of those women's getaway things. They shared a room. I assumed it was separate beds. I have no idea. I don't care. Although, come to think of it, when they went to conferences together they always got one room. Of course, with women that doesn't have to mean anything. I guess it doesn't have to with guys, but you hear of women doing it more often and people raising fewer eyebrows."

He was being a little more forthcoming than some of the others, so I wondered how loyal he was to Spandrel. He was in that faction, and I had to assume he was.

I said, "I also heard that Peter Higden was upset about someone on the staff using the n word, but that he made some kind of deal."

"You do hear a lot."

I said, "Murder has happened. People become more forthcoming."

Schaven said, "I thought it would be the other way around, people would clam up."

"I'm just saying what I've gotten. Now I'm checking with you. I want to make sure the things I find out are accurate."

"And you think someone using the *n* word to Peter could be a cause for murder?"

I said, "I wouldn't blame him for being really angry. My source says he got tenure because of it."

Did Schaven really not know the person who had used the slur was Spandrel?

Schaven said, "No, I think Mabel was going to give it to him anyway. He is on our side, after all. To be honest, have you known any of the young teachers who, as long as they are loyal to Mabel, didn't get tenure? It isn't their teaching that makes a difference, it's their loyalty."

A refreshing bit of honesty. "So some not-so-good teachers are getting tenure?"

"You know they do. You know the system is flawed. Not for the reasons the politicians think. No, it's flawed because we're human, not because the unions want power. I care about children. I have no idea if Peter was a good teacher or not. I do know he was given tenure. Others? Well, as we both know, most of the staff are aware of who are good teachers and who aren't, and it isn't test scores. That's easily fixed."

This was true. All you needed was an administrator who didn't like you, and you'd get all the kids who had low test scores in your class. Your test scores would be lower. I'd seen administrators do that to people.

I said, "I heard he was part of the group planning to push for a strike before negotiations even began last year."

Schaven said, "Nobody ever took that seriously. Rumors blew that all out of proportion. I never heard about Peter being part of that planning. Gracie, sure. She was always an activist. Give her a cause and she'd put up a picket line around it."

I couldn't tell if he was lying. I'd heard Schaven had been blaring about a strike since the last contract settlement. "Did you hear about other people being part of that faction?"

"No. I'm a loyal union member. I voted for the contract." Several sources said that at the last ratification meeting, he had waved his ballot in the air with the *no* prominently circled.

I said, "Did Gracie's activism go so far as to be willing to picket Peter when he made anti-Semitic remarks?"

"She never said anything to me."

"How come nobody else besides me objected when Peter made anti-Semitic remarks?"

Ludwig sighed. "I'm Jewish. He never said any of them in front of me. I did hear rumors, and I mentioned them to him. He denied them."

"He made remarks in front of me. I told him to stop."

"Are you Jewish?"

"Why would that make a difference?"

"I guess it doesn't."

"I'm saying it's true."

"I did hear him make homophobic remarks."

"And no one spoke up?"

"No."

"Why the hell not?"

"I guess no one's gay in our group."

"And so it's okay to be prejudiced against anyone who isn't represented in the group?"

"No. We were friends. Everybody just kind of knows each other. We let those things roll off our backs. No one takes it seriously."

I said, "And whoever speaks up makes the group feel uncomfortable?"

"Well, yeah."

"And you're saying that if he'd made an anti-Semitic slur in front of you, you'd have said nothing?"

"No, but like I said, he didn't."

I gave up the debate. I said, "I thought we were beyond this."

"We who?" Schaven asked.

"Society. Educated people."

"Are you saying prejudice led to these two murders?"

I said, "Somebody was pretty angry. Prejudice can make people pretty angry."

"Maybe it was jealousy or money."

"Money? In a school system?"

"People are ambitious. They want better jobs."

I said, "Yeah, I heard lots of the younger people wanted to move into administration."

"The money is better there."

"Do you think anybody was ambitious enough to kill for a job?"

Schaven said, "There's not much point in killing Gracie and Peter. They didn't stand in anybody's way. Not that I know of. I don't know why everybody isn't just sad. These people are worse than children."

I said, "Did Peter get along with all the members of your faction?"

"Of course, we all got along."

"I heard there was dissent. That some were turning on others."

"Impossible."

"Why is that impossible?"

"No one is like that. Everybody got along."

"Two members of your faction are dead. Obviously somebody didn't get along."

"Most likely the killer is someone from the old guard."

"Any notions on who?"

He shrugged. "Jourdan's pretty obvious, but I'm not ready to make an accusation."

I said, "Have you noticed anything about the administrators acting strange?"

"Who?"

"Towne, Bochka, Graniento?"

"I never see them much."

I asked, "Do you know where Carl got his statistics on who traveled to conferences?"

His eyes flicked back and forth. "No."

If I were a betting man, I'd have said he just lied.

I said, "I will never understand you people."

His response was quick and angry. "We were united on one thing. Nobody liked you, but it wasn't because they were homophobic. You always wanted to fight and challenge what administrators wanted to do."

"They needed challenging. I was responding to legitimate complaints."

"Yeah, but you always wanted to fight. We newer teachers were fed up. We wanted to get along with the administration."

"At the price of your souls? Your dignity? All the things we've fought for years to have?"

"But we haven't fought for them."

"But you get the benefits."

He returned to staring out the window.

I left.

25

Schaven said they'd been united in dislike of me. I hadn't been aware of this much animosity on the staff. I thought I was pretty self-aware. I'd missed something. Or being homophobic had been forced deep into the closet.

I headed for the gym and Steven Frecking. The field house was dark, the large and small gyms empty. The emergency lights were on. On my way to the PE offices, I heard the sound of raised voices coming from the locker room. I eased forward. I didn't actually stop to listen—that would have been unprofessional and at the level of a teenager in a bad soap opera. I just slowed down. Very, very slow.

I recognized Morgan Adair's and Steven Frecking's voices.

Frecking was saying, ". . . can't be seen with you. You shouldn't have come down here. What if someone shows up?"

"I locked the door."

"You shouldn't have. If anybody came down here, it would make it look more suspicious. The other coaches are getting ready for tonight's football game. I've got to get there, too."

This was the same game I'd promised Fred Zileski and a couple other kids I would go to. I was never eager to attend, and this was an awful day, but I'd promised.

"Were you really making out?" Adair asked.

"Do you believe what Mason told you?"

"Tom has never lied to me."

"He ever make out with you? I did. Who are you going to trust, him or me?"

Morgan's pause appalled me.

Finally Morgan said, "You didn't answer my question." I breathed a sigh of relief.

Frecking said, "I'm not going to answer it."

"How can you be like this?" Morgan asked.

Frecking said, "You don't understand."

Morgan said, "You're right. I don't understand. You were making out with Brandon Benson? He's married, for Christ's sake. You and I were good together."

"I'm a slut. Okay. So what? Get a life. Go away."

Silence.

"Get out," Frecking said.

I knocked on the door.

More silence.

I said, "It's Tom Mason. I'd like to talk to you."

I heard the lock click and the door open. Tears streamed down Morgan's face. I thought this was a bit much—he'd only been dating the guy a week. But Morgan's infatuations were strong: his desire to find a life partner was intense, and his need to get married bordered on the irrational.

He said, "I. Tom. I . . ." He looked over his shoulder. "I can't . . . I'll talk to you later." He rushed past me.

I entered the room.

Frecking had a defiant look on his face. I thought he most

141

resembled a teenager who'd just been accused of doing something unwise.

I said, "I need to talk to you."

He said, "Nope. Not going to happen."

"Ah, but I have a few things to say to you."

Frecking wore low-rise jeans that hugged his hips and bulged out his basket. If he wasn't stuffing his crotch, it was impressive. The former quarterback wiped his hands on the apparel in question.

He marched toward me and the door and tried to brush past me. I slammed the door and stood in front of it.

"Move," he ordered.

I said, "I'm not going to fight. Maybe you won't talk, but you're going to listen. Your lie is going to cost you. The sex you had is going to cost you. They asked me for DNA. They'll be around to ask you. If you left traces of yourself of any kind in that room, they will find them."

His face turned ashen. "Maybe I was in there before."

"For what?"

"I . . ." He stopped.

"And you lied about being there."

"Let me past."

"It's all going to come out," I said. "What you were doing in there, who you were with."

"You should never have said anything. This is your fault. You're the traitor. You're the one who shouldn't have said anything. You found the body. Why couldn't you leave it at that?"

I said, "I didn't murder anybody. I wasn't having sex in a venue that was fraught with peril."

Stubborn silence. He clenched and unclenched his fist. He was strong and about my size. I did work out, but if he chose to physically attack, it would be a challenge. A fistfight, however, was nonsensical. We were adults.

142

I asked, "Why mess around with Benson and at school? You are the cliché other man."

Frecking frowned. "He's hot. He's funny. He's masculine. He knows sports. He keeps his mouth shut."

"Is he getting a divorce?" I asked.

"We haven't talked about it. Why would I want him to? I'm not going to marry him. We can't anyway."

"I can understand his dilemma," I said, "although I'm not particularly sympathetic to it. Why can't you come out? It would be safer than getting caught with your pants down in the storeroom."

"We've never gotten naked at school."

I said, "That's an awfully fine distinction for the activity that was going on in that storeroom."

He looked confused.

"Do you ever not sneak around?" I asked him.

"He's married. We've got no choice. It's just such a hassle. You guys are safe." He pointed at me. "Your lover's famous and rich."

"So by that logic, anyone who isn't a wealthy couple is condemned to a life of shame."

"I can't come out."

I said, "And you've got Morgan Adair, who is not married. Why not stick with him?"

"He told you about us?"

"Obviously."

"He should know to keep his mouth shut."

I said, "He was happy and in love."

Frecking had stopped moving forward. Now he stepped back and leaned onto the desk and squirmed his butt on the edge of the top. He placed his hands behind him and shifted his weight from one butt cheek to the other. The effect jutted out his crotch even farther. I wondered if good-looking people were aware of what they looked like when they did this. My guess is that most of them were. Was he switching into seduction mode? Asshole.

The office had two desks. Sports equipment dotted the floors. Clipboards and whistles and stopwatches hung from nails along the corkboard walls.

Frecking said, "I'm not responsible for Morgan Adair's jumping to conclusions. If you'd kept your mouth shut, what Benson and I were doing wouldn't have come out."

"You chose to lie about being there. And you were two-timing Morgan—probably with more than one person. The key, however, is that you were making out at a murder scene."

"I didn't kill her."

"You think your presence there wouldn't come out? Are you nuts?"

"Shit. At least Benson knew it was just fun. Morgan Adair was so clingy. It's probably better he knows, I guess. This way I won't have to tell him it's over."

"Hell of a way to live," I said.

"That's my choice. As soon as I hook up with a rich lover, I'll jump out of the closet, too. For now, being out could affect my job."

I said, "Illinois has a gay clause in its equal rights law now. Even if they wanted to fire you for being gay, there's legal protection."

"You don't know the head of the PE department. He is a total Nazi. He retired from the Marines and decided to teach. He hates fags. He's head of the Fellowship of Christian Athletes. The head football coach calls guys who miss tackles homo and queer and sissy and fag. Even in gym class he calls the wimpy kids names."

"And you put up with it?"

"What choice do I have?"

"Why don't you call him on it?" I asked.

"I'm not tenured."

Ah, the coward's defense. I heard it over and over again from young teachers: I can't take a stand because I don't have tenure—when I get tenure, then I'll take whatever stand I'm too much of a coward to take now. Ha! In all the years I'd been teaching and union building rep, not one teacher who swore they'd make their brave stand once they got tenure actually took a stand, brave or not. With or without tenure, they're cowards. It's an excuse not to do their job, or an excuse to suck up, or an excuse to do nothing, or a way to hide.

I said, "I understand leading a closeted life."

Frecking said, "The other coaches would crucify me. They'd use rumor and innuendo. And you can afford high-priced attorneys. I'm a first-year teacher. Sure, you can be in all the headlines. The kids make fag jokes in the locker room. They wouldn't trust me."

I said, "Tell them to stop making fag jokes."

"Then they'd know I was gay."

"You don't have to be gay to be offended by homophobic slurs."

"They'd know, and I'd be ostracized." Still a real possibility in most high schools, among a lot of kids and more teachers than I'd care to admit.

He was continuing. "Even the women who are lesbians wouldn't support me."

"We have open lesbians in the PE department?"

"No."

"You're sure they're lesbians?"

"Well, duh," he said.

"It's the cliché," I said, "but if there are any, none of them have come out to me. Nor are they required to. Say there are lesbians in the department—how do you know they wouldn't be supportive?"

"They separate themselves from us guys. They despise us. I can't say anything. I just can't."

I said, "You do realize your job could be in real jeopardy if the cops mention your indiscretion to the administration?"

He sat down on the edge of the coach's desk behind him. "I got to that room first. I was there a minute or two before Brandon showed up. We were going at it for fifteen minutes, probably a little longer. We have to grab our time together when we can."

"Being the other man is okay with you?" I asked.

"Sure, yeah. We hadn't been caught before. We usually go to the PE office but there was a meeting of head coaches in there yesterday. We like the storeroom because the door makes that creaking noise. We figure we'll be warned, that we'll have time. We were just kind of more involved yesterday."

I said, "You should worry about someone walking in. What if one of the kids had caught you?"

"We were careful."

"Not careful enough," I said.

Frecking said, "I am so fucked. I know they're going to ask for a DNA sample. You've got to help me."

"After the lie you told about me?"

"I'll try to make it right."

"Do you think you have any credibility with the police?"

"I've got to try something. I can't lose this job."

"It's a little late to worry about that."

"I might have left signs of sexual activity. My pants were wet. They rubbed up against some boxes when you startled us. Maybe there's like DNA or something left."

"Might be," I said.

"But I can't come out. Can't you do something? You're the union building rep."

"Which does not mean I'm able to wipe up after members who blow their loads in their underwear and smear it all over a crime scene. And who would tell any lie to save their own skin."

"You gotta help me. Please."

I was not about to tell lies for this man. Hot he might be. Cute covers a multitude of sins, but not one like this.

I asked the obvious question. "Did you kill her?"

"No," he said. "No, I . . . Is this what I'm going to face? Are people . . . ? No. I didn't. You were there. It was awful just seeing her. It's worse thinking about what we were doing while she was lying there. Maybe she wasn't dead when we started. Maybe we could have done something." He got tears in his eyes. "I've never been close to death like this. I don't know how I got the courage to follow you up to her. I guess I thought she was breathing. I figured maybe she was just passed out. You don't expect a dead body. I . . . just . . . I. Will the police think I did it?" He put his face in his hands. "I got up yesterday morning and my world was okay."

"How well did you know Peter Higden?"

"The dead guy under your car?"

"Behind the back wheels. He wasn't under the car."

"I never met him."

"Really? I heard you played poker with him every noontime. You and a bunch of the other coaches."

He got very pale.

"And there was some problem with the PE coaches double dipping."

"Everybody did that. It wasn't just me. That's what they told me they all did. I assumed it was okay. Nobody ever said it wasn't."

"It struck you that being at one job and being paid for another that you weren't at was okay? This isn't the city of Chicago. And you knew Peter. You're still telling lies. You screw with married men, which has got to be a strain. You cheat at your job. You're gambling on school premises. Is there something here about you that is supposed to be redeeming?"

His response was a defiant, "Fuck you."

I said, "Well, no, that's never going to happen. However, your attitude needs to change. You're the one who's in deep shit. You're the one who's done all these questionable things."

"Other people did them. People with tenure. I was just doing what they were doing."

"You think that's something we can engrave on your tombstone or something that's going to save your ass?"

He seemed to deflate.

I said, "How well did you know Peter?"

"He was one of the assistant football coaches. Mostly I'd just see him when he played poker."

"Did he ever make anti-Semitic remarks when you were around?"

"I never paid much attention. We were just guys playing cards. Nobody cared what anybody said."

"Did he make homophobic comments?"

"Nobody got mad about anything. We got along great."

"You ever go drinking with him? You ever go out with the crowd to Chicago on Friday nights?"

"Maybe once or twice."

"Did you know Peter was screwing Mabel Spandrel and Gracie Eberson?"

"I was never part of that."

"Part of what, exactly?"

"Look," he said, "can't we stop this? What's the point?"

"Somebody died. You guys made it look like I might be a suspect. This is real, serious, adult stuff here. You can't just have another drink with your buddies and hope it all goes away. You do realize that you should consider quitting before the administration finds out what you did?"

"I can't quit."

"You want to take a chance on being fired?"

"You've got to help me."

"Then I want better answers."

"About what?"

"What can you tell me about Peter? Did he help you change grades?"

"Yeah, we knew he was the one to go to for that to happen."

"Who said he was?"

"I don't know. It was at poker. It was just discussed as something that got done."

"The other coaches trusted you."

"It wasn't a matter of trust. We don't rat each other out."

"Did you know Gracie Eberson?"

"Never met her."

"What else can you tell me about Peter and these guys?"

"They didn't like you."

"Why not?"

"Duh. You're openly gay."

"They never said anything to me."

"You expect them to? You've got a hot, famous, rich lover. No one would dare take you on. You're safe. Maybe the rest of us aren't."

I didn't like Frecking, and he was a lying sack of shit, but I didn't think he was acting now. I was still furious about his lie to the police. His job was in deep trouble.

"You need to tell the police the truth," I said.

"I can't. It'll mean my job."

"You complicated your lives when you guys decided to lie."

"Brandon wasn't sure you'd leave out what we were doing."

"Well, they're hunting for DNA right now, and you guys are going to have to give DNA samples unless you get really good lawyers."

"I can't do this shit," he said. "Just let me go. I can't talk to you."

"Why?" I asked. I thought I knew the answer. He was a closet case desperate for the world not to peek in.

"Don't come near me," he ordered. "Maybe I could tell people you came on to me. That's sexual harassment. That might save my neck."

Speculation about a new set of lies. Right in front of me. He had to be on extra-strength stupid pills.

I said, "Added to all your others lies? Who is going to believe you?"

"The administration will."

"Allies in high places? Good try. You need a witness, which you don't have."

"Maybe they'll tell lies for me."

"You think people would go that far out on a limb for an untenured teacher they hardly know? Unfortunately for you, the police are involved. They only care about catching a killer."

"I didn't do it. Now get out of my way."

I stood aside. Was he going to attempt to tell more lies and get people to lie for him? Disturbing but not plausible. Still, it gave me a chill. The man was a menace.

He was the second person to report that others disliked me, either for myself or for the job I was doing as union rep. The prickle down the back of my neck turned into a grotesque shiver. Fear blossomed brighter in my very bones.

26

As I made my way though the darkened gym, I heard my name called. I glanced around warily. Edgar Cauchon, the athletic director, hustled across the floor toward me. Cauchon, like so many PE coaches, had let his body run to a barrel belly, which he clad in an array of sweatpants and T-shirts that must be sold on an Ugly Gym Teachers' Clothes Web site. Today's outfit was maroon.

He asked, "Are they going to cancel the football game tonight?"

"I have no idea."

"They can't do that. It's all set up. I've got parents calling me insisting we play. I'm sure there's no danger to the kids."

"If something bad does happen, are you planning to pay out of your own pocket for any lawsuits that are filed?"

"We've got to play the game."

I said, "I don't care if you play the game."

"You're the union rep. You've got to handle this."

I said, "Talk to Teresa Merton."

"She won't listen. She never does."

I said, "I heard you and a bunch of the guys play cards at lunchtime."

"Huh?"

I waited.

"Well, sometimes. It's not a crime. It's not a lot of money."

"You guys have an argument this week?"

"No. Who told you that?"

"Just a rumor I'm checking."

"It's not true."

I said, "Did you know Peter well?"

"He was real friendly. A great guy."

I said, "Do you know anyone who would have a reason to kill him?"

"No."

"He never talked about other people in the English department?"

"No offense, but who cares about the English department?"

Over the years the PE department had become known for opposing every contract and for being the biggest complainers. They'd gotten nothing in our last contract settlement. You want to be the continuous, unreasoning opposition? Yeah, well, welcome to getting nothing.

I said, "I got a rumor that you guys had a pretty organized way of double dipping. Was Peter in on that?"

"What?"

"You heard me."

"District office is responsible for checking pay sheets."

"Actually, you would be. You're the one who has to sign off on all the coaching assignments. It's likely that the secretaries don't have the season schedules memorized."

"Double dipping doesn't happen."

"You sure? You're in charge. If you haven't done it, but you know about it, you could still be in trouble."

152

He said, "Nobody keeps perfect records."

I said, "Maybe one of your colleagues has been keeping track behind your back. The English department might not be the only one with vicious backstabbing beyond reason. If one person has records and is planning to go public, then you could all be in trouble."

"I know who it is: it has to be Emily Haggerty. She's a lesbian who hates the rest of us."

"I'll have to talk with her."

"Do you really need to bring all this up?"

"Peter was an assistant football coach. Was he double dipping?"

"Maybe. I guess. I'm not sure."

I waited some more.

Finally, "Peter might have, but nobody would be angry enough to kill over it. And that Eberson woman wasn't even a coach."

"Did Peter take somebody else's coaching position?"

"Nothing like that happens."

I said, "You guys rigging grades for athletes?"

"Hey, that's out of line. We don't do that. Are you going to get us investigated?"

I hesitated.

He turned red. "That's why we don't like you. Nobody can ever slide by. You find every fucking thing and mess it up for everybody. Why don't you back off?"

I said, "I prefer to play by the rules. I have no desire to bring trouble to you, but I won't cover for you either. If somebody catches you, find your union rep."

"That's you."

"Yes, I know."

"Fuck."

I said, "Talk to Graniento or Teresa Merton about your precious game tonight." I left.

And this was the third person to tell me I was generally disliked. Maybe my being under suspicion made me vulnerable in their eyes and let them feel like they were free to attack. Or maybe they were homophobic pigs.

27

I found Meg in the library and told her the upshot of my conversations. She said, "Take them out and shoot them."

"I thought we were against the death penalty."

"Not today."

I said, "That's three people who said they don't like me and/or the job I'm doing. It bothers me."

"Do you care what these people think?"

"Not really, but sort of. And it's so odd. Three I-don't-like-yous. Two murders."

"And a partridge in a pear tree," Meg added.

"I wish I knew what it all meant."

"Danger and death," Meg said. "Until the killer is found, we all need to be on guard."

Luci Gamboni rushed into the library. She slumped into the chair behind Meg's desk. She put her chin in her hand. Tears slipped down her cheeks.

Meg and I settled into seats next to her. Meg asked, "Luci, what's wrong?"

"Here!" She pulled a crumpled eight and a half by eleven–inch piece of paper out of her purse. She thrust it into my hands. I uncrumpled it. In boldface thirty-two-point type it said, "I know what you did."

She said, "I snuck around with Peter Higden. No one knew. Absolutely no one knew. There was no one I could tell. I'm married. Happily married. But he was kind and friendly."

Meg and I spent several minutes comforting her. When her tears were under control, Luci said, "I know he was in the other faction, but I couldn't help myself. I didn't betray anyone on our side. Never. I never gave away our secrets. I know he'd go out with others, but he was always kind to me. What do I do at the funeral? Go up to his wife and say, 'I had a great time having sex with your husband'?"

Meg said, "I wouldn't."

I said, "I heard he was having three-ways with Spandrel and Gracie?"

"Those were just vicious rumors. He fooled around a lot before he met me. He was faithful to me."

She was in for a jolt.

Meg said, "He cheated with you faithfully."

A trifle cruel but accurate.

Luci said, "Once I got this note, I had to tell somebody. I had to let it out. I'm scared. Meg, you've always been a friend. You too, Tom. I've known you both for years. I've never cheated on my husband. Not before this. Never. He's a good man. What are my kids going to think?"

"Are you going to tell them?" Meg asked.

"How would anyone ever know?" I asked. "We're certainly not going to tell anyone."

She shook the note. "This. It's going to come out. All of it. The police have been asking about Peter all day. Someone's going to blab."

"Did anyone else know?" I asked.

"I never told."

"Did Peter?" I asked.

"Who knows? Everything else is coming out. Look at that stuff about Mabel and Gracie. I know it isn't true."

I said, "I've had confirmation of it from a pretty reliable source."

Meg said, "And Peter was involved with them intimately."

Luci gaped. She drew ragged breaths and wiped at tears. "He told me he loved me. Are you sure?"

Meg said, "I'm sorry, yes."

"A traitor and now this." Luci threw the note as hard as she could. "Who would send such a thing?" she asked. "I'm just so frightened. Is someone going to try and kill me?"

Meg said, "Kids do this kind of thing. It's a game."

"You think a kid did this?" Luci asked.

"Or a demented adult," Meg said. "Remember Pinyon got those hate notes, which everybody thinks were made up. This could be designed to do exactly what it's done. Scare you."

Brook Burdock, who'd been cheering Gracie's death on Thursday, bashed open the library door and rushed up to us. "Mabel Spandrel called me into her office. She recited chapter and verse of what Schaven and his cronies claim they overheard me saying. The nerve of those people! I didn't say anything criminal. She started to threaten me. I said I wanted a union representative. She threatened me some more. She called me uncooperative. She told me I wasn't a team player. I told her I made comments protected by free speech rights. She might not like them, but she can't stop me from saying them. Again, I said I wanted a union representative. By this time I thought she was going to have a stroke. Frankly, I was hoping she would. I just kept repeating I wanted a union representative. She threw me out. I want that woman crucified."

Burdock paused in his recitation long enough to notice Luci's tears. "What's wrong? Have those suckups done something to you? Did Spandrel threaten you?"

Luci showed him the note. She left out the part about Peter. When she was done, Burdock glanced around the library. He lowered his voice. "I'm glad Gracie is dead. I'm glad Peter is dead. I wish Mabel Spandrel was dead. I hated the two dead ones. I hate the live one. They are moronic, fucked-up people who deserve to die."

Meg said, "Tell us how you really feel. Don't hold back."

Luci said, "Brook, I think you're going a little too far."

"They were cruel and vicious to me. They tried to turn my students against me. They tried to tell them they didn't have to do homework I assigned."

"What?" Gamboni asked.

"Tom knows the story. At the beginning of last year, I kept having kids not do their homework. I couldn't figure out why. Finally, one of the little darlings confessed. He was on the football team. Higden had told him he didn't have to listen to me and do my homework. The kid told his buddies and word spread."

"Did you confront him?" I asked.

"I went to Mabel. She brought him in. He denied it. The kid came in. He denied saying anything to me. The parent came in and demanded her kid be taken out of my classroom. They all just lied, and they got the kid to lie."

"That's sick," I said.

"Got that right," Burdock said. "About Mabel, just now, do I need to be worried? I am protected, right?"

"Yes," I said. "I think any of us who is still breathing is a step ahead."

"Is it that dangerous?" Luci asked.

"It is to them," Burdock said. "I hope they all die, painfully."

I said, "A couple people have mentioned to me that they aren't fond of the way I do my job as building rep."

Burdock said, "Some people can't stand you. Sure. It's

pretty much the suckup faction. You're terrific. You stand up for us. You do what's right."

Luci said, "It's a few malcontents who you've given reality checks to. You do wonderful work. Don't worry about it."

After reassuring them both as best I could, we arranged it so that Luci and Brook walked out to their cars together.

Scott showed up a few minutes later. We decided to dine at Francesca's Fortunato in Frankfort, a wonderful place to have a meal. While we ate, I told him what I'd learned this afternoon.

When I was done, he said, "They claim lots of teachers don't like you?"

"That bothers me and it doesn't. I don't do this to be popular. I try to be fair. I also refuse to lie to them. I try and make bitter pills easier to swallow, but sometimes they have to take some tough things."

Scott said, "I know this kind of thing does bother you. Try not to let it. You do a great job."

"I always thought so. You know, those people don't seem to have the same kinds of self-doubt."

"They do," Scott said. "They just don't tell you about it."

"I think they're oblivious."

"Nobody's accusing them of being smart. Is that note Luci got serious?" Scott asked.

"I don't know. If the murders hadn't happened, I'd be inclined to give it less weight. Now? Who knows? It is the kind of thing kids would do."

◣ 28 ◢

We sat in Scott's Porsche on Kansas Street in Frankfort.

I said, "I promised I'd go to the game."

Scott said, "You're upset. It's been an awful day. The kids will understand."

"No. Teenagers don't. I can't explain to them I'm hip-deep in murder. I always keep faith with the kids. You know that."

"I'm more concerned about you than I am about them."

"I know. I know. It'll be easier to keep a promise. It'll feel normal."

Scott said, "I'll go with. I've got my hat. We'll take blankets." We drove back to school. As we walked through the parking lot, he said, "Be nice to anyone you meet. Do not confront any administrators."

"I'll be good. I promise. I'll make sure the kids see me. We'll watch for a while. Then we'll go." I'd played on this same field as a kid. It had good memories for me.

The stadium was a cheapo conglomeration of a concrete structure built in the 1920s, plus an ultramodern press box and uncomfortable aluminum bleachers. These last two were thanks to the sports boosters who refused to support any building referendums for their children. They were quite willing to dun to death the unwilling members of the community with sales of mounds of pizza and candy. They'd proceeded to erect the so-called improvements. Can they say *priority*?

The night was cool. Besides the blankets, Scott had hooded sweatshirts. Some day that man is not going to be prepared for something. On that day I'm going to dance in the streets and cheer, although not while he's watching. Well, I do love him, and it is awfully handy to have someone around who makes the Boy Scouts look like unprepared pikers, but sometimes Mr. Ready needs to screw up.

The crumbling concrete that formed the walls of the stadium provided numerous nooks and crannies for teenagers to make out, do drug deals, smoke, and engage in nefarious things teenagers have found ways to do since forever.

We used the faculty entrance. The most run-down of all. As you walked up the concrete ramp, a yellow, two-story, concrete-block concession stand barred the view to the field. The aluminum stands that were less than three years old loomed up on both sides around us.

As we neared the field, the crowd erupted in rhythmic stomping on the bleachers and obscene chants interrupted by fits of booing. Scott and I made our way around the edge of the stands. I could hear the stentorian tones of the public address system, but I couldn't make out the words. I could guess what it was about. Graniento had probably just made his usual appeal for no booing, no obscenities, and no stomping on the bleachers. After he did this, the kids always booed, chanted obscenities, and stomped on the bleachers. Graniento hadn't caught on yet to the cause and effect.

Parents and kids were streaming in and out of the stands. The lines for food and drink were ten deep. Scott had a baseball hat pulled down low and his hood pulled close around his face. It's amazing how often this leads to lack of recognition.

I usually went by myself to the games, and I seldom stayed long, just long enough to let the kids know I was interested. Teenagers love it when you notice that they are the center of their universe.

The teachers' section was near the fifty-yard line. Before I was halfway there, teachers were stopping by, asking how I was doing and adding other kind words. The LD teachers who I worked most closely with came up as a bunch. We exchanged hugs and comfort. Our progress was slow, but I thanked each one.

When we got to the teachers' section, we stood to one side. Mr. Zileski and a group of parents were conferring about twenty yards away. He was always at the games, always sat in the same place. Mr. Zileski looked kind of like his son. He was a big man with receding brush-cut hair. He wore blue jeans, work boots, and a heavy flannel shirt that hung open, showing a long-sleeve white T-shirt underneath. He spotted me and marched over. He glanced at Scott and held out his hand. "It's an honor to meet you, sir." Then he turned to me and asked me if I was okay. I thanked him and said I was.

"They booing Graniento's usual announcement?" I asked.

"Yeah, they love stomping on the bleachers and booing. Typical administrative moron. Never give a command you know they can't or won't obey—or worse yet, that you can't enforce. Idiot."

I smiled. I liked Mr. Zileski. Even more now that he'd not made a big deal about meeting Scott.

He said, "I was just talking to a couple of the parents. We want to know why there is a game tonight and why there isn't more police presence here now. My idiot ex-wife should have announced precautions and then actually taken precautions that people could see, or canceled the game. I don't see extra police." He rubbed his hand over his brush cut. "I don't think the kids are really in danger, but you can't just leave things like this. I know why she hasn't done anything. She is petrified of getting bad publicity." Several parents had joined our group. They were paying attention to Mr. Zileski and not Scott. Good.

Scott said, "You'd think she'd be afraid of the bad publicity that would come from not acting." People nodded.

I said, "Or the hideous possibility of something bad actually happening."

"Will it?" one parent asked.

Mr. Zileski said, "I sure doubt it, but a bunch of us have stationed ourselves around the stadium. We've got cell phones with us so we can contact each other or the police if we see anything wrong or out of the ordinary. A few of us are going to confront my idiot ex-wife and those moron administrators. Stomping and booing! They've got the safety of children to worry about."

He and his group marched off.

Scott said, "I like him."

I glanced around the stadium. The band was on the field. Lots of high school bands had turned themselves into precision machines in the past ten years or so, competing for coveted spots in bowl parades over the holidays. Not Grover Cleveland. Like the football team, they swung between relentlessly average and not quite that good.

Kids said hi. A few stopped and said a few words. Scott stayed in the background. Just as our team trudged onto the field, one of the kids, a slender young man, approached us. Stanley Connors was in my senior honors class and in the gay student group. His acne had begun to clear up, but he still hid his braces-filled smile by ducking his head. He was with another boy I didn't recognize. Stanley leaned a little more closely toward me than the other kids and whispered, "This is my boyfriend, Joel." Stanley's eyes flitted to mine, and he almost smiled. Joel was a skinny kid with long blond hair.

I said, "Scott, I'd like to introduce Stanley and Joel."

Stanley looked at Scott and did a double take. Then he looked at me and back to Scott. "You brought him to the game. That is so cool. I wish I had a relationship like yours."

I said, "Maybe you will someday."

Scott said, "Good luck."

The two boys moved off. I hoped they wouldn't broadcast Scott's presence.

The teams were ready for the kickoff. The underclad cheerleaders bounced up and down the sidelines. Scott and I spread one blanket on the cold seats and one over our legs.

I said, "The rule is, I get to leave when I notice the cold."

Sitting at a high school football game on a fall night in Chicago can be dull, and the cold seeps in quickly. A few minutes into the second quarter, Mr. Zileski came back. He saw us and came over. I made room for him next to me.

He said, "My ex-wife is in a perfect position in life."

"What's that?"

"President of the school board. Her gift for stupidity matches the job." I smiled. He leaned toward me and asked in a whisper, "Do they really call her Bitch Bochka?"

I whispered back, "Mostly it's Kara the Terrible, but they avoid saying either one to her face."

Mr. Zileski said, "A few of the parents want school called off on Monday. That's too extreme. People need to take sensible precautions. My ex claims the police are already planning an extra presence for Monday."

I said, "I'm sure things will be fine."

The crowd roared. We stood up with them. From underneath a huge pile of muddy teenagers, Fred Zileski emerged with the ball. He played defensive line, so I assumed he must have recovered a fumble. He handed the ball politely to an official.

"Go Fred!" Mr. Zileski yelled.

29

Midway through the second quarter, we decided to get to the washroom and leave before the half ended. As we got up, the crowd was chanting and stomping their feet.

The sports boosters hadn't spent a penny on the washroom facilities. They rented portable toilets from a fly-by-night company in Kankakee. These might have been modern in the depression. The stench was a killer. They'd been plunked past the concession stand in the dim shadows under the bleachers. You had to squeeze past the concession stand to get to them. I always wondered if it didn't violate some health code or other to have them this close to the food. I never ate any of it anyway. Too much junk food and not enough chocolate.

Finishing quickly, we began making our way back. As we neared the shadows of the concession stand, I could see two people waving their arms at each other. As I got closer, even with the din of the crowd, I could hear them shouting. When we were about ten feet away, the taller person rushed off. Whoever it was turned the corner of the concession stand before I could recognize him or her.

The other person was Mabel Spandrel. She didn't notice us until we were nearly upon her. I made no move to stop, but she held out an arm.

She said, "Are you sure you should be here?"

The crowd noise had ebbed. A voice behind us said, "What's going on?" Kara Bochka emerged from the darkness under the stands and planted herself next to Spandrel.

I said, "I promised the kids I'd come to the game."

Spandrel said, "I'm not so sure someone under suspicion of murder should be here."

"Do we know someone like that?" I asked. I could play the ignorant asshole as well as any.

"You," Spandrel snapped.

Bochka said, "Do you know if the police have found out anything?"

I said, "I assume they know by now what colossal assholes many of the people who are running this place are. I assume they know people hated each other. I assume they know that Spandrel and Eberson were having an affair."

Bochka's mouth gaped open. She glanced at Spandrel.

"That's bullshit," Spandrel said.

Gone was any trace of the lecturer who bored us beyond enduring at meetings. She was pissed and ready to fight.

"I'm not here for a debate," I said. "You asked what they know. I'm telling you what I assume they know. You want me to stop?"

The crowd erupted in mad cheers. The bleacher stomping started again.

Bochka said, "I thought I told Graniento to put an end to them stomping on the bleachers. Can't he do anything right?"

I said, "I also assume—and so should you, for that matter—that the police have heard the rumors about the constant warfare in the English department. That each side

166

in the disputes has attempted, in the past, and presumably will in the future, plot against, smear, tear down, slander, and destroy each other. I assume the police know that the administration was trying to cook the students' grades and test scores to make the administration and board look better. Also that Peter Higden was boffing as many of the women on the staff as he could, perhaps even Ms. Spandrel."

Spandrel let fly. "You lying asshole. How dare you attempt to smear me?"

I didn't lose my temper. I was concentrating on being articulate. I said, "I have no idea if any of this is true. You might. I was asked a question. If you don't want answers, then don't ask questions. Were you having an affair with Gracie or Higden?"

"I don't answer to you."

"You've got to answer to somebody," I said.

"Certainly not to a faggot."

The slur pushed me over the edge. I began, "You homophobic—"

Scott put his hand on my arm. He glared at them. When he spoke, his voice was at its deepest thrum. I knew two things from that tone: he was deeply angry and in icy control. He hadn't pitched in the World Series for nothing. He said, "We need to keep a sense of decency."

Spandrel rounded on him, "Don't you start."

Scott laughed. It was the most refreshing sound I could have heard. When he spoke, his voice still thrummed. "You have no power over me. If I had a bucket of water, I'd be tempted to throw it on you, just to see what would happen."

I couldn't suppress a smile.

Spandrel turned to Bochka. "Do something," the head of the department demanded of the board president.

Bochka said, "I'm sure none of the teachers were engaged in unprofessional conduct."

I said, "No, it looks like it was mostly administrators—or if not, the administrators were heart and soul, part and parcel, of the whole screwed-up operation. But Ms. Spandrel still hasn't answered the question."

Spandrel said, "You miserable excuse for a human being."

I said, "You've made people miserable for no discernable, rational purpose."

"Good," she said, "I'm glad I made them miserable. I hope I've made you miserable."

I said, "Is that a management technique you learned in school, or do you come by your Nazi instincts naturally?"

The crowd was going nuts. No one else was around us. The rest of the attendees were focused on the action on the field. The dim lights played off Spandrel's beet-red face.

Spandrel said, "People don't like you, and we have proof they don't like the job you're doing."

"Proof where?"

"You'll see. You think you run this place. You push yourself forward and try to tell everyone else what to do."

I said, "Name once."

That stopped her.

I said, "If I've been telling people what to do, then you would have evidence of that."

"You do all those union things."

"Yes, that's correct. Next point?"

Bochka said, "The union can't do all the things you do."

I said, "If you are accusing me of an unfair labor practice, file a complaint. Have you talked to Teresa Merton, complained to her? What exactly don't you like? That you have to follow the union contract? If you don't like the contract, say something at the negotiations table."

Spandrel said, "I've had it. You don't listen. You do the same things you accuse administrators of doing."

168

I said, "No, your problem is that people listen to me more than they do to you. Even your suckups know I have more direct effect on their pay and their working conditions than you do because I'm part of the union leadership."

Spandrel said, "How dare you call teachers suckups?"

Bochka said, "That's totally unprofessional."

I said, "Speaking truth to power can always be a problem."

Spandrel said, "No one likes you. No one likes the job you do as union building rep."

I said, "As long as I'm irritating you, I'm satisfied."

Spandrel said, "I think we should settle this now. He's been criticizing the administration behind our backs since the first day I started."

"What exactly did I say? I assume you have dates, times, and exact quotes. And of course, you'll need to tell me who told you I said which things."

"I'm not going to tell you who told me."

I said, "If you're not going to tell me who, then it doesn't exist."

"Are you saying I'm making this up?"

"Yes."

She shook her finger in my face. "I don't have to make things up about you. I know you for what you are. You're a fag."

Scott put his hand back on my arm. I said, "Yes, I know. To whom is that news?"

The crowd groaned. Moments later they began chanting an obscenity. Bochka said, "Where are Graniento and Towne? I told them I didn't want any more obscenities chanted at these games. I'll cancel these games if I have to."

Spandrel's finger still wagged in my face. I was pissed, but Scott's touch was reassuring.

Scott stepped in front of me. Although the crowd was

chanting loudly, I could still hear that wonderful thrum. I moved close enough that I could catch a whiff of his deodorant. He said, "You two are the most pathetic excuses for human beings I have ever seen or heard of. You have no sense of proportion or decency. You have no common sense or common courtesy. You make me sick. Why don't you both quit and get out? You certainly don't care about children."

Bochka said, "Who the hell are you to say anything to us? How dare you? We do care about children."

Scott said, "Then why is there a football game going on? If you cared about children, there would be no game, or at least there would be hundreds of police. Two people have died, and yet you are playing this game? Are you mad? Is there no mourning for those have been murdered? Is this the appropriate way to honor those who died?"

Spandrel said, "Tickets were sold."

Scott interrupted. "And could have been refunded. Is your message here that sports are more important than murder? Or money is more important than people? Aren't you planning to do something before Monday to reassure the parents that the children and teachers are safe? I see no evidence that you have taken action to protect anyone at this game."

Spandrel said, "We haven't had problems at games."

Scott said, "People are dead, and you're having a football game."

I looked up. The stands were now at a normal buzz. Numerous people were looking over the edge of the bleachers down at us. Kids were pointing and calling out to different ones of us.

Spandrel, who didn't seem to have noticed the noise reduction, screamed, "You and your faggot lover are the problem."

Scott's voice was very soft, "That's the last time you get to say that."

Scott towered over her. I knew he wouldn't physically assault her. If she was in the batter's box, she'd have to duck the next pitch, but Scott was one of the most gentle of men, sort of a Gregory Peck with extra muscles.

Bochka said, "Mabel, we should leave."

Spandrel looked pissed and ready to keep fighting. Bochka put her arm through the crook in her employee's arm and escorted her away.

"Let's go home," Scott said.

"Yeah. I don't want to be near these people for a whole weekend."

We returned to our seats, picked up our blankets, and trudged out.

As we passed the concession stand, Scott asked, "Why haven't they fired your ass?"

"They must want something—or think that I know something or that I have some power over them that I'm not aware of. That last makes no sense, but yeah, something is out of control here."

"Before you said it just now, did Bochka know all that stuff about Spandrel and Higden?"

"I couldn't tell. They're homophobic creeps, and I guess Spandrel is a sexual athlete, but I'm not sure how that all connects to murder."

He said, "I'm worried about you."

"I'll be better when we get home."

30

The cops had been around all day. They had set up a command post in the school. I'd heard they'd been interviewing people nonstop.

As we neared the parking lot, Gault and Vulmea, the detectives, strode toward us. Vulmea was eating a corn dog with lots of mustard. Gault said, "We need to see you for a few minutes." His tone was rough and acerbic.

I nodded.

"In the school office."

He stood aside.

I didn't move. "What's this about?" I asked.

"We need to talk to you in the office."

I felt my pulse racing. Scott gave me and the cop puzzled looks. I said, "My attorney has advised me not to speak with you without him present."

Vulmea gave me a dirty look.

Gault said, "We have a witness that saw you coming out of the supply room at 4:45, long before you claim to have gotten there."

I gaped at him. My mind flashed to the scene in the

movie *The Producers* after the play *Springtime for Hitler* has started and the audience sits, mouths agape, in absolute stunned silence at what they are hearing and seeing. A jumble of thoughts and emotions swept through me. All reminders of my attorney's advice or being remotely sensible were gone. I could argue with Spandrel, but this was blatant irrationality, a lie without basis, and it was a threat.

I managed to gasp out, "Who?"

Gault asked, "Where were you at 4:45?"

"I already told you. I won't repeat myself. I came out of the supply room with Brandon Benson and Steven Frecking when I said I did."

Gault shuffled through a notepad. "We got that at 5:10."

"That's about right."

Gault said, "And now we've got someone who says they saw you coming out of the room at 4:45."

The pit of my stomach had taken a vacation. My mind reeled. I got misty-eyed. I was shaking.

Scott said, "Tom, do you want to sit down?"

It was like a dream. I said, "I was nowhere near the supply room at 4:45."

"Why would someone lie about that?" Vulmea asked.

"I don't know. I wasn't there."

"Do you have a witness to that?" Vulmea asked.

"I already gave you a statement of my movements. I don't need to repeat them. I was where I said I was. I'm sure you've checked it."

"As far as it was checkable," Vulmea said. "The parent said she did talk to you. She doesn't know exactly what time it was."

"Phone records will show exactly what the times were."

"But were they 4:45?"

"Why would I kill her?" I asked.

"You tell us."

"I have no reason to. Who told you I was there? I need to know that. I have a right to confront my accuser."

"That's in a court of law, not in an investigation."

"Bullshit. I have a right to know. This is bullshit." I was frightened and furiously angry.

"Why would people lie about your movements?"

"To protect themselves. Because they're homophobic creeps who are trying to destroy me."

"Why destroy you? What do you have that they don't?"

"A life? Someone who loves me? A life as an openly gay man who is comfortable with himself? Is it an attempt to wreck me because they're nuts? Because I have a lover who is a rich, famous baseball player? People can be insanely jealous. Some people want to tear down, hurt, and destroy just because they can. Because they want to bring others down to their level. How the hell should I know why? I just got told someone saw me near a murder scene. I'll need my lawyer here before I say anything else."

"If you could just go over again what happened," Vulmea said.

Again Scott put his hand on my arm. He said, "Tom will want his lawyer. He's not going to say any more until his lawyer gets here."

"Don't interfere," Vulmea said.

"Am I under arrest?" I asked.

"Not at the moment," Gault said.

"Then I'm leaving." I stumbled toward the parking lot. Scott kept his hand on my arm. They didn't try to stop us.

Before we were out of earshot, Vulmea called, "Don't leave town."

I was pulling my cell phone from its clip as I eased into the car. Trembling, shaken, and angry, I called my attorney. I got his voice mail. I left a message.

Scott started the car, turned to me, and took my hands in

his. "Okay, you're not arrested, because you're here with me. It's going to be okay. If you don't want to talk, fine. We're going home, or we'll do whatever you want."

I pulled in deep breaths. He put his arm around me. Feeling his touch was calming and a comfort. His eyes sought mine. He is a treasure of calm in any storm.

When he saw that my breathing was under control, he said, "I've never seen you so upset." He caressed my hand. "It's going to be okay. We'll get through this."

I said, "I'm furious. I've never been this furious. Deliberate. Absolute, deliberate, lies." I shook my head.

"We'll figure it out," he said.

"I've got to find the killer. I've got to be proactive. Someone lied. Deliberately, bald-faced lied."

.31.

It was late. I didn't want to stay at my place. I wanted to be as far away from Grover Cleveland High School as I could get. We drove to the city to stay at Scott's penthouse. As the warmth of the car spread over me, and the more I thought about the day, the more pissed off I got. Whatever was between towering anger and a stroke, I was there. I was fed up with anything remotely resembling a suburb or an administrator or a police detective.

I ranted about the vicissitudes of the world until Interstate 57 ended and the Dan Ryan Expressway began. I drew deep breaths and stared out the window from Ninety-fifth Street to Twenty-second. We inched toward the Loop in the construction traffic on the eternally-being-rehabbed stretch of road. As we eased off the Ryan onto Lake Shore Drive, Scott took my hand. That felt good.

If I was a get-drunk-and-hit-people kind of guy, I would have gone out and gotten drunk and hit people. Instead, I worked out for an hour with Scott, mostly in silence. We showered in his sunken tub.

We mounded the chocolate–chocolate chip ice cream with marshmallow sauce, chocolate sauce, and cashews and got down to serious eating. Another workout would be necessary in the morning.

As we were piling dishes in the dishwasher, I said, "I don't know how someone gets over being this angry. I don't remember this kind of fury."

We repaired to the living room. We each wore jeans, white socks, and white T-shirts. I walked to the floor-to-ceiling windows and stared out at the waves lapping against the lake shore. He stood next to me.

I said, "We don't believe in conspiracy theories."

"No, we don't."

"Unless it's Republicans."

"Well, of course."

"River's Edge is a very conservative area. Maybe it is a vast right-wing conspiracy. Maybe they're all Republicans."

"There are a lot of lies, but to be a conspiracy they'd have to be organized. You usually sneer at them for being too stupid."

"Maybe they're taking lessons or classes. Maybe there's a book: *The Rush Limbaugh Guide to Concocting a Brainless Conspiracy.*"

"Even for you, that's a little paranoid."

"Depends on which side of the conspiracy you're on."

"I'm on your side."

"I know. I meant them."

"But who would 'they' be? And a conspiracy to do what?"

"Isn't that one of the benefits of a vast conspiracy? You need to not be able to name specific people specifically conspiring."

"But we do know at least some names. Frecking and Benson lied. Someone lied about where you were. The superintendent, the head of the English department, the president of the school board, and the principal are acting suspiciously."

"And we've got two dead bodies. Both of which I discovered. I am depressed and pissed off."

Scott said, "You have every right to be."

"I think I'm the most pissed off at Victoria Abbot, the assistant superintendent."

"Why?"

"Because she knows better. Because she knows what people are up to—and it's not good. And she won't tell what she knows, but she gives fire-alarm-level warnings. Hell, she could be part of the conspiracy trying to make me more frightened. 'We've got the guy on edge, let's see if we can't make him more miserable.'"

"Did she seem honest?"

"I couldn't tell. After all the lies I've heard today, I'm not sure I'd believe god himself if he showed up."

"And you don't believe in god."

"How many supreme beings can you fit on the head of a pin?"

"Not as many as I used to."

It started to rain again. I watched Lake Shore Drive dampen. Traffic was light. It was long after midnight.

"What's worse is that somebody I work with is a killer. Attempting to pin it on me adds excess anxiety to my life, but to think that someone who teaches in the same corridor is a killer is spooky."

"Might be a killer. We don't know who did it."

"Definitely a liar."

"The police seemed to believe you."

"I'm afraid that was more Frank Rohde's support yesterday than anything I said or did. That young cop is a menace."

"We've got the weekend to relax."

"Or brood."

"You are very good at that. I'd hate to deny you the chance to enjoy something you're good at. We've had ice cream and chocolate, and I'll do what I can." In bed he massaged my back for quite a while. We do that for each other for tension release, for pleasure, and for the hell of it. I took my turn massaging him. I wasn't in the mood for much more. In a short while, he fell asleep. He almost always falls asleep quickly and seldom wakes up during the night.

I tossed and turned. I tried reading. I went straight to my surefire "get to sleep" book, a volume of Wordsworth's poetry. Not a smidge of luck.

I returned to the living room. Got a blanket and a mound of pillows and cushions and sat them in the middle of the couch. I made a snug spot for myself, and I watched the rain. I must have slept. I awoke and it was dark. Scott had my head in his lap. His head was wedged against several pillows and cushions. He was snoring softly. I snuggled close and made sure the blanket was covering us both. I slept again.

32

Saturday we did our grocery shopping online. It's a pain in the neck to try to go out shopping with Scott. If he's recognized, it becomes a madhouse and can get dangerous. While a cap pulled far down on the eyes and sloppy clothes are often enough to throw off casual observers, as they did the night before, use his credit card and all anonymity goes out the window. I switched sites and ordered a few things for my nephews for Christmas. Saturday night we put in our latest NetFlix DVD, *Secondhand Lions,* a great movie. Saturday night I finished the Agatha Christie and managed to get a little sleep.

Late Sunday morning Meg called. I was doing some laundry, mostly socks and underwear.

She said, "The assistant superintendent wants to meet with you. I talked to her again. She said she felt bad for the way she treated you."

I said, "This isn't going to be one of those 'I've got something to tell you' moments and 'Meet me at three,' and I go to the appointment and the person I'm supposed to meet is dead."

Meg said, "Don't you hate when that happens?"

We agreed to get together late that afternoon.

I called Todd Bristol, our attorney. We'd played phone tag most of Saturday. Todd said, "Do not confront those people. Do not say anything to them. If they come talk to you, take out your cell phone. Call me or get in touch with your union representative. Do not be alone with any one of those people. If there are two or more, turn around and walk away immediately."

"Do I have to be paranoid about walking down the halls?"

"Yes. Look to see who is where. You might want to get in touch with your friends and see if they can provide escort service."

"This is absurd."

"You're the one who called me for advice."

"I didn't mean the advice is absurd. I meant having to follow your sensible advice is absurd. An escort in my own building? That's nuts."

"That place is dangerous to you."

"Should I quit?"

"It's going to be nerve-wracking for a while, but my advice is not to quit. You need to take precautions. So, take them."

Scott nudged me. "Ask him if anything these people are doing is specifically illegal."

I asked.

Todd considered. "It's complicated. Partly it depends on what you can prove, and you can't prove anything. It doesn't sound like you can count on Victoria Abbot. You've got proof on that one grade-changing mess, but that's not a major felony. They'll never admit to a conspiracy to get you. Giving false statements to the police is a crime, but how often do cops prosecute that?" He answered his own question. "That depends. Saying negative things about you to the police is not illegal."

I said, "They're masters of innuendo and character as-sassination."

"You have my permission to talk to your friend on the po-lice department. He might know what's going on."

I asked, "Are you saying that if I didn't have a friend on the police force, I'd be in more trouble?"

"You're not actually in trouble. You haven't done any-thing wrong."

I promised to fill him in if we found out anything. We called Frank to set up the meeting for early Sunday evening.

33

Much as I hated to return to the suburbs before Monday morning, we hustled out for the meeting with the assistant superintendent and Meg. We met at a Brew-Ha-Ha coffee shop in Park Forest, far from the River's Edge school district.

Victoria Abbot wore dark glasses, a black sweatsuit, and a beret pulled down low over her eyes. She clutched her car keys in her right hand. I only recognized her because she was with Meg.

When the assistant superintendent took off her sunglasses, I could see that red lines shot through the whites of her eyes, which had big bags under them. Her face was pasty gray. She said, "You can't tell a soul about this meeting. Only Meg can know. I'm almost sorry I talked to her. I'm probably going to regret talking to you, but I've done wrong. I should have told you everything Friday morning. I'm going to tell you everything I know or have surmised. I can't take the pressure anymore. I can't take the lies and deception. I can't stand this nonsensical secretiveness. I can't stand the cruelty. This madness has gone on long enough."

I said, "I appreciate any help you can give me."

"Help?" She leaned close to me. "What you need is a tank battalion."

"What the hell is going on?"

She glanced carefully around, taking her time examining all the patrons. Then she leaned within inches of my face and said, "It was their idea to try to accuse you. Bochka, Towne, Graniento, and Spandrel, especially Spandrel. They made one of the teachers go to the police and lie about seeing you. I don't know which one."

I got the same chills I had on Friday when the police had first told me the news.

I said, "They're insane."

"Very desperate and very determined and very angry."

I made a guess. "They threatened to keep the teacher from getting tenure."

"Oh, dear, yes. They are willing to go quite far to make you miserable."

"Why?"

"You know why."

"Being gay?"

"Not just being gay. That you are comfortable being gay. You are out of the closet. You aren't dying from some dreadful disease. You aren't suicidal. You don't party until you puke. You are what they might consider normal if they didn't hate you so much. They don't like you because you have a successful lover who is an attractive man. They don't like you because they don't have power over you. They can't bully you or intimidate you."

Scott said, "But they can't discriminate. That's illegal."

Abbot said, "They're trying to get Tom accused of murder—at the very least, ruin your reputation."

I said, "Do they teach being a moronic bully in some administrative class at some university?"

Meg said, "Probably only at the PhD level."

"Why?" I asked.

Scott said, "Remember what Larry Kramer said in that recent speech? They all hate us."

"But everyone doesn't," I said.

"But these people do," Abbot said. "They really do."

I said, "They're the bosses. They have power over me."

"But that's not how they see it," Abbot said. "They are angry because they can't make you respect them."

"I don't respect them."

"Exactly. They know you have disdain for them. They feel that spreads among the staff and hurts their power over them. If you can disdain them, ignore them, not take them seriously, laugh at them, they don't have power over you, and they have less power over the others. It's that way with lots of bosses."

"I guess I knew some of these things, sort of," I said, "but I'm seldom aware of them on a conscious level, certainly not of how much of a danger Bochka, Graniento, Spandrel, and Towne are to me."

The assistant superintendent said, "They are a distinct danger. They planned to come up with every suspicion possible they could about you and give it to the police."

"Were there a lot of those?"

"They didn't let me in on the final meetings. I'm in on many of them, but not all. They think I'm one of them. I've never spoken up against what they do. I'm a coward."

I said, "Friday night before I had a confrontation with Spandrel and Bochka, Spandrel was fighting with someone. I couldn't tell who it was."

"Graniento, the principal. I don't know what was going on, but there is now some kind of bad blood between them."

I wished I knew what that was. I asked, "Has Bochka met with the suckups?"

"They all meet and plan together. Eberson, Higden,

185

Pinyon, Schaven, Spandrel, Bochka, Towne, Graniento. They are endlessly plotting. Even when something could be done simply, they come up with convoluted methods of doing things and complex ways to implement them."

Scott asked, "Were the teachers in on plotting to get Tom accused of murder?"

"Except for the teacher who actually told, I don't think so."

"That had to be one of the people you just mentioned."

"Probably, but not necessarily," she said. "Any non-tenured teacher they could bully would do."

"They're nuts," Scott said.

"Why are you coming to me now?" I asked. "What happened after we talked Friday morning?"

"They want you fired. They will tell any lie. This is a further warning."

"Maybe I should assume your meeting with me is part of their conspiracy."

She drew back and breathed hard for several moments. "I suppose I deserve that."

"Will you help me expose them?"

"I can't. I'll lose my job."

I said, "I won't stoop to their level. I'm not going to threaten to tell them you told me if you don't help me. I won't. I promise. You've tried to help, but I'm not like them. I won't become like them."

Abbot said, "Maybe you'll have to, to win. I wanted to warn you to help my own conscience."

"But your conscience doesn't go so far as to try to expose them or put a stop to them?" Meg asked.

"If there was a way to do it without me losing my job, I'd do it. I swear I would."

I asked, "How did this get started?"

"Bochka began it."

I said, "She's already an all-powerful school board president. What more does she want?"

"But don't you see?" Abbot said. "She isn't all-powerful. That's one of the things that pisses her off."

Meg said, "Does she want tanks and guns and torture and prisons? The board does her bidding in a heartbeat. How is she not all-powerful?"

Abbot said, "She keeps making promises to her friends in the community. One parent or a group comes to her, and Bochka makes a promise to get a thing done. Then another group comes, and she makes a different promise to them. Sometimes it doesn't make a difference who she promises what to, but sometimes the promises are contradictory or just silly or stupid. Towne, as superintendent, gets driven nuts. Bochka calls and gives a command, and Towne is supposed to obey. We all are. I have heard that her style has finally begun to catch up with her. She may have a lot of opposition in the next school board election. She's petrified of that. She's worried about losing her position."

"But it's only a small district," I said. "Why does she care so much?"

"She's ambitious. I've heard her talk about running for the state legislature. Her ego is involved. She's been a part of this community for thirty years. The funny thing is, I'm not sure she knows what she wants. She mostly waits to react negatively and pick at people. Why do you think some teachers haven't gotten tenure and others have? Why do you think Jourdan has had so much trouble the past few years? Word came down from on high, and she's as high as it gets in this district. One of the few people she hasn't been able to cow or intimidate or make miserable is you."

"Should I be honored?" I asked.

"Very frightened," she replied.

Meg asked, "How did you get involved?"

Abbot said, "I got dragged in by Towne. She said she wanted witnesses. I assume to protect herself in some way. She made no objections to any of the proposed schemes. Bochka has hated you for years. Probably since your first public appearance as an openly gay man. That woman would connive at anything. She is mean-spirited and vicious. She's got a political agenda behind everything she does. I don't blame her husband for divorcing her. She is vile."

"If it's so awful," I asked, "why don't you go to another district?"

"I've been trying. I've only been here a year. It looks odd if you switch jobs after being in one for such a short time. I can't wait to get out and find a place where real professionals are in charge."

I said, "I appreciate your coming to me."

"You're not going to say anything?"

"I said I wouldn't, and I always keep faith."

Meg said, "What do you know about the cheating on the state test results?"

Abbot now began to sweat. She leaned forward and whispered. "We are in so much shit. It's not just test results. They've been faking graduation rates. They've been changing grades."

" 'They' who?"

"All of us. They've ordered me to. I had no choice but to comply. Administrators don't have tenure. These people are ruthless. You know what happens if they don't keep the test scores and the graduation rates up and meet all the guidelines?"

I said, "Not much, as far as I can see."

"Oh, but yes. Among administrators and on the board it is a big deal. They compare themselves to other districts. And parents go nuts and call to complain about their kids not doing well."

One of the great lies we'd been told when the new state testing system came out was that the test results would never be used to compare districts or kids.

I said, "The parents could always vote for a referendum. Their kids would get a better quality education."

Abbot said, "They don't see a direct connection between a new school and higher scores."

I said, "It's new textbooks. It's better, more up-to-date computers. Did you know one of the science textbooks they use still talks about going to the moon someday?"

Abbot said, "I don't believe that."

"I've read the passage," Meg said.

Abbot said, "Parents won't budge. It's like they're spending their own money in the middle of the Great Depression. They just won't do it, and they will do anything to protect their low taxes."

Our district was notorious for having the second lowest per-pupil spending among K–12 districts in the state of Illinois. What did they think was going to happen when they didn't spend any money?

I asked, "Is there some kind of investigation going on?"

"People from the state have been in looking at records. Teachers aren't supposed to know how to get into the program, but someone's been leaking information. Bochka and the rest are desperate to find out who. They think it's you or one of your friends."

I wasn't about to reveal the actual source. I said, "I've helped a couple teachers who were interested in learning the system. I've taught them password controls. We came in before school started last summer."

"They better not find that out," Abbot said. "You'll be blamed for that and everything else. If there's a union problem, then it's Tom Mason's fault. If a teacher disagrees, then it's Tom Mason who put them up to it."

"I don't," I said.

"But you listen to people. And both factions listen to you. You've had more effect on the teachers' lives in the past few years than these administrators. They hate that. They hate your influence. They hate your untouchability. Do not underestimate their hatred."

"Who exactly is doing all this hating?"

"Graniento, Spandrel, Towne, Bochka, and I don't know how many of the teachers in the suckup faction, but my guess is at least three or four. The teachers in general do respect you."

"Do you have proof of the cheating?" I asked.

Abbot said, "I kept detailed records and logs of times and dates of what I did. I kept printouts before I made changes and after I made changes. I haven't told anyone that. I've made backup copies. If they try to harm me, they will never find all the copies, and my husband has orders about what to do if something happens to me. He's furious. He says that if I'm in real, physical danger, I should go to the police, or I should quit."

Meg said, "I'd think about that seriously. Murder has been done."

Abbot said, "These people are dangerous. These people are insane. If I could find a way out, I'd take it."

34

Scott and I checked in with Frank Rohde to make sure he wasn't out on a case. As the new guy in the rotation, he had to work most Sundays. I asked about my car. They didn't know when I would get it back.

Frank greeted us warmly. A few cops at the desk recognized Scott. He signed autographs. I wanted to tell Frank what I'd learned and find out from him what the police knew. If he told me anything, I had no intention of revealing it to those disparate factions who'd asked desperately for me to get them information.

Rohde said, "I used to spend Sundays with the kids. I'm not sure this is such a good thing. Pay is better."

We chatted briefly, then I filled him in on what I knew. As I spoke, the only thing I left out was Abbot's name. I ended with the big question. "Who told Gault and Vulmea that I was outside that door at 4:45? That is not true. I was petrified I'd be arrested."

"It's your word against your accuser. They do need confirmation from at least one more person. They don't have a second person. It's tough to get two people to tell the exact same lie."

I said, "I've seen it happen."

"Maybe they haven't worked it out," Scott said. "Yet."

Rohde said, "They can't keep coming up with a string of witnesses at their convenience. It looks too odd. 'Oh, by the way, I was there, too, saw the same thing, and decided not to say anything because I didn't think you were interested.'"

Scott said, "I can imagine one of them saying that kind of thing."

Rohde said, "But it's got to be believable."

"You really don't know?" I asked.

He gazed at me evenly. We'd been friends for a number of years. We'd done some good things with a lot of tough kids. We'd had some spectacular failures. But he was a cop and I was a civilian. Had I gone too far? He said, "Tom, if I knew and I told you, what would you do?"

"I'd be pissed. I'd want to confront whoever it was."

"And what would that accomplish?"

"I'd know who was trying to frame me. I'd know who to avoid. I could fight back."

"How? What could you say?"

"I'd ask him why."

Frank asked, "And if he told you he did it because he hated you, what have you gained?"

"The knowledge that an evil person knows I know they are an evil person."

Scott said, "If they cared about that, do you think they would have lied in the first place?"

I thought about that for several moments, then said, "I guess not."

Frank asked, "Could you stay calm?"

After another hesitation, I said, "I'd hope I'd be able to." I glanced at Scott. "I think I could. Maybe." Scott put his hand on my arm for a moment. I said, "I'm not sure what would happen."

Frank said, "All that lying trying to get you in trouble has actually been to your benefit. That many lies nobody can believe. They also have to be believable lies. Something odd is going on at that school."

I said, "They're frightened and frightening people."

"Afraid of what?"

"I'm not sure. Looking bad?"

Scott said, "Their egos are caught up in their jobs to an unhealthy degree. They've got a passion for all the incorrect things in education. If they had that kind of passion for kids, I bet they'd be great."

Frank said, "I'll try to help any way I can. Conspiring against you is bad, but they've done nothing provable so far that I can arrest them for. They're rotten, but so far, not criminal. I think it should make you very wary, but you are that already. If they were sane people, I'd tell you to sit down and talk to them."

"I'll be calling the union president tonight to fill her in. The shit is going to hit the fan. I'm worried for people's physical safety. We've had two murders already."

Frank said, "That assumes at least one of the people at the school committed one or both murders."

"I assume they all could." Unbidden into my imagination came a scene near the end of the movie *A Shot in the Dark*: Peter Sellers, as Inspector Clouseau, confronts all the suspects and attempts to explain the murder. It's the best comic-crime-resolution scene ever. Then all the suspects get blown up with a bomb Clouseau's boss planted in Clouseau's car. It turns out all the suspects were killers except one who was a blackmailer. The one his boss suspected, who does not get in the car, was innocent. Frankly, at that moment the ending of the movie was a pleasant thought. All of the rotten conniving people jammed into one car and getting blown up. An appealing picture. But sane adults don't think these things. Well, actually, they do, it's just that we don't act on them. I wasn't ready to go to jail for murdering any of these people. They weren't worth it.

I said, "Did they find out anything about Eberson having an affair with a student?"

"They have no confirmation on that. The source says it was an anonymous tip and they've given it no credence. The husband went nuts when it was suggested. He seems to have genuinely loved his wife. Gault said the three older boys were in tears. The littlest one is still a baby."

"That is sad," I said. "Poor little kids."

Rohde said, "Right now, we have nothing we can tell the family. We have no suspects."

I asked, "Why did they take Mabel Spandrel to the police station that first night?"

"As far as I can tell, it was excessive zeal mixed with missteps by Spandrel. At first she said she had no witnesses to where she was. By the time they got her to the station, she had several witnesses."

I said, "She lied and got the others to lie."

"If she did, they were convincing enough. Gault and Vulmea couldn't shake their story."

"Who gave her the alibi?"

"I don't have the names."

"I know who," I said. "Or I can make a good guess." I told him the names.

He said, "I can try and check that for you. I can't interfere with their case. Sometimes it was easier being a plain old detective."

We discussed the argument I'd seen between Graniento and Spandrel and Abbot's comment that it was a sharp disagreement of some kind but that she didn't know about what.

I said, "Maybe they're starting to turn on each other."

Rohde said, "If there is some kind of conspiracy, maybe it's starting to unravel. That's actually kind of a lot of people to trust to keep their mouths shut. The more who know about something, the possibility increases exponentially of someone telling."

I said, "We got rumors that Peter Higden gambled a lot."

"Gault has that as well. So far we've got respectable bookies who never heard of Peter Higden."

I added, "And the PE coaches were double dipping." I explained.

Rohde said, "That doesn't sound like a motive for murder."

I said, "It's a pattern of things done on the sly. Things that aren't seriously illegal, or seriously immoral, just skating on the edge of getting away with—"

"Murder," Frank said.

"Did they get any information about the hate notes Pinyon reported getting?"

"Nothing useful. Pinyon says he got them, but other people said he might have done them himself. I don't understand these people."

"Join the club," I said.

Scott asked, "Did they get any results on what killed Eberson and Higden?"

Rohde said, "Yeah. Someone held that eraser in her mouth until she stopped breathing. It was wedged surprisingly far into her throat. Somebody was pretty angry, pretty strong, or both. Higden was run over with his own car."

"Smart," I said. "The killer was planning. No traces on his or her own car if Higden's is used. But using his car brings up several more questions. How'd the person get in the car? If Higden was in the car, how'd the killer get him out of the car and in a position to be run over?"

"Those are the right questions," Rohde said. "He was run over twice. The first time, they got his legs. He was still alive when they got his upper chest and neck."

"My god, that's awful," Scott said.

"Hell of a way to die," Rohde said. "But none of it gives us much of a clue to who did it. We've got lots of possibilities. Everybody here had a good laugh at the descriptions of the fights within the English department. Are these really adults? Teachers? What kind of idiot administrators are these that countenance that kind of shit?"

I said, "It takes a special brand of stupidity. If I weren't living it, I wouldn't believe it."

Scott asked, "When did Peter die?"

"Not long before you found him is all I know. Nobody saw Higden after he was questioned—or at least, if anybody saw him, they aren't admitting it. So far, Gault and Vulmea are the last ones who admit to seeing him alive."

I said, "I don't think Gault and Vulmea killed him."

"They've got alibis," Frank said. "They were questioning everybody."

Scott asked, "Is Tom off the hook?"

Frank said, "Yes. That doesn't mean you shouldn't be very careful. We found some interesting things when we searched their homes. Mrs. Eberson had an office in her home. The screensaver on her computer was a picture of Ann Coulter with quotes from her speeches superimposed along the edges."

I said, "That homophobic, right-wing, Nazi bitch."

"Eberson or Coulter?" Rohde asked.

"Both," I said.

Rohde said, "One of the quotes said that she was just trying to be funny and outrageous."

Scott said, "That has to be one of the most moronic and insensitive things anyone has ever said. That woman shows nothing but stupidity and ignorance every time she opens her mouth."

Rohde said, "Eberson obviously revered her."

I said, "That is sick shit."

Scott said, "These people hated you. This is all about you. These people are all homophobic pigs. Someone is trying to pin the murders on you. They lied about where you were. I'm afraid for you. Maybe you shouldn't go back there."

I said, "It's their faction that's dead."

Scott said, "But it's you they hate."

I asked, "Is there really a sexual angle to this?"

"Gault and Vulmea think so," Frank said. "We've got rumors and denials from several sources. Higden isn't married and as far as we can find out was not dating anyone. He lived in one of those condos just south of the Loop in Chicago. You know, the new places. According to Gault, the parents didn't seem to have a clue about their kid's life. He didn't have brothers or sisters. They didn't know of anyone he was dating seriously. Eberson's husband seemed genuinely confused and upset when they suggested the possibility that his wife was unfaithful. He claimed their sex life was fine and that his wife would never cheat. You told me one of the teachers confirmed that she was having an affair. Gault and Vulmea will have to check again."

I said, "Some teachers were worried about being safe in school. I assume they are also worried about the kids being safe. We do have two unsolved murders."

"You know, it's odd. The administrators didn't call us about that. We had to call them. We had reporters asking us questions about safety. We're going to have a police presence at the school. Only one entrance is going to be available for the kids, one for the teachers. At the beginning and end of the school day there will be cops at all exits and entrances. Cops will be patrolling the halls. It's a volatile situation."

I asked, "Did the administrators say why they didn't call?"

"They said they were trying to avoid publicity."

"Avoid publicity?" Scott said. "Are they out of their fucking minds? Publicity? They've had two murders."

Rohde said, "You're not going to get an argument on that from me."

Scott asked, "Are the police planning to tell the administration about Benson and Frecking trysting in the closet?"

"I'm not sure what Gault and Vulmea told them. As far as I can tell, what they were doing has nothing to do with the murder."

I said, "I can't imagine they did it. Who can make love after doing something like that? They lied about me, though—doesn't that make them more suspect?"

"But Gault isn't totally convinced yet that they're lying and you're not. It's complicated. They've found more evidence of sexual activity."

"There were more people in that storage closet?"

"I don't know yet. Right now they're checking to see if it's old or new residue. Also, Peter Higden had fresh semen stains in his underwear."

"I'm finding this hard to believe. They don't need to get hotel rooms, they could just rent out a wing of the school."

Rohde said, "I've seen some killers do some pretty insane things. But Benson and Frecking didn't strike Gault and Vulmea as killers. From what they said and from your description, I agree."

"Would their lying implicate them in a larger conspiracy?" Scott asked.

I shook my head. "It marks them as desperate and not too bright, but I'm not sure they'd be in on it with the administrators. Maybe."

Rohde said, "Gault is an honest, hard-working cop. I've

talked to him and his partner a couple times. Vulmea doesn't like you."

"I don't like him either."

"Neither do I, but Gault is a good cop."

As we got ready to leave, we thanked him. He said, "I'll say it again: be very wary, very careful."

35

We headed back to Chicago. As we drove, we talked. I said, "I have no idea what to do. I am completely stumped. Abbot is frightened out of her mind."

"You're not going to say anything to the other administrators?"

"I gave her my word, and I'm not sure how much good it would do anyway. If they know I'm onto their conspiracy, it could drive them to more desperate measures or further underground. If I can keep getting information from Abbot while they think I don't know, that might be best."

Scott said, "If one, some, or all of them are killers, then Abbot could be in danger if you told."

I said, "I think every person at that school is in danger while that administration has anything to do with running the place."

He said, "You could just quit. You don't have to work."

We'd had this discussion numerous times. Yes, he's got plenty of money and high school teachers in Illinois don't make bad money. I wouldn't have to give up eating chocolate if I quit. But early in our relationship I'd sworn to myself

I would never live off Scott and his fame. I have my pride, and he seldom pushed it. At the moment he was trying to give me an alternative to a horrible situation.

I said, "I'm not going to quit. Leaving would be an admission of guilt. It would cede the field to them. I'm frightened, and I'm angry. I want to beat those motherfuckers. I want them to suffer and be miserable."

"Tom, I'm worried for you. They can push any number of your buttons. You need to stay calm at all times."

"I'll be careful."

"Maybe you should have a security guard."

"Maybe."

"Don't be alone with them. You need a witness or a lawyer or somebody. Remember what Todd Bristol said about having an escort in the building."

"I'll talk with Teresa Merton tonight."

When I got home, I called Merton and told her the whole story leaving out only the name I'd promised to keep secret. She said, "I know you will anyway, but I urge you not to worry. You've done nothing wrong. I'll contact the union legal service first thing in the morning about all the issues. It's time we brought the cheating on statistics to a head."

I said, "I'll do whatever I can to help with that."

She added, "Brandon Benson called. He doesn't want you as his rep." She gave a comfortable laugh, then said, "I hope that son of a bitch is squirming and miserable every step of the way as you represent him. Traitors don't get to pick who talks for them or who represents them."

I said, "Thanks."

"No need to thank me," she said. "I'm doing what's right. Those who feel they are above the rules don't get to dictate to the rest of us our behavior or our reactions to their behavior.

We don't have to cower in the presence of the assholes in the universe, and in this case Brandon Benson is one of the sillier."

I said, "The administration might not find out about them being in the room."

"And sometimes the assholes get lucky. You might encourage him to quit before they get a chance to find out."

"I already did."

She said, "That's why I like you as building rep. You think of the basics and tell them honestly. Thanks."

I told her about the suggestion that I have some kind of escort in the building.

She said, "I'll work out a schedule. You've got Morgan Adair in that third-floor corridor with you. Set something up with him, and then we'll cover for any other times."

I called Morgan. He readily agreed. "Should we all be scared?" he asked.

"They are frightening people."

"Got that right. I've given up on Frecking. I'm never going to date someone I work with again."

I thought this was a sane notion.

Scott and I worked out, took showers, then sat on a mound of pillows in front of the fireplace.

Scott said, "I desperately want to say everything is going to be okay. I know I have no control over that."

"These people are dangerous and vicious. They're out of control. I think they would try anything. They would tell any lie. It's like watching people having a tantrum and not being able to stop them. And all that leaves out the fact that two people have been murdered."

"These people have tried to pin everything on you. They've failed."

"Not from lack of trying."

Scott said, "You've got good people in your corner making plans and giving support."

"You're the most important one."

He put his arms around me, and I leaned my head back onto his shoulder.

He said, "You know I'll do anything."

"I know. I wish I could count on the assistant superintendent taking a stand."

"You and I will stand together, no matter what it takes."

I took great comfort in his arms that night.

36

Monday morning I felt a little better, but I was still tired from lack of sleep. I arrived at school about an hour early. On normal days I did that to be able to grade papers left over from the days before (a perennial problem), to make sure all my technology requirements for the day were set (any sensible teacher always assumes the technology in his classroom will break down), to double check the plans for the slow kids (if they didn't have enough to do they could get restless; if they had too much to do they could get restless), and finally to sit, sip coffee, and think (sanity check).

Georgette Constantine met me at the teachers' entrance. She motioned me into a nearby janitor's closet. She was shaking. Her eyes held mine as she said, "Amando Graniento told me to keep you busy. He is down in your classroom. Spying. Sabotaging. I don't know what all. It can't be good."

"I won't tell him I saw you."

"You can tell him I met you with bagpipes and a brass band and escorted you to your classroom. Don't worry about me." She took out her cell phone. "You'll need a witness. Call me now, and leave your phone in your pocket.

When Teresa Merton and Meg come in, I'll send them down to your room."

I said, "You think of everything."

She said, "This is murder, and we all need to take precautions."

I thanked her. As I hurried toward my classroom, I repeated to myself my pledges about remaining calm. I was angry. Were these coordinated attacks? Maybe. I wondered if Graniento's presence represented the second team. I'd had a confrontation with Spandrel and Bochka—was it going to be Graniento's turn?

The building was mostly quiet. I nodded to the few other early teachers. Through the window in my classroom door, I could see that the computer monitor light was on. I paused at the doorway. I took deep breaths until I was under control. I took out my cell phone and checked to make sure it was on. I put it in my shirt pocket and pulled my jacket tighter to cover it.

Graniento sat at my desk. He was going through the drawers. Every few moments he'd tap several computer keys, then go back to searching. Occasionally, he added a piece of paper to a pile in the middle of the desk. I'd left no such pile last Friday. I thrust the door open and strode in. I made sure the door didn't shut all the way.

Graniento jumped about a foot. I loved the simple-minded gape on his face.

"What are you doing here?" he demanded.

I said, "I work here." I laughed. Really. I felt a little of the tension drain away. If he was that stupid, how much of a threat could he be? A lot, I warned myself.

I walked up to the desk and around to the side that he was on. As I moved, I got a continuous glare. I looked at the monitor. He tried to reach to turn it off. I grabbed the keyboard and moved it out of his reach. "The bigger questions are, what are you doing here, and why would you be at my computer?"

"We have a right to look at how you've been using the Internet."

"Do you?" I tapped several keys. "And here's the recent history. Let's see, for the past ten minutes someone has been attempting to access pornographic Internet sites on this computer."

"You've been doing that."

"Too sad for you, Tiger Lily. Georgette met me at the door. She knows you were here and what time you left your office to come in."

"Georgette will be fired."

"She's got a union, and she's got protections, just like I do."

"You can't prove I did that. You probably have it set on a timer."

I laughed. I said, "Good try on getting into the pornographic sites. I, however, let the students in my classroom use this, and I've got the most sophisticated blocks and firewalls possible on this computer. Weren't you beginning to wonder why you couldn't get to any site?"

He stood up and moved around to the other side of the desk. He was wearing the most godawful combination of a brown suit, a green tie, and an orange shirt. The colors may have been supposed to suggest autumn but looked more like someone had ingested a Hawaiian flowered shirt and puked it up.

I sat down. I picked up the papers he'd placed in the middle of the desk.

"Let's see what you've been looking through, or perhaps trying to plant."

"I can look through your things."

"What were you expecting to find here?" I asked. "A secret

stash? You could have brought drugs to plant, but then you'd have to bring them to school yourself." I checked each drawer. Only the one on the top left seemed to have been disturbed. I said, "In here you would have found my lesson plan printouts, copies of my notes to parents, and copies of weekly progress notes on each of the kids with learning disabilities."

I kept separate files on each kid and made daily notes on significant progress or problems, as well as a record of discussions with parents or LD teachers. These included times and dates for everything.

"Why are you here?" I asked.

"I can be here."

"At the moment, I'm not disputing that. I asked why?"

"Looking for clues to solving the murder."

"Really, in my desk? How odd. Did you expect to find a smoking eraser? Or perhaps an extra automobile?"

"I don't answer to you."

"But what you've done is suspicious."

"You're the one who's the problem," he said. He put his fists on the edge of my desk and leaned toward me. "You're the one who can't get along with people. You're the one who causes trouble. You're the one who stops anything from happening in this department."

I said, "I rarely say a word at departmental meetings, which you don't attend."

"I get reports."

"Do you? And you've done what to solve the problems?"

"I know all about you. You ignore all the directives."

"Name a time and date when I have not complied with every single one of your memos, e-mails, commands, and directives. Produce a scintilla of evidence."

"I don't have it with me."

"You don't have it at all. Unless you plan to make it up. How would you do that? You couldn't have a witness. You don't attend our meetings. Even the superintendent never attends meetings. Until last Thursday, he'd never been to my classroom. Bochka hadn't either. Until then, I'd never met with you and any combination of them together."

"They will vouch for me."

"They who? And vouch for what?"

"Everyone. All the trouble you cause."

"And what trouble would that be? Try to be specific."

He leaned back and crossed his arms across his chest. "You know what I'm talking about."

I said, "Nope. Not a clue."

He said, "You're always defending the teachers."

I said, "Yes, that's what a union representative does."

"Even when they're wrong."

"Right or wrong, they're entitled to representation. When they've done something wrong in the past, I've worked with administrators to try and help them improve their teaching, or to get them to stop doing what they weren't supposed to be doing. You're the ones who felt the need to be autocratic and bid and command. I was willing to work with you. You're the one that wanted to run roughshod over the union."

"You were against every change I've tried to make."

I said, "You pick the curriculum or the teachers pick the curriculum, I don't care. The kids in my classroom will learn. You can have a lovely power trip or you can work collaboratively with the teachers. I don't have time for your nonsensical politics. You're the one who's been a traitor to the teachers and the kids. You've taken bullying and backstabbing to new heights. All to what earthly purpose?"

"You don't understand how real businesses work. If this was a real business, you'd have been out on your ass the first day I was here."

"Really? How could that have happened, even in a real business? I didn't even speak to you the first day."

"People confide in you."

"A hanging offense in this jurisdiction. Or is it that they wouldn't go talk to you? I thought the suckups did come rushing to you."

"You older teachers have had a wild run of this place for years. You've driven it into the ground. You need to be reined in. You teachers don't know how to run a school."

I said, "So this is what running a school has felt like. Gosh, I missed that all these years. I wish I'd have known I was running the place, I'd have gotten paid a ton more, and I'd have fixed things up better and more efficiently. Nobody tells me these things."

"Don't try and make light of this!"

I was surprised at how calm I did feel. Scott would have been proud.

I said, "Humor is not your strong suit."

He said, "You're not in charge. You'll never be in charge."

"But I don't want to be in charge. Never have. Never will." I tried the abrupt topic switch tactic. "Who did Spandrel get to lie about where she went after the meeting? You?"

"How dare you?"

"I figure it could have been the usual triumvirate of you, Towne, or Bochka, but more likely one of the teachers."

"Her alibi is perfect."

"Then why didn't she have it set when the police first questioned her?"

"How do you know that?"

"I'm in charge, remember? I know everything. How do you and Spandrel get people to lie for you?"

"We don't lie."

"It's one of your most used administrative techniques."

"How dare you?" Graniento said. "No one speaks to me like that."

I said, "I just did."

"And gets away with it. That's insubordination."

"Actually, I'm kind of tired of going over that with you." I reached into my union files. Graniento hadn't reached this drawer yet. I pulled out one of the files. "Here's a copy of the page from the school code with the relevant section which defines insubordination circled in red." I tossed it on top of my desk.

"Insubordination is what I say it is," Graniento said.

"No," I said, "it's what legislators, attorneys, judges, and the state school board say it is. You don't have much say in the matter."

"I do in this district."

I asked, "I don't remember when I've ever seen you here at school this early, much less being in this corridor anytime before nine o'clock. Did you come by to help Spandrel spy this morning?"

Graniento said, "I've never spied on anyone. No one I know has spied on anyone."

"Why not come in over the weekend to do this? You people don't know I come in early?"

"I wasn't here to spy."

"Or you're not as organized as you think you are? Or you're lazy? Or not too bright?"

"Insults may not be insubordination, but they are inappropriate."

I asked, "Why did Spandrel imply to the police that Eberson was having an affair with a student? What does that gain her?"

"I'm sure she did no such thing."

I said, "It would divert suspicion if she needed suspicion diverted. And why would she need to divert suspicion? Unless she's a killer."

"Mabel Spandrel is an excellent administrator."

"What were you and she fighting about at the football game just before halftime?"

"I have no idea what you're talking about."

I said, "Can you really keep this many plots and lies going at the same time? You remind me of a juggler who's trying to keep flaming swords in the air. I can't imagine you'll be able to keep going indefinitely. You'll drop one."

He said, "You've got no proof of any of this."

The door banged open. Meg stomped up to the desk. "Would you like chapter and verse, dates and times?" she asked.

"Were you listening to us?" Graniento demanded.

"Yes," Meg said. Daring him to make something of it.

Graniento said, "You have nothing to say in this, librarian."

Meg said, "I do believe the tone you just used implied that being a librarian is something less than a dignified thing to be." She drew herself up to her full height. She jabbed a finger at him. "You listen to me, you overstuffed piece of shit. You need to look in the mirror at your own incompetence. Two people have died at this school. Two teachers. I may not have liked them, but the atmosphere around here is poisonous. That poison comes directly from you and your cohorts. You should not be near children. You should not be near a school building."

"We'll deal with you later," Graniento said.

"You can 'deal with' me whenever you like," Meg said. "You aren't what I care about in the world. Your judgments are not the ones in this world that are important to me. You are slime. People have been murdered, and you're down here spying. You're sick."

Teresa Merton entered the room. Behind her was Riva Towne, the superintendent. Merton came and stood next to me. She asked, "Is there a problem?" She glared at Graniento.

"What's going on?" Towne demanded.

I said, "Graniento was in here spying and trying to access pornographic sites on my computer so he could claim I had done so. He was going to use it as an excuse to fire me."

Towne said, "Pornographic sites? This is an outrage. There will be an investigation."

I said, "Look at the computer." She did. I pointed. "Watch. See these." I called up the firewalls and the time recorder. "No inappropriate sites have been accessed, although someone tried to get to them. This keeps track of everything on the computer. I have a witness from where I was when Scott dropped me off to when I ran into Georgette in the hall and to the time I arrived here."

Towne said, "You can't have."

I pulled out my cell phone. I held it up. "This has been on the whole time."

"It's illegal to record conversations," Graniento said.

Merton said, "While you are actually right about that, Mr. Mason is not saying he recorded you. He's saying he has a witness who heard everything. The phone records will also have the time that call began. Someone trying to put pornographic sites on a teacher's computer to get them fired is a serious charge."

Graniento said, "I was not. I don't know how those got there."

My mind reeled at how outrageously blatant this lie was.

Towne said, "I'm sure no one was trying to get anyone fired."

I get saint points for not guffawing hysterically at this.

Meg said, "Graniento's been threatening me, too."

"I have not," Graniento said.

I said, "I'm her witness."

Graniento said, "You'd lie for her."

I said, "Not all of us have turned lying into a lifestyle."

Towne said, "This is too much."

Merton said, "I agree." She turned to Meg. "What did he threaten you about?"

Meg told her.

Merton said, "And have you been making threats to Mr. Mason as well?"

"That's absurd," Graniento said.

"So why are you here?" Merton asked.

Stubborn silence from Graniento.

I said, "He was going through my desk as well as attempting to log onto the Internet."

"I have a right to do those things," Graniento said.

Merton said, "Is there a problem with Mr. Mason's teaching?"

Graniento said, "Well . . ."

"Good," Merton said, "because if there were, I'm sure you'd have it documented with dates, times, and specifics about what the problems are. And you'd have been documenting it for quite some time. And you'd have copies signed by him that show he received such data."

"Well, no," Graniento said.

Towne said, "He's part of a murder investigation."

"Have the police charged him with anything?" Merton asked.

"Well, no," Towne said.

"Is he in any way a suspect?" Merton asked.

"He might be. Or might become one," Towne said.

Merton said, "He might flap his arms and fly to the moon. He might do or become about anything. Come see me when you put 'might' in his job description. My impression is that you have been trying to bully and intimidate one of my teachers and one of my staff. I'm here to tell you to back the hell off. If you are going to bring charges, do so, and we will confront them in the appropriate forum. You are both out of line. If you don't want unfair labor practices up your asses all the way to your eyebrows, you'd best stop."

"We'll be consulting our attorneys," Graniento said.

Merton replied, "I'll be happy to have mine call you."

Noses in the air, the two administrators stalked out of the room.

Merton turned to us. "Actually, they're going to have unfair labor practices up the ass anyway. I'm going to keep those two so busy, it will drive them nuts. They've got to learn to stop this. If I've got to slap them around every time, I will."

"Good," I said.

Merton said, "This is kind of early, even for them. If there are any more problems today, get word to me immediately. I'll be speaking with the union attorney this morning." She gave an evil cackle. "I love doing this to those assholes. I love it every time they screw up. I'm going to rub their faces in it. These assholes have lost every fight with the union since they started."

"You'd think they'd learn," Meg said.

"They haven't yet," Merton said.

Meg chuckled. We gave her quizzical looks. "They remind me of the scenes in *It's a Mad, Mad, Mad, Mad World* when the characters in the movie try to organize themselves. These administrators rival those people for ineptness."

I smiled. Merton gave a rueful chuckle. She said, "They are a sad bunch."

We discussed the escort issue. Merton said, "The LD teachers have agreed to a rotating schedule to help you out. They and Morgan Adair should be enough."

I thanked Merton for her help. She said, "I've got to get to class. Call me if there's a problem." She left.

Meg said, "You look exhausted."

214

I sat down at my desk. "I'm not sure," I said.

"Do you want to take the day off? They'll get you a sub. You're under enormous pressure here. What they're doing is so sick and so out of line and so unprofessional. If I were a murderer in this building, Gracie and Higden wouldn't be dead, those two would."

37

Grief counselors flooded the building. They called the seniors down to the field house first. One of the administrators spoke to the entire restless assemblage. I didn't hear sobbing until they announced it was time to go to class.

Grief counselors also came around to all the classes in the English department. Most of my kids looked bored.

My morning classes were reasonably normal. Good.

38

Two minutes after the kids left at lunch, Teresa Merton entered with Steven Frecking. He wore the same low-slung jeans that emphasized his crotch and the belt with the enormous buckle that said, "Look here! Look here!"

Merton said, "Mr. Frecking came to talk to me. Seems he has a bit of a problem. It's part of what's been happening, and I think you have a right to know."

Frecking hung his head. He muttered, "I had sex with Peter Higden on Thursday."

"You did what?" I asked.

Frecking snapped. "You heard me."

Merton said, "And now you want legal help from the union?"

He nodded.

"Then lose the attitude and talk."

Frecking said, "Fine. I did have sex with him. It started the first week. We were all put on these stupid committees. I sat next to Higden. Him and me had been discussing the sports we'd played in college. He saw me staring at his crotch once or twice. I didn't look away quick enough. Him

and me went out to lunch together. We got it on in his car."
He shrugged. "We both enjoyed sex. There was no commitment. He dated women as far as I knew. We'd get together during lunch and have a little fun."

"Every day?"

"No, once in a while."

"And you did Thursday?"

"Yeah."

"And you met with Benson in the storage room later the same day?"

"Yeah."

"Don't you get tired?"

"Not often."

I said, "I'm finding this a little hard to believe."

"I don't care what you believe. I'm telling you what happened. Higden told me he did it with Benson once. That's how he kept Benson in line. Threatening to tell. That's how I knew Benson was available."

"And you were dating Morgan Adair?"

"He thought we were dating. I was having a good time."

"Did he know this?"

"I don't know what he knew. I'm not responsible for him or what he thinks. Peter knew exactly what we were doing and what it was about."

I said, "The police mentioned to me that they had evidence of sexual activity on Higden's part."

Frecking said, "You do have an in with the cops. That's what everybody said."

"Everybody who?" I asked.

"Different people around."

Merton asked, "Are they going to find evidence of you on Peter?"

"I don't know."

"Why are you telling us this?" I asked.

"I was afraid I'd get in more trouble. I don't know what's going to come out. I can't give them a DNA sample. I need help. What's going to happen to me?"

Merton said, "The police are going to have a million questions. You're going to need an attorney. They'll provide you with one. I'll help as much as I can."

"Maybe we can just not tell them," Frecking said.

Merton laughed gently. She patted his arm. "My dear, at this point, nothing is going to be easy for you."

I said, "Maybe if you answer a few questions, we'll let the police find out about what happened on their own."

Merton gave me a quizzical look.

I said, "Was there a fight among the poker guys last week?"

Frecking said, "I'm not supposed to tell."

I said, "Get real."

For a few seconds, Frecking looked stubborn. Then he snorted and said, "Fine. People fought. Sometimes Peter could get on people's nerves. He always gloated when he won a hand. That day he was more irritating than most. Edgar Cauchon, the athletic director, threw his cards at Peter. We had to pull them apart. Edgar was pretty pissed. He said Peter was going to be out of the loop on assignments for coaching and to not bother to try to double dip. Peter threatened to go to the administration about the whole thing. It was ugly. The game just sort of broke up. In fact, that's why Peter and I had time to go out Thursday. There wasn't going to be another game until everybody cooled off."

I said, "If you've got information on the grade fixing and the fights, we'll do our best by you." I also knew another conversation with Edgar Cauchon was in order. Frecking gave us what he remembered about people taking names to Higden and him fixing the grades.

I asked, "How come the teachers who gave the grades didn't notice they'd been changed?"

"Nobody ever said anything. You know that to view the grades from the previous quarter you've got to go through all those steps."

I knew it was complicated. The grades from the quarter before didn't appear on the screen as you were working. I rarely saw the report cards of any of the kids. They were mailed home. The goal was to get them sent home electronically.

After giving us the information, Frecking left.

Merton rubbed her hands together. She said, "I'm glad you told me about the grade fixing last night. This is going to be too much fun. I'll talk to Luci. We may need a committee to go have a chat with these folks, probably tomorrow. We'll get all the data today. Leave it to me." She left.

I found Meg and told her the news.

She said, "Having sex doesn't make him a killer. He qualifies as a philandering boob, sort of. He's not married, so I guess he isn't committing adultery, is he? How does that work? Is the married one the only one committing adultery? If the other person involved isn't married, which sin have they committed?"

"Not sure," I said.

Meg said, "Nor is it important. The key is, not all philandering boobs are killers. If they were, half the planet would be accused of murder by morning—and the other half would be dead, I guess."

"Are all these people randy trash?" I asked. "And does being that way have anything to do with murder?"

"Sex and money, dear: those are often the answers."

I returned to my classroom.

39

I was halfway through wolfing down my sandwich when the classroom door crashed open and banged against the wall. Tammy Choate, the sponsor for the GLSEN chapter, swung into the room. She slammed the door shut and rushed to my desk. I stood up. She was crying.

Before I could say a word, she burst out, "I shouldn't have told you. I shouldn't have told you. This is awful. So awful. They've been after me all weekend." She gasped and began sobbing. "I'm so frightened. They're going to fire me. I know they're going to fire me." She collapsed into a student's desk.

I grabbed a box of tissues and hurried to her. When the sobs had finally subsided, I asked, "Tammy, what's happened?"

"I was meeting with the gay student group a few minutes ago. We were planning a bake sale to help raise money for Third World AIDS Awareness Week. Mabel Spandrel and Riva Towne came into my room. They told the kids to leave." She dabbed at her eyes and blew her nose. "Riva Towne told me the gay student group is disbanded until you're cleared of murder charges."

I said, "I'm not a suspect, and she can't just disband a club."

"That's what she said. Then she left, but Spandrel stayed. She was mean. She told me I should never have told anybody about her and Gracie being at my apartment. She said she knew I was the one spreading the rumors. She said I would never get tenure. She said terrible things about me. I don't want this kind of pressure. I can't handle this kind of pressure. What am I going to do? I thought I was just telling you gossip. I was telling another gay person. I didn't think you'd use it against me."

"Wait a sec," I said. "I never used your name. You weren't the only one with the rumor. It could have been any one of a number of people."

"But they know it was me."

I said, "You and I will discuss this with Teresa Merton. I need her advice on this one, and she'll be able to give you better assurances than I."

"I don't want to fight," Tammy said. "I can't stand the pressure. I want nothing more to do with any of this. Can they just disband the gay student group? I'm frightened."

"We'll talk to Spandrel and Towne."

"No," Choate wailed. "If you tell them I told you, I'll get in more trouble. I don't want you to do anything. I'm so frightened."

There isn't a lot I can do if a union member decides they don't want to do something about what's been done to them. They've got to at least go with you. Or at least, they've got to let you tell others that they talked to you. Tammy was frightened. I was in enough of a mess. I didn't need to pressure her. I said, "Tammy, you let me think about it, and I'll have a talk with Teresa. The police would have said something. We won't talk to anyone or do anything without your permission."

222

"You won't?"

"You're going to be okay," I said. "They won't be able to get away with this much longer."

"Are you going to stop them?"

"If I can."

"But don't mention my name."

"I won't. Do you want to go home?"

"No. It would look odd."

"Okay," I said. "I suggest you stop in the washroom. Pull yourself together for your afternoon classes. Can you do that?"

"I'll have to try."

She left.

Morgan Adair appeared in the doorway as Tammy left. "What happened to Tammy?" he asked.

"Administrators," I said.

He nodded that he understood.

He took the desk that Tammy had vacated. He said, "I thought I'd stop by and see if you needed me to escort you anywhere. Or maybe you wanted me to get you something."

"I made it to the library earlier without a problem. A trip to the washroom at the end of lunch should be okay. It's only halfway down this corridor. I'll be fine."

"I'll stand in the hall anyway." He hesitated.

I said, "Any gossip going on?"

"Word is, the administrators have been meeting all morning. Bochka's here as well. They've got to be cooking up some bullshit." Then he "ummed."

"What's up?" I asked.

"Ah, I think I maybe should, uh . . ."

Now what?

"Did you talk to Frecking again?" I asked.

"No, I don't ever want to see him again. I, uh. I guess I should just say this."

I waited.

"Brandon Benson?"

"Yeah."

"The week before he got married? He got married the week after school let out his first year?"

"Yeah."

"Well, you know that swimming party the suckups organized?" I nodded. "A few of us in the old guard went. The end of that first year, we were sort of getting along. And I knew he was going. And he's hot. And I kind of made it my business to be changing into my swimsuit when he was. One thing led to another."

Was I the only one not getting into everybody else's pants?

I said, "I find this hard to believe."

He said, "It's not just the gay guys. The straight people are humping each other and dating each other and running around."

I asked, "Did you guys date? Did you think he'd stop his marriage for you?"

"No. That time it was just fun. He's hot. It was only once." He sighed. "I figured I'd better tell you. There's enough secrets around this place. I had sex with both guys who were in that room. Quite a while apart, but still. I should have told you sooner. I'm sorry."

I said, "I don't think it's connected to the murder."

"Something must be."

"Yeah, but I'm not sure what."

After several more apologies for not telling me sooner, he left.

40

During my planning time I checked the halls carefully, then made my way to the office. I didn't see any of the suckups or administrators. Georgette asked, "How's your day going?"

I nodded. "I'm heading to the gym."

She said, "I'll walk you over, then send Meg to wait at the doors so you've got someone with you when you walk back to class. You shouldn't have come down here alone."

I filled her in as we strolled the halls. She patted me at the gym doors and said good luck. I made my way to Edgar Cauchon's office. The smell of rancid jock strap and mold were a great backdrop to the rotting tiles, dented lockers, and water stains on the ceiling.

Cauchon was behind one of the desks. He stood up. "We had the game Friday. Nothing happened."

I said, "You and Peter had a fight last week."

"Who told?"

I said, "Do we live in a mafia-ruled world? Every time a secret gets out, someone's going to die?"

"I didn't kill anybody."

"But you had a fight with one of the people who was killed."

"I didn't even know Gracie Eberson."

I said, "Do you want the police to talk to every person who was at the poker game?"

"Fine. Higden was an asshole. He'd gloat, and I'd been losing. He'd gloat the closer the hands were. If he had a flush to your pair, he was kind of okay. If he had a higher four of a kind than you did, he'd get nasty. Doesn't mean I killed him."

"You threatened to end his double dipping?"

"I told you, we don't—"

I interrupted. I was angry. "Will you cut the shit? How much of all this do you want to come out? Talk to me and I'll do what I can to keep it quiet. Keep silent, and I'll report it now."

"Who to? The administrators all hate you."

I said, "I just have to find one honest one. Are you sure they're all crooked?"

He hesitated.

I said, "I want to solve the murders, not destroy you. Although I am going to suggest you guys clean up your act."

"Fine," Cauchon said. "Fine. I threatened Peter. He might have been going to rat on us. I don't know if he did before he was killed. No one has talked to me. I always knew Peter was a two-timing backstabber. That fake cheerfulness was a crock of shit."

"Would you have cut him out?"

"No. We'd have talked. I never got the chance. You've got to believe me. I've covered my tracks here pretty well. Peter might have given us some problem, but I'd have weathered it."

"You sure?"

"I think so."

Not certainty. "Did anybody lose serious money at these games?"

226

"No, but Peter used to brag about his gambling in the city. We always heard about the convoluted bets he made and how much he won. He never told us about the losses. Anybody who gambles as much as he claimed had to be losing."

"Anybody on the staff who would know?"

"I suppose his suckup buddies in the English department."

"Who else didn't like Peter?"

"He was okay most of the time. He just set me off that day, that's all. It really wasn't a big deal. You're not going to tell?"

I said, "Not as long as you were honest with me."

"I told you everything.

Meg met me at the gym doors. Teresa Merton was with her. Teresa said, "Tomorrow during your planning time, we're going to have a little meeting. The union attorney is going to be here. Someone from the regional office of education will be present. I've been assembling the data all day about the grade-fixing problems. You'll want to be there."

"You have what you need?" I asked.

"Oh, my, yes."

227

41

That day I had my usual tutoring class after school. I wasn't much in the mood for teenagers, but they do have a positive side at crisis moments. The vast majority of them are totally caught up in concern about themselves, their world, their emotions, and their egos to the exclusion of all else. This is normal. I'd have to pay attention to their needs no matter how I felt. This was actually good, because then it could take my mind off of how pissed off I was.

Fred Zileski came in first. He found his work folder and the day's assignments I'd prepared for him. I had his work for each week from each teacher organized and set to go. Any writing or reading assignment, we would go over. He sat in the back as he always did. A few others drifted in and began muttering and grumbling as teenagers do. Desiree Delaney bustled through the door and banged herself into the front desk in the first row. Having gotten our attention, she began to weep and blubber. "They're dead. They're dead."

From the back, Fred said, "Shut up, Desiree, you didn't even know them."

A harsh but honest assessment. Desiree said, "Don't be mean. It's sad."

I said, "Fred, don't be mean."

He gave me a teenage grumble that was just soft enough that I could ignore it.

Spike Faherty bashed open the door. Late, as usual. He walked to the row of desks by the window, plunked himself into his chair, and flipped his textbook off his desk. It banged against the metal cabinet near his left foot and flopped to the floor. Everybody gaped at him.

Spike was six feet tall and might have weighed 140 pounds. His goatee was sparse. He kept his hair spiked in deft swirls. He tended to change the color from week to week, although he sometimes did one-day dye jobs. He was perhaps the angriest kid that I'd dealt with who still showed up for school. The book throwing hadn't happened since the second day of school. It was his mom I'd been on the phone with last Thursday afternoon.

I said, "That cabinet has feelings."

Spike glared at me. He said, "These people are effed up." At least he'd remembered to use the initial and not the word.

I said, "You want to talk about what happened?"

"No."

I got everybody settled and mostly on task, then re-trieved Spike's work folder from the pile and brought it to his desk.

I said, "You gonna be able to get any work done today?"

He looked up at me. He said, "What's wrong with my hair?"

Today's color was a pretty awful magenta. I'd asked him once how he fit his hair under his motorcycle helmet. He just shrugged and said it worked okay. Today, I said, "I'm not real fond of that color, but it looks pretty normal."

"That goddamn gym teacher, Frecking, gave me a hard time about my hair today. He made all kinds of comments and picked on me about it. And Milovec hassled me and made comments. They're going to suspend me."

"Why does Milovec care?" I asked. "He doesn't have you for class."

"He supervises lunch detentions."

Among the first things Graniento and Spandrel had spearheaded when they started was an anti-teenage-hair campaign. I couldn't imagine whatever for. In this day and age, pestering teenagers about their hair struck me as stupid. There were plenty of other more important things to pester teenagers about. Most of them desperately want to be individuals as long as they don't stand out from the crowd. One way to do this was hairstyle. It was also another way to say, "Look at me, look at me, I'm a person." I've generally found that if a teenager is crying out for attention, giving them some can sometimes avoid larger problems. It's funny. With some kids, if you make sure to greet them every day, acknowledge their existence in some way, they tend to respond better in general. This works with adults as well. With Spike, I usually made some mention each time his hair color changed. I had a great art teacher for a class once. At the time, I'd been proving to myself and the world that I had no artistic talent and was never going to be a Picasso. The art teacher would walk in and marvel and exclaim, "How interesting," no matter how awful the product I or any of her other students was creating. It's not hard to be harmlessly effusive and neutral; ask any kindergarten teacher.

I said, "Haven't they hassled you about your hair before? What was different about today?"

"They said if I didn't get it cut, I'd be suspended. They said it was disruptive to the educational environment."

I didn't laugh. I'd like to have beaten whoever told him

that. People had used that same catchphrase during Vietnam when kids wore armbands protesting the war. They use that same phrase whenever they don't have a logical reason to disapprove of something some kid is doing. The other kids in class usually don't give a rat's ass about the alleged disruption. It often becomes a disruption because some idiot administrator overreacts. It's the adults who are disturbed and who should learn to get a grip. What Spike didn't know—but that I did, from a friendly LD teacher—was that Graniento, Milovec, and company had conspired to make the claim that his hair was disruptive.

Today of all days, I didn't need such a nonsensical distraction. But Spike was in a mood, and he wasn't getting work done until he calmed down. I took out my cell phone and said, "What's your mom's number?"

Mrs. Faherty and I talked at least once a week so I could give her updates on his progress. She was normally at her wit's end about her recalcitrant teenager. "Are you going to tell on me?" he asked.

I said, "Sort of."

"I don't care." He filled the three words with teenage despair and defiance—a neat trick. He rattled off the numbers.

Mrs. Faherty knew my voice. I said, "Spike's got a problem today. The principal, the head of the department, and several teachers are conspiring together to get him in trouble about his hair."

Spike gaped at me. The other kids gave each other puzzled looks.

She said, "They what?"

I know that school personnel, like so many government officials—police are a major example—are supposed to stick together and lie to the public. What's the point, especially over such simple stuff?

I repeated what I'd said.

She said, "I'll take care of this."

I knew she would.

Spike said, "They did what you said?"

"Spike, I need you to get some work done today. We can talk about the hair problem after I see two paragraphs of to-day's essay."

He gaped at me again. He fiddled with his pencil a minute, then broke it in two.

From the back Zileski said, "Give him a break, Spike. He's on your side."

Spike picked up his pencil parts and started working.

Mrs. Faherty arrived at the classroom door about five min-utes before the tutoring session was to end. Mrs. Faherty was gargantuan. She wore an immense, heavy overcoat that covered enough acreage to keep warm the members of the football team sitting on the bench on a Friday night. Her hair was a ratty mess. She wore what, when I was a kid, we would have called combat boots.

Spike looked at her for a second, then returned to work on his essay. She swept on up to my desk. We exchanged greetings.

I said, "I didn't expect you to come in."

She spoke in a voice that matched her heft. She said, "He getting anything done?"

She saw what he'd done that day, and then I showed her the essays he'd worked on since the beginning of the year. I pointed out the changes and improvements. She said, "He's never done this much."

Spike was turning red and looking out the window. The bell rang for the end of tutoring. They hurried to leave. Spike mumbled as he rushed by, "I gotta go."

"Wait," his mother commanded.

He stopped.

She held out the essays. "These are good."

He nodded.

I said, "He's fairly bright." And he was.

She said, "That isn't news. That he's doing some work is. Good. Don't worry about your hair. I've taken care of it."

Spike grinned.

His mom said, "Don't be late for dinner."

He left.

She turned to me. "My kid is in your class because I'd heard of your reputation for teaching even the most delinquent."

I said, "Spike knows a great deal. And my guess is, much as he might deny it, he would like to graduate with his classmates."

She said, "Hard to believe. Hassling him about his hair? I gave that up in third grade. What's the point? Even though I'm on the board, they pester him. I guess I don't speak up enough. Perhaps it's partly my fault. I had a little chat with Graniento before I came up here. That man's pitching stupid with a steam shovel."

She plunked her more than substantial butt on the edge of my desk. "Sit," she said. "We need to talk."

I sat.

She said, "Meg has been sworn to secrecy, but this situation is out of hand. I'm one of her secret sources. I've known her for years. My kid needed help, and so do you. I agreed to let Kara Bochka put me on the school board because she promised it would only be until the spring, when they have elections. They do hate you. Kara tried to get me to join one of their conspiracy clubs. She wouldn't tell me much, but there is no question she is meeting with teachers. She wants to undermine you and Teresa Merton. And she would love to destroy the union. I know she had Higden, Eberson, Schaven, Pinyon, and Milovec over to her house. She has parties with them and the administration."

"Why?"

"Maybe she's lonely. I do know they discuss you. Isn't there a gay-rights ordinance in this state now? If they were conspiring to get you, couldn't you sue their asses off?"

"Yes. Bigtime. I'd make a lot of money out of their conspiracy."

"You might want to talk to a lawyer, if you haven't already."

"What is it they want?" I asked.

"The anti-union stuff is big, but I can never figure out exactly what they want. They seem to be enamored of power. Whatever gets them more power, they want to do. What precisely they're going to do with all this power is beyond me. I think Kara wants to be a state legislator. She and I have been part of the same bridge club since time out of mind. Those gossips in the bridge club are back in the Stone Age. I may stop going. It isn't fun anymore. All they want to do is gossip. All I want to do is play cards. And I don't have time for that anyway." Abruptly she stood up. "Check with me through Meg. I'll do what I can for you. Anybody who can handle my kid and get him to work is okay by me."

I stopped to see Meg. "I met with Mrs. Faherty." I explained.

Meg said, "I wish I could have told you."

I said, "We both keep faith. I understand."

42

At home that night, Scott and I talked while he made dinner. He made a gorgonzola sauce with milk, sage, and cheese, then poured it over some kind of chicken. Any cheese sauce I make always comes out grainy. His are always smooth and silky. I watched him work while I filled him in on my day.

Scott said, "It sounds like it's all starting to unravel."

"No question. Tomorrow's confrontation about the grade fixing should be telling."

"Merton didn't warn you to tone it down with the administrators?"

I gave him a quizzical look.

He said, "You've been under a lot of stress. You've said some important things, but these people are your bosses. They can make things difficult for you."

"I know," I said. "It's funny. I couldn't be having these conversations if I didn't have you. People are right—you are my safety net."

He stopped stirring for a moment and took my hand. I gazed into his blue eyes. He said, "Please be careful. I'm really worried about you."

"My friends are rallying around. Look at what the LD teachers were willing to do."

"You've gone out of your way for them and the kids they serve for years."

I said, "It was the right thing for me to do."

He smiled at me, then said, "All this leaves aside the fact that somebody committed these murders."

"It's gotta be administrators or suckups or some combination of both."

Scott said, "I don't get how the timing was supposed to work on this."

"How so?"

"Okay. For them to get you implicated, the murder had to happen first. Unless they planned the murders just to get back at you."

"Maybe they did. They put the second body behind the wheels of my truck."

"Okay," Scott said. "Scenario one. They planned the murders and they planned to implicate you in them. The murders were all about you."

"Unlikely, but theoretically possible."

"So they organized everything ahead of time and waited for their chance. Seems a little far-fetched that they would be able to monitor your movements on this one day. That there would be this one fight at the faculty meeting. That this one woman would happen to walk out."

"Not real possible."

"The second scenario is that the murder happened, you found the body, and they realized they had an opportunity and went into action"

I said, "So the superintendent and head of the board and all the others were in on it together?"

"Obviously they were in on conspiring to screw you. The question is, did they commit the murders?"

236

"So somebody kills two teachers. Meanwhile, the super-intendent and the school board president, seizing an opportunity to destroy my life, try to frame me. What if the cops had caught the real killer?"

"They haven't so far. And remember, the accusation can sometimes be enough."

"But why?"

"They're homophobic pigs? Because they can? Because they're sick sacks of shit? This is all going to come out. All of it."

"But who killed these people and why?"

43

Jourdan found me in my classroom first thing Tuesday morning. He said, "This place is a madhouse. The police questioned me again yesterday. They finally gave up late in the afternoon."

I said, "I'm voting on the murderer's being one of the administrators."

He nodded. He sat on top of one of the kid's desks. He said, "You know, I was thinking about what Pinyon said about traveling to conferences. I went yesterday and checked my files. I wasn't at any conferences back in the eighties. They were making it up."

"That would be so like them."

"I called Sandra Barkin. She keeps records of everything. And she has them at home. By year and alphabetically. Class lists, phone lists, travel vouchers. She never went when they said she went."

I repeated what Scott said. "It's all going to unravel."

Jourdan said, "I talked to Luci. They were really trying to fix grades?"

"We're going to try to prove it."

"Excellent. I can't wait to see them fall."

Francine Peebles bustled in a few minutes after Jourdan left. She said, "The funerals are Thursday and Friday. You'd think they'd have them on the weekend so we all can go. Are you going? I should be one of the representatives from the faculty who go. They shouldn't be charging us for sick days if we go."

I said, "Francine, how well did you know Gracie and Peter?"

Francine said, "I didn't like Peter. Not because I'm racist. That manner of his. That sucking up. He was always friendly, but really, there should have been limits. But he's dead and it's sad."

"You've heard the rumor that Gracie might have been having an affair with a student."

Francine said, "I heard that. I can't believe it. I'm sure it's not true. I know it's not true. I worked with Gracie with a lot of her kids. We shared duties after school sometimes. She never, ever did anything untoward."

At lunch, Meg joined me in my classroom. She had a woman I vaguely recognized with her. Meg said, "This is Emily Haggerty, my source in the PE department. She is reluctant to talk to you. I've insisted that it's vital."

Haggerty was a tall slender woman. She wore an orange and brown warm-up outfit. She said, "I don't see why this is so important."

I said, "We're dealing with murder."

Haggerty said, "Nobody who was a friend of mine died."

Meg said, "We need to find the killer. Who knows where he or she might strike again?"

Haggerty plunked herself into a student desk. "Whatever. If I didn't hate those male gym teachers, I wouldn't even be here."

Meg asked, "Why do you hate them?"

"They're all misogynists, racists, homophobic pigs. Any woman who disagrees with them is accused of being a lesbian. They are assholes."

"Why didn't you ever report them?" I asked.

"Ha. The administrators in this district loves those idiots. Those sports boosters are all-powerful."

If she had information about possible suspects, I would listen to her ranting about her colleagues. I said, "Anything you can tell me would be helpful."

"Yeah, right. For a while I dated one of those schmucks who plays cards. They always think you're still interested. He'd come around and confide in me. Jesus, crap he used to tell me. I am so not interested. Men and their egos!"

"What did he tell you?" I asked.

"Those guys had everything set for their double dipping. Let me use your computer for a second." She sat at my desk. Meg joined me in looking over her shoulder. Haggerty called up her e-mail, opened one, transferred an attached document to my desktop, then clicked on it. A spreadsheet appeared on the screen. She said, "This lists the coach, the sport, the time, and the date of every one of the incidents when they were double dipping. This is for the past three years."

"How'd you get all this?" I asked.

"The women watched. We knew what the men were trying to do. What really pissed a few of the women off was the men wouldn't let them in on their cheating. We've been planning this for a long time. Most of us, anyway. A few of the women are cowards. All the men are cowards. Assholes! Ha! They'll be sorry now. Will this get all of their asses fired?"

I said, "It's going to depend on how much money was involved and how much of this can be proved. Will the other women in the department back this up?"

"Just ask the sons-of-bitch men. They can't deny it all. Hell, call up their outside jobs. Some of them just went home or went drinking, but some went to other jobs or took classes. They can't cover up this many lies."

I searched for Peter's name, found it. I said, "Peter and Cauchon, the AD, had a big fight. Peter threatened to tell on them for double dipping."

"And he's dead, I know."

I said, "It'll be obvious that insiders gave us this information."

"As long as it gets them fired. Higden should have been."

"Why's that?" I asked.

"I turned him in for doing drugs. Why the hell wasn't he fired?"

I said, "Mainly because it wasn't on school grounds, and they had no physical evidence of drugs."

"No," she said. "It was because he was a suckup and a man. Graniento would protect any man who was in trouble. The suckups always win. I thought for sure I had him when we saw him. I was with a couple parents. We all know what we saw."

I said, "Well, he's dead."

"He was an asshole," Haggerty said. "He tried to come on to me once. He got a big fat rejection. He claimed it didn't matter to him. Ha!"

I said, "With this information you've given me, the double dipping should stop."

"And all the other unfairness in the PE department? They try to lord it over us . . ." She ranted for several minutes. The English department wasn't alone in having divisions. I wasn't sure that was a comforting thought.

When Haggerty left, I asked Meg, "How did she ever come to confide in you?"

"Ah," she said, "magic. The same way both sides in the

department come to you. I listen. Then I say some version off, 'How interesting, tell me more.' It's amazing how many people just want someone to talk to."

As we'd arranged yesterday, during my planning time Morgan Adair escorted me to the central office. Georgette said, "They're in the conference room." She smiled at me. "Get 'em, tiger," she whispered as I passed her and entered the room.

The gang was there: Towne, Graniento, Spandrel. Our guys were there: Merton, Luci, me, and the union attorney, Marguerite Seymour. At the far end of the table sat a man and a woman who were introduced as being from the regional education office.

Towne said, "What can we do for you people? This is all very mysterious. We should have been notified about the existence of this meeting and the topic and been given an agenda. The union can't just decree."

Spandrel produced an eight and a half by eleven–inch sheet of paper and shoved it across the table. She said, "We've had complaints about the union, specifically Tom Mason."

Seymour, the lawyer, glanced at it and said, "This isn't signed."

Spandrel said, "It doesn't need to be."

"Who wrote it?"

"I'm not at liberty to say."

Seymour picked up the paper and ripped it up. She said, "If it's not signed, it doesn't exist."

"We have lots of copies," Spandrel said.

Seymour said, "You can have a mountain of copies. This union doesn't deal with unattributed accusations. If you do, you're a fool."

Spandrel gaped. I'd seldom felt more pleased at the look of frustration and fury on her face.

Seymour said, "Now that we have that settled, let's move on. We have evidence of cheating on state tests, grade fixing, and altering of statistics for state and federal reporting."

That got a round of silence from the assembled administrators.

Seymour went on. "All three of you are implicated."

"You can't have proof," Spandrel said.

Seymour picked up a box next to her chair and placed it on the table. She said, "In here are copies of statements by various teachers, copies of grade books, copies of the grade sheets, copies of just about everything that you people have done." Bless Georgette.

Towne said, "I'm sure Mr. Graniento has an explanation."

Graniento rounded on her. "I have an explanation? I have nothing to explain. We'll need the district's attorney here."

Seymour said, "I called him and asked him to be here. He had a schedule conflict. I'm sure he'll be happy to go over all of this with you. Page by page."

"We'll need those," Graniento said.

"These are copies for you," Seymour said. She shoved the box toward them. The assembled administrators looked at it like it was a pile of living shit.

Spandrel said, "Those are confidential school documents that you have obtained illegally."

Seymour said, "You have a law degree? You haven't even seen the documents. You don't know precisely what they are. The representatives of the regional education office have copies. Inspectors from the state will be here this week. They will also have copies."

"How did you get all this?" Spandrel said. "Someone must have broken into the system. Someone is a traitor."

Seymour said, "Why don't you wait for your attorney and talk to him?"

After the meeting, Luci, Seymour, Merton, and I met briefly. I told them about the double dipping and the attempted dissolution of the gay student group. The attorney said, "I'll talk to their lawyer. He's got sense."

I thanked her.

"How's the escorting working?" Merton asked.

"Great. Everything's organized, and Scott's coming by to pick me up after school."

44

After school, Spike sauntered into the tutoring session first. His hair was bright yellow with swirls and spikes nearly six inches high. Celebrating, I suppose. He rapped his knuckles on my desk. He said. "I think something's wrong with Fred. You better talk to him." Spike had his skateboard with him. Bringing those to school was against the rules, too. I didn't care. At least it wasn't his motorcycle. He and his toy took their seat and got to work. Good enough for me.

At five minutes to four, Fred Zileski sidled into the room. He'd never been late before. I had wondered how the after-school-tutoring kids would be on this second day of upset. Until Fred's appearance, only Spike had showed up. Fred saw the emptiness and shook his head. I remembered parent conferences when his father said, "You'll go to that tutoring. You'll go every day. You won't complain. Or you're off that football team. Off completely." Fred's dad had worked a deal with the coach so the boy could be late for practice. It helped that Fred was one of the best players on the team.

Fred didn't take his usual seat but plopped into a desk

near the door. He took out his grammar notebook, turned to a page, and started to cry. Getting Fred started on his work was usually pretty easy. The crying was unique.

Spike gaped.

I said, "Something's wrong." Pretty obvious, but I've found with teenagers it's usually better to start with the basics.

Fred wore his letterman's jacket open over a T-shirt and jeans. The T-shirt had the logo and picture of a band I did not recognize. The number of obscure rock bands I didn't recognize was legion.

I grabbed the box of tissues on my desk, walked over, plopped them on his desk, and leaned my back against the wall.

"Is there anything I can help you with?" I asked. I figured it was a relationship problem, although usually the criers were teenage girls, and usually it was at a dance, and usually they were in the washroom having their teen tragedy. Boys tended to do their crying alone in their rooms.

Fred shook his head, sobbed, grabbed a tissue, blew his nose. I waited. Giving teenagers time was a trick I'd learned long ago.

Spike walked over. "What the f—"

I glared.

"What's up?" Spike asked.

Fred just cried. I said to Spike, "Let's go easy on him."

Finally under some degree of control, Fred spoke in a tone of teenage doom, "I don't want to be here."

"That's pretty normal," I said.

"Not today. Today's different. I got nobody to talk to. Nobody never asked me to lie."

"Who asked you to lie?"

He snuffled a huge amount and settled his feet flat on the

floor. He stared at the *Lord of the Rings* poster on the wall. He said, "I can't talk in front of Spike."

I glanced up at the other teenager. He was unabashedly gazing at Fred and me.

There were only a couple minutes left in the period. I said, "Spike, you can wait in the office for the final bell. Go directly to your locker and then the office. No side trips."

He muttered, "I know." Before he left, Spike made a detour to pat Fred on the shoulder.

I turned back to Fred.

"Who told you to lie?"

"My mom."

"What did she want you to lie about?"

"My dad hates her. I do, too. She asked me to lie. Adults aren't supposed to do that. It's bull. My dad would kill me if I lied."

"Must be something pretty important."

Snivel. Wipe.

"I'm supposed to lie about you."

Alarm bells began to clang in my head. Over the past few days a cardiologist would have had a field day with my heart rate.

"About what?"

"They told me I'd never have to worry about grades again. I dunno. I didn't want to come here today, but I had to. My dad said I had to come here for tutoring. I dunno what to do. I gotta have that note signed by you every day. I can't tell my dad."

"Tell him what?"

"What they told me to say."

"What did they tell you to say?"

He sniveled and gulped and looked away. His voice was barely audible as he said, "They told me I should say that you showed me porn on the Internet. That you tried to get me to go home with you. That you talked about sex. You never talk about nothin' but grammar in here. Grammar sucks. No offense." He met my eyes for a moment, then glanced away. "And that you tried to do stuff."

"To whom were you supposed to tell this?" I asked.

"I dunno. They were gonna set it up. I dunno. Reporters. Or the cops. Or somebody. I thought about it, but I ain't lyin' for those assholes. I'm supposed to learn somethin'. You taught me stuff I never learned before. I gotta know this stuff. I gotta get a real grade. I'm never gettin' into college if I don't know this stuff. It's probly too late, but I gotta try. Lyin's for shit. Oh, sorry."

I ignored the expletive. I was reeling. I eased over to my desk, got the edge behind me, and sat gingerly.

"You said 'they.' Were there other people besides your mom?"

"Old Lady Towne. Sorry. Mrs. Towne, and Mrs. Spandrel, and a couple others."

"When did they ask you this?"

"My mom talked to me last night. Today, I got called to the office. This time there were four of them, Spandrel, Towne, Benson, and Graniento. They said they'd talked to my mom. They put a lot of pressure on me. They made a lot of promises. They were going to transfer me to Benson's class. The kids make fun of him. He doesn't know stuff. Not like you do. I had him for class as a sophomore. Nobody ever even listened to him. Are you gonna be in trouble?"

I said, "I have nothing to fear from the truth."

"Am I going to be in trouble?"

"No."

"Are you sure?"

I said, "Fred, you have nothing to fear from the truth."

"What do I do?"

I had the same question. I wasn't sure what I should do next for myself, but Fred had to be helped. That I could take care of.

I asked, "Do you want to leave?"

"No. I've got that stupid history paper. It's due tomorrow. If I don't get it in I'll flunk."

"If you're uncomfortable, I'll get someone else to watch you."

"Uncomfortable about what?"

While he got up to get his work, I called Mr. Zileski. When I finished, he said, "Bullshit. I'll be there as soon as I can."

"Do you want me to get someone else to watch him?"

"What the hell for? You haven't done anything wrong."

I handed the phone to Fred so he could talk to his dad. Fred gave a series of yeps, then said, "I'll get it done." He pushed the button to disconnect and gave the phone back to me. He began writing his paper.

I called Scott. His phone was off, which meant he was still in a meeting. I left a message to call me.

I called my lawyer and left a message on his voice mail.

I tried to call Frank Rohde. He was out. I called Detective Gault, who said, "Doesn't sound like that has anything to do with murder."

"It's another lie about me."

He assured me he'd check into it. I wanted him to rush over and arrest people.

Then I sat down and stared out the window, drummed my fingers on the desktop, and tried not to begin slamming objects around the room. I didn't want to leave Fred in this state, or I'd have walked down to Meg. I certainly wasn't going to talk to Meg about Fred in front of the boy. Fred simply picked up his daily folder and got to work. Habit can be a good thing. He sniffled on occasion and barely looked up at me. My mind raced and swirled. Baseless false accusations.

Lies and shit. I would take care of Fred, and then adults were going to answer questions.

Mr. Zileski worked half an hour away. He was there in less time than that. Fred saw his dad and began to cry.

Mr. Zileski put a hand on the boy's shoulder and said, "Tell me the story."

Fred did.

When he finished, Mr. Zileski said, "I'm so sorry to have brought this on you, Mr. Mason. Is there anything I can do to make things right?"

I said, "I think taking care of Fred and seeing that he's okay will be enough."

"My wife is a shit," Mr. Zileski said. "I keep trying to get full custody. Fred will be old enough soon to just leave that bitch."

Fred said, "I don't want to talk to anybody. Am I going to have to talk to the police?"

I said, "What they did is criminal."

Fred said, "The stuff they wanted me to lie about would have sent you to prison. That's sick."

Mr. Zileski said to me, "There must be something you can do. How about your union? There's gotta be rules against that kind of thing. You must be able to sue the bitch."

I said, "I'll work on it. Fred, you did the right thing. Thanks."

"Are you guys mad at me?"

I said, "I'm not."

Mr. Zileski said, "You didn't lie in the face of terrible pressure. I'm proud of you. I'm going to confront your goddamn mother."

"Please don't," Fred said. "It won't do any good. She'll just lie. That's what she always does, lies. She'll tell any lie to get her way. She lies to me all the time. She lies about you, Dad."

"Got that right," Mr. Zileski said. "She lied her way through the divorce proceedings. Luckily, I had a great lawyer. After this, I'll get full custody. He can visit her in prison." He turned to me. "This isn't over. I will do what I can to bring that woman down. You don't try to destroy a person's life. No one gets to get away with that. Are you okay?"

I said, "I don't know."

Mr. Zileski said, "If I can be of any help, call me."

They left.

45

My name, my career, my job, and my reputation had been saved by a kid's honesty. I felt vulnerable and sick. And the adults were going to pay. And they were going to pay bigtime. I didn't know how yet. I called Scott. He'd just gotten out of his meeting.

When I heard his voice, I began to cry. Comfort, safety, someone who loved me.

"What's wrong?" he asked. I felt his concern and caring wash over me.

I got myself under control and told him Fred's story. He said, "Hold on. Stay calm. I'll be there. Call our attorney. You're okay. You'll be fine. I'm on my way. I love you. Go see Meg. Stay with her until I get there." He reassured me over and over until he was confident that I'd pulled myself together. He said, "I'll be stuck in traffic, so it will take me longer than usual. I wish I was there now. I'll be there as soon as I can. I love you. I'll be right there."

After talking to him, I was calmer and didn't need tissues for the moment.

As I hung up, once again my classroom door crashed open. It had been through a lot of that lately. Meg burst in. In one hand she swung her cane wildly. The fingers of her other hand clutched Basil Milovec's left ear. I liked Meg and no question this looked important, but I'd just been through something shattering.

Milovec squawked and said, "Quit that." He flailed at her with his arms. She twisted his ear with one hand, whacked his shin with the cane, and shoved him forward. When they reached my desk, Meg took one look at me and said, "What's wrong? Do you want me to dump this piece of trash?"

I said, "I'll tell you about it when we're finished."

She nodded, then asked, "Where are the cops?"

I said, "They were downstairs earlier."

Meg said, "We're going to have a little chat with them." Again she hit his shin with the cane.

"Ow, that hurts."

"Good," Meg said.

"What's up?" I asked.

"This is the person who told the cops you were outside the supply room at 4:45."

My anger flamed instantly to fury.

I snapped, "You lying sack of shit."

He snarled, "You can't prove anything."

I said, "Why?"

He said, "Fuck you."

Meg said, "Follow us. We're going to the police." She began to prod her captive toward the door.

I said, "Wait."

Meg stopped.

I said, "The cops already know he told them."

Meg said, "They don't know he made it up."

"Hold on," I said. They waited.

Here was a chance to get information. I said, "We know he lied. Maybe he'll give us information in exchange for not going to the police."

Milovec said, "Fuck you."

I said, "Meg, what happened?"

She said, "Not more than ten minutes ago, I heard this dirtbag as he passed by the library. He was plotting and planning with someone I could not see. He was talking about the police investigation and about duping Tom into helping the suckups. He then said he was the one who lied to the police about you being at the storage room earlier. Then whoever he was talking to laughed and agreed that it was a perfect plan."

Milovec snarled, "I said no such thing."

Meg said, "I know what I heard."

"Who was I talking to?" Milovec asked.

Meg said, "I didn't see. I thought it was a woman's voice, but I'm not sure. We'll go to the police. Everyone in the school will be questioned before you can warn them. That person will confirm they were with you. They won't know they need to lie. And you need a witness to say that isn't what you said."

Milovec said, "And I'll say you're making this up because he's your friend."

"Oh," Meg said, "perhaps in the excitement, I've forgotten. When I heard what you were plotting, I made a call." She took out her cell phone and spoke into it. "Georgette, if you could step in, please."

The classroom door opened and Georgette Constantine walked in. "Did I forget to mention?" Meg asked. "I have a witness who heard everything."

Georgette smiled. "Mr. Milovec said that he was glad Tom was being set up and that he was making it up about Tom being outside the storeroom at 4:45."

Milovec's face turned red. He said, "I'm leaving."

I said, "And we'll go straight to the police."

He hesitated. "You can't make me talk."

Meg said, "We will tell the police you lied. They will find out who was with you in the hall. That person won't know there's a need to conceal that you were together."

I was thinking fast. I said, "Milovec, I don't like you, and the police will probably find out you were lying, but maybe they won't. We'll agree to keep quiet if you give us some information."

"I'm not talking to you people."

Meg said, "Lying to the police and impeding an investigation is a crime. You're in deep shit, you fool."

I said, "Let's all sit down." I held in my anger. Here was the possibility of real answers. Finally, there would be a break in the monolithic suckup faction. Somebody had made the mistake of blabbing, and witnesses had heard. Now, he might break under pressure and betray all the conspirators' secrets.

Georgette said, "I've got to get back to the office. Let me know what happens." Meg and I thanked her for her help. She left.

Milovec said, "I'll talk, but I'm not talking with a witness present. I've got to see all cell phones. No tape players can be plugged in. We need to sit away from the intercom so we can't be overheard. I've got to see the librarian walking across the parking lot and getting into her car. I'll talk, but you'll get no proof on me. It won't do you any good, but I'll talk."

Meg said, "You comfortable being alone with him?"

"If he doesn't talk," I said, "he knows I'll call you, and we'll get Georgette, and we'll all go straight to the police."

Milovec and I watched Meg stride across the parking lot in the fading light. We saw her car lights go on. We saw her pull out. Both Milovec and I checked the hallway to make sure no one was lurking. I figured he might try and bolt, but he didn't. We returned to the corner of the classroom farthest away from the intercom. We sat in kids' desks. I made sure I sat so that I could watch him and the door. We each placed our cell phone on a desk next to us.

Milovec said, "What if I talk, and you still go to the police?"

I said, "You know my reputation. I always keep faith. Does anyone else know about your affairs?"

"No."

"I've never told. You know I'll keep my word to take you to the police. And at this point, I'm not sure how much of a choice you have." He was on the edge of the precipice between being ratted out for obstructing a police investigation and trusting me. "What the fuck was going on?" I asked.

He said, "We should have had someone go with me to rat on you, but we thought it would look odd if two people hadn't come forward."

I said, "And you couldn't find someone else to lie so blatantly."

"We tried," Milovec said.

At least someone had a conscience.

I said, "With whom did you plan the lie about where I was?" I tend to get grammatically rigid when I'm angry.

He wiped his hands on his black jeans.

"You can't tell anyone I told. They'll kill me if this gets out."

"Who will kill you?" I asked.

He blanched. "I didn't mean kill me dead. I meant it metaphorically. If I tell you, I'm betraying them."

"You tried to get me convicted of murder."

"Yeah, well, you're a—"

I said, "It won't take long to call the police."

"Fine." He drew a deep breath. He loosened his tie and undid the collar of his white shirt. He said, "We met at a bar both last Thursday and Friday nights. That's when we planned everything."

"Who is we?" I asked.

"Bochka, Spandrel, Pinyon, Schaven, Graniento, Towne. All of us."

"What was the plan?"

"To get you accused of murder. To get you fired."

I said, "You weren't worried that one of them might be a murderer?"

"We figured one of the old guard did it."

"Who was pushing that notion?" I asked.

"Nobody was pushing it. It was logical."

"But accuse me of sexual abuse?"

"You know about that?"

"Obviously."

"We were ready to do whatever it took."

Blind fury swept through me. He made his statements so calmly and almost without concern. My conscience, my love for Scott, his love for me, my parents' training, my sense of self—I'm not sure what it was that kept me in my seat and kept me from hurting him. I don't know if I could have killed him. At that moment I frightened myself.

"That's easy for you?" I asked.

"This is a fight. We do whatever we can. You do whatever you can." I almost thought I saw a smirk on his face. Was he enjoying my discomfort? I rubbed my hand across my face and focused. I'd get the information from this son of a bitch. Added to what we had from Fred, it was possible I could bring all these people down. That would bring intense satisfaction.

I said, "Were you part of their sexual trysts?"

"No. I haven't dated anyone from Grover Cleveland since, well, since the women I told you about. I'm going to be married soon to a woman I went to college with. I went out with these guys. I never had sex with any of them."

I said, "But you're always talked about as the stud of the staff."

257

"I am a stud. I just don't screw anybody from here, not anymore."

"Were Eberson and Spandrel having an affair?"

"They were just having fun."

"Peter, too?" I asked.

"I guess he had sex with them, but he was supposed to be a lousy lover. Had a small dick, too, according to Spandrel."

"Did the husbands know?"

"Not until the murder. Mabel told us that her husband walked out on her over the weekend. Took the kids."

"Nobody believed in being faithful?" I asked.

"I'm not responsible for their behavior. We were having fun. Something you guys know nothing about."

I said, "Perhaps we have a different definition of fun. Who else was screwing whom?"

"That's it, as far as I know. It's only three people. Out of a whole staff of nearly fifty, counting administrators and members of the department, that's not a lot, is it?"

I had no idea.

I said, "Why was Spandrel fighting with Graniento at the football game Friday night?"

"That was nothing."

"What?" I demanded.

Milovec said, "Spandrel wanted to add your boyfriend in the plot. Graniento told her no, that everything was getting too convoluted. When you weren't arrested Friday after what I told the cops, we knew we needed to take more action."

"Why do all this?" I asked.

"First, everybody dislikes you. Second, you're the heart of the old guard."

"I never say anything."

He said, "You don't have to. Your silences are deafening.

When you don't support our causes, the other side has more confidence. Whoever you do speak up for, or whenever, they listen to you. They don't listen to us. You had to go. And you're gay. And none of the administrators like that. Bochka hates you. Hates you. We worked out the final details that Friday night after the game."

Still I kept my temper. There was a homophobic conspiracy. My paranoia was justified. Destroying these people would hardly be enough.

I asked, "Who wrote the Pinyon hate notes?"

Milovec said, "We set it up to try and get sympathy from some of the teachers who were sitting on the fence. Some people were put off by Peter being anti-Semitic and prejudiced."

I asked, "He's African American. Why would he be prejudiced?"

"Same reason Clarence Thomas is against affirmative action, I guess. I don't know. He was. It was funny."

"Were you involved in the double dipping and gambling?"

"No. Graniento was pissed about that. He didn't know it was going on. He also didn't know that Spandrel had gotten us into the files to find out all that information Pinyon had."

"Graniento wasn't aware of that either?"

"He knew a lot, but Spandrel and Bochka did most of the planning before this week. I think Spandrel wanted Graniento's job. She's tough."

"Was Higden in debt?" I asked.

"He owed tons of money to bookies. He even owed nearly a thousand to the guys in the PE department."

"Why didn't you play?" I asked.

"My girlfriend would kill me if she knew I was gambling in school. She's a teacher, too."

"Peter was double dipping?"

"Sure," Milovec said. "My understanding is that it was the common practice. More common than not. Why is it a big deal?"

"It's cheating," I said.

"Everybody does it at all the schools I've ever heard of."

"Where did Pinyon get his statistics from?"

"A bunch of us went on a Saturday with Spandrel and went through the files."

"That's illegal," I said.

"Have the file police arrest me," Milovec said.

"Why bother?" I asked.

"Huh?"

"Why bother doing all that work in the first place? What is so fucking important about going to conferences? Whose idea was it to gather all the statistics illegally? Why even take such a useless risk?"

"I was told to."

"Bullshit."

"I didn't have a choice."

"Of course you did," I said.

"Fine," he said. "Spandrel didn't want to let any of the old guard out of the district. She figured if she had the statistics, she could give her people permission to go to all the conferences and never let the old guard go anywhere."

"So people were right. It was fixed so the old guard was screwed. And you rigged the statistics."

Milovec licked his lips. "A little," he admitted.

"Frank Jourdan said he couldn't remember going to any conferences in the eighties. We've talked to a retired teacher who knows you were making stuff up. Why bother to go through the files if you were just going to make things up?"

"Okay, fine. At first it was going to be legitimate, but it took too damn long. We had to have enough to make it look real. Who would remember that far back?"

260

"If you twisted those statistics, what other crap have you been making up these past few years?"

"Spandrel switched things to meet her needs. We had to take action. She wanted to call Homeland Security on you and get you in trouble. She even suggested putting dope and drugs in your car or in your desk in your classroom."

"Call Homeland Security?"

"And say you were a terrorist."

"Why didn't you?"

"We couldn't figure out how to make a call that couldn't be traced. The government can get records of everything. We needed to do it anonymously. We thought of trying a pay phone in Chicago, but so many places have security cameras now. We couldn't be sure of where it would be safe. We thought of all kinds of things."

I said, "If I wasn't so pissed off, I think I'd be honored to have been that much of a threat to you guys."

"Spandrel hated you. She'd have done anything to destroy you."

And now was he bailing on her, trying to save his own ass? Blaming someone else in an attempt to save his job? He had to have been really frightened of us going to the police with his lie.

"Teachers spying on teachers is pretty low. Why did you guys agree to that?"

"We never knew what you were up to. We knew you were plotting and planning against us. We had to find out what you were going to pull."

I said, "I never met with anybody to plot and plan. As far as I know, the old guard never met. They never got themselves organized enough."

"So you say. In public you were always neutral or pretending to be. Maybe they never invited you to their meetings."

"Did you find evidence of their perfidy?"

"No, but we knew they were fighting us. When we spied, we were supposed to get materials on whether they were obeying all the school rules. You know, doing lesson plans. Check their computers to see if they'd been used for personal things."

"It was okay with you to spy on us?" I kept harking back to that because it was such an astoundingly traitorous thing to do. In the pantheon of things they'd done, it wasn't up there with murder and what they'd tried to do with me, but I was dealing with one shock at a time.

"Hey, Spandrel said it was okay to spy. She said it would help her."

"Did it?"

"I guess not enough."

Spandrel was not the brightest. All that time and work of professionals spent on spying. What a waste.

"Why try and claim that Eberson was having an affair with a student?"

"That's where Spandrel got the idea about you."

"Why turn on Eberson?"

"The funny thing about Gracie is that she was the most homophobic of all of us. She hid it better than most of us, but when she and Peter were together it was something. They hated you, but on Thursday, she was dead. We had to make sure nothing reflected back on us. She could be smeared and blamed if things started to go bad."

Or Spandrel had more in mind and didn't confide her entire plan to Milovec.

"But she was having sex with Spandrel?"

"So what? That didn't stop them from hating you."

I asked, "Did you see Peter after the meeting?"

"We all did," Milovec said. "Schaven, Pinyon, and me. We met to discuss what to do next. The meeting didn't last long."

"And you didn't tell the cops this?"

"We knew to keep our mouths shut."

If he was telling the truth, the three of them could surely vouch for each other about where they were at the time of Gracie Eberson's death. Unless he was lying or covering now. I asked, "After the meeting, you didn't see Spandrel, Graniento, Towne, Bochka, or Eberson?"

"No. It was just us guys."

"Who was the last to see Peter?"

"I guess I was. He asked me for a few bucks to tide him over."

"How much?"

"A hundred. I couldn't spare it. My girlfriend would notice. We live together, and we're kind of in debt, paying back our student loans, and we've got an expensive condo together. We have a lot of bills. The wedding is going to cost a fortune."

I said, "And whose idea was it to get Fred Zileski to lie?"

Milovec shuffled his feet. "Spandrel and Bochka cooked it up. Bochka was sure her kid could be trusted."

I said, "He could be. To be honest."

"Yeah, well, you guys weren't all saints."

I said, "You don't see the difference between making things up, telling vicious lies, ruining people's careers, and having philosophical differences over educational issues?"

He said, "All's fair."

I held myself very still. I stared out the window for some time. The sun had nearly set. The lights were still out. Gloom gathered in the shadows.

Milovec asked, "Are we done?"

Without looking at him, I nodded.

Milovec scuttled out.

46

I sat on a low cabinet in the back of the room. I leaned one arm on a stack of books and stared out the window. Dark grays and browns were fading rapidly to black. I didn't bother with the lights. The gathering shadows matched my mood. I watched darkness envelop cars and trees. I'd calm down for a moment and then become upset anew.

I called my attorney. He said he'd come out for a meeting. Scott called on his cell moments after I hung up from the attorney. He was merging from the Stevenson Expressway onto the Dan Ryan. He'd gone ten feet in the last twenty minutes. He told me he loved me and he'd get here as fast as he could. Frank Rohde was still out on an investigation. I called Meg and told her what happened.

"Do you want me to come back?" she asked.

"Scott will be here soon."

She reassured me over and over.

After we hung up, I continued to stare outdoors. Depression and anger warred for mastery. Fred Zileski told the truth, and I was free. I had the goods on these people, and they would pay. Pay for the rest of their lives, if I could help it. I'm not the kind of guy who dedicates his life to revenge, but at that moment, I could have been convinced.

The shadows deepened. I shivered.

My classroom door opened. Brandon Benson was a third of the way to the front before I moved to get between him and the door. He hadn't turned on the lights. He heard the movement and turned back. I flipped on the lights. I said, "What are you doing here?"

He started to rush toward the door, but I was between him and it. He said, "I have to go."

"You in the habit of sneaking into teachers' rooms after you think they've gone home?"

"I wasn't sneaking."

"You in the habit of going to board members' houses?" I asked. "Or going out drinking with them on Thursday and Friday nights?"

"I can't talk to you."

"You don't have a choice."

"You can't make me."

"Why would you take part in such a conspiracy? Why would you agree to be part of so many lies? Your current crime is that you were making out with a guy. That is no longer a felony in this country. It would be frightening to a married man, but even if you aren't gay, you must be able to sympathize with a teacher who is being lied about."

"I'm not part of a conspiracy."

"And you're in here sneaking around."

"You can't prove anything," he said.

"Ah," I said, "but I can. People are blabbing. All the lies are going to come out. All the conspiracies are going to be unmasked. All of it. You and your cohorts' day is over."

He began to cry. I let him find his own goddamn tissue. "I can't do this," Brandon Benson said. He sobbed mightily.

I didn't care. The son of a bitch had lied and been part of

all the planning. If they wanted my vote, Benson could join the corpse count.

"Why?" I asked.

He wiped his eyes, blew his nose, then said, "Maybe I'd be next. They are ruthless, vicious. I'm afraid of them. I'll always be afraid of them. I don't have tenure. I need my job. I've got bills. We've got a kid coming. I need the family coverage insurance. They made me lie. They said they'd tell what I'd been doing in that room. That I'd been having an affair. With a guy. They threatened me." He sobbed again.

It would be great to think that giving tenure actually had something to do with teacher competence. Mostly I'd seen it used by administrators to get even with teachers they didn't like—teachers they couldn't cow, or bully, or intimidate.

I asked, "How'd they find out what you were doing?"

"The police told them."

So the cops had tattled.

My voice rose over the histrionic weeping. I said, "So you'd prefer to lie and destroy my life."

"Better you than me. I don't know you. Well, okay, I know you're rich. You're famous. You've been on talk shows. You sit there at those faculty meetings as if you're better than us."

"I may or may not be better than you are, but you are moral poison. You'd tell lie after lie after lie, and you wouldn't care how much it hurt someone else. And if they weren't lies, they were distortions. Did you kill Eberson or Higden?"

"No. I didn't know Gracie was in there. I swear to god, I didn't know she was in there."

"Who told you to lie?"

"They all did."

"They who?"

"The superintendent, the head of the board, the head of the department, the principal."

"Did they tell you why?"

"No. They just told me what to do. I had to do it. I didn't have time to think. I couldn't discuss it with anyone outside that group. I couldn't tell my wife any of this. How could I tell her I was cheating on her?"

"Weren't you frightened that one of them might be a killer?"

"No. They just told me what to say. I guess I assumed one of them might have done it, or they were all in on it, but everybody kept saying it was the old guard. I didn't want to think about it. I wanted to save my skin. Maybe somebody would kill me. I was scared. I'm still scared. Why aren't you yelling at Milovec? He's still here. I saw him heading down to the office. He's a big part of this. Some of them are still here. Go confront them. They said they were going to meet after school today. They're really pissed at you about the grades and test scores thing."

I said, "I didn't do wrong."

"But you brought it out in the open."

"That was a group of us."

"But they blame you," he wailed. "I was supposed to come up here and see if you'd gone. If you had, I was supposed to download everything from your computer onto my flash drive. They were determined. They are determined."

"Still planning?"

"Supposed to be."

I thought for a while.

"Am I going to lose my job?" he asked.

"You will if I have anything to say about it. Are you going back to join them?"

He stood for a moment in silence. "No," he whispered. "No, I'm going home. I'm going to talk to my wife. I love her."

I didn't hold out a lot of hope for that relationship.

⟍ 47 ⟍

Anger trumped all my other emotions. These people were plotting their lies even as I stood in my classroom. I told myself, Wait for Scott, wait for your lawyer, wait.

But I was furious.

The honesty of a single teenager.

I told myself I should be able to be calm.

But I wasn't.

My tears earlier were gone, replaced by steely resolve to fight anyone and everyone. I stalked out.

First, I hunted for the head of the department. All the classrooms I passed were empty. No one was in the English department offices. I stomped down the stairs to the main office. The conference room was dark. The district offices were in an attached building next to ours. Unlike the main building in the school complex, their air-conditioning worked in summer and the heat system kept them nice and toasty in the winter. They were steps ahead of us in the high school on both counts.

I found the superintendent, Riva Towne, still in. Her secretary barred the way. I said, "I have important information about the murders. I've got to talk to her."

"I was told to keep you out," Harriet Smithers said. She smiled grimly. "However, you've done wonders for the secretaries since we got into the union. And Georgette is a friend. She told all of us to help you if she wasn't around." She nodded her head toward the double doors.

I didn't knock.

Towne looked up from her desk. She was on the phone. She said, "I'll have to call you back," and hung up. I realized that I should have called Scott on my cell phone and left it on. Anger had trumped planning.

"What are you doing here?" Ice and anger radiated in her tone and manner. I didn't note the slightest trace of professionalism.

I stood in front of her desk. I said, "I'd like to take a picture of you sitting here. I'd like to sell it on eBay so that people can see what 'evil incarnate' looks like."

"That's insubordination," she said. "You're fired." Her eyes were flinty, her lips compressed into a sharp line.

"Really? We'll have to have an insubordination seminar. Do you have a witness to what I said? Oh, of course not, it's just us. Or maybe you could get somebody to lie about it. That seems to be your management style. Get people to lie and hate each other and fight and get nothing done. The same ploys the other administrators in this district use. Unfortunately for you, the jig is up. Everything is going to come out. The statistics rigging. Teachers spying and lying. Having a teenager make false accusations. All of it."

For the first time she looked wary, but she wasn't ready to back down yet. She said, "I'm surprised they haven't arrested you. You'll be lucky to have a job here. You run around being insubordinate because you've got a rich boyfriend." She stood up. "Get out."

"It's not that easy," I said. I was breathing hard. I was

nearly speechless with wrath. It was difficult to form the words, but I intended to get all of this out in the open.

She said, "You look like you're out of control."

I said, "I don't believe you're ever going to meet someone as angry as I am now. And you're going to listen. Let's start with Fred Zileski."

She bit her lip.

I said, "Never trust a teenager to keep his mouth shut."

She said, "No one's going to believe what a teenager says."

"Which would work against people believing what you wanted him to say about me. Your larger problem is that you've got to be more careful when you're concocting a massive conspiracy. Somebody might wind up telling the truth. You're amateurs. You involved too many people."

"You intimidated that boy. You can't harass students."

"You won't be able to turn this back on me. Mr. Zileski knows everything. He was here. He'll be talking to his ex-wife. And the police."

"So, some kid is making up stories. Why should I care?"

"We'll let that go for now. What you don't know is that now we've got real live teachers starting to tell the truth."

"Who talked to you?"

"Milovec has told all, or if not all, at least enough to incriminate you in all the lies."

She said, "If somebody implicated you in the murder, it wasn't my idea."

"You were part of the plan to get me accused of murder and of inappropriate conduct with a student. I'm sure you knew about the attempts to sabotage my computer. My attorney is on his way. Charges will be filed. You will be the one who no longer has a job."

She laughed. "You think you've got some kind of power around here? You think you've got some kind of immunity?

You think you can claim discrimination? You think you can get away with anything?"

"What precisely is it that you think I've gotten away with?"

"Breathing. Being gay. You should have been fired as soon as it came out. That would have been before the gay-rights ordinance in the state."

"What you're saying is that you're a coward and a bigot, and you're looking for an excuse to get rid of me. You wanted me accused of murder to get me out of the classroom."

"Morals charges don't work anymore."

"And you'd suborn a student?"

"His father has twisted that boy."

"Sounds like the kid has an honest streak. Something you seem to lack. Did you commit both murders?"

Towne said, "You've got a hell of a nerve coming to my office."

"Let's see, you tried to destroy my life, and you're upset because I'm in your office. My lawyer will be interrupting your evening."

"I don't know what you think you can prove. Your job is going to be gone."

"Wrong again, you moron."

"Name-calling isn't going to help."

"Really? After what you've done, you're worried about name-calling?" I was, however, going to have to stop it. I was so furious and was breathing so hard that I had to speak between deep inhales. "Did you kill Eberson or Higden?"

"That's absurd."

"Not this evening, it isn't. At the least, weren't you worried that one of the people you were meeting with might be a killer?"

"That's absurd, too."

"You might need to change your absurd index meter or get a new one."

"The old guard killed them."

"Who?"

"Proof will come out. There is much more to be said. No one will trust you. No one likes you."

I said, "Blow it out your ass."

She picked up her coat. "Unless you intend to physically restrain me, I'm leaving."

I didn't attempt to stop her.

48

Spandrel wasn't to be found.

I ran into Morgan Adair. He was in his coat and hat. "What's up?" he asked.

"Deceit and murder."

"Are you okay?" he asked.

My upset must have shown on my face. I asked, "Have you seen Spandrel?"

"I think she went home."

I said, "I've got to find her. I'll tell you about it later."

I passed darkened empty classrooms. I couldn't get a handle on my emotions. I was almost dizzy with anger. Through the window of my classroom door, I could see moonlight filling the room. The full moon was rising. I'd turned out the lights when I left. I entered. The door clicked shut behind me. I reached for the light switch.

A voice called, "Stop."

Mabel Spandrel sat in the chair behind my desk. She held a gun pointed at my chest.

She said, "Stand there." She waved the gun toward the front of the classroom. I moved carefully to where she pointed. I wound up in front of the windows with my back to the moon. Shouting would be useless. No one was on this floor. I'd be dead before the echoes died.

I said, "This whole thing was about me being gay?"

"No," she said. "You just don't get it, do you?"

"Maybe you can explain it."

"We have a few minutes. We need to wait until everyone is out of the building."

Would it be long enough for Scott to get here, realize something was wrong, and come looking?

I said, "You're going to kill me. Did you kill the others?"

"No. I'm not sure who did those. No, right now, I just want to get even with you. You've cost me my job, my career, my husband, my kids."

"It would be nice to think I accomplished that," I said. "You ruined your life all by yourself. While that does please me after what you tried to do to me, I can't take credit for it."

"Don't get snotty, motherfucker."

"How did I accomplish all that?" I asked.

"The scandal about the test scores is going to come out. I don't know who you suborned in that office. They are a tight-lipped bunch. I don't know why they're so loyal to you."

"Do you think you've done something to earn their loyalty?"

"I bring them doughnuts on Fridays."

I said, "Give them back their twenty-five cents and tell them to go to hell."

"Huh?"

"The punch line to an old joke. Skip it. Doughnuts didn't cut it?"

"Those secretaries know everything. My husband is going to sue for custody of the kids and probably everything I've ever earned."

274

"And he'll win," I said. "Good for him. You did have sex with Eberson and Higden?"

"Of course, you dope. Sometimes one at a time. Sometimes both at once." While she talked she waved the gun around. Eventually it would get heavy. She'd have to rest it and her hand on the desk. Would it be enough of an opening?

"How did you get the gun into the school?" I asked.

"Who doesn't have to go through security? Who has a key to every door? The administrators. Only the main entrances have metal detectors."

"Why try to make all of us so miserable?" I asked.

"I was hired to do that. The day I signed my contract, Towne and Bochka met with me. They told me to 'get into that department and clean house.' They specifically targeted you and the union."

"But you failed every single time. You didn't have one success. Every time you violated the contract, you lost. I never pestered you as long as you didn't screw something up connected with the contract. They gave you direct orders to be miserable to us? You and they could have brought about changes without being Nazis about the whole thing."

"You were just angry because you weren't in charge anymore."

"People keep saying that. I was never in charge. All I did was check the contract and help people."

"Hah." She rested hand and gun on the desk. The weapon was still pointed at my midsection.

I said, "You were part of the conspiracy to get me fired."

"Getting you accused of and convicted of murder would have been perfect. Short of that, getting you fired would have been the next best thing. It was fun making shit up about you. How did you get Bochka's dope of a son to blab, tickle his torso? We never should have trusted him. We

275

should have gotten Spike Faherty to do it. He'd have been tough enough. I called Spike into the office. I asked him if you'd ever done anything. The stupid kid is loyal to you. He said you'd never touched him. That all you did was try to teach them grammar and writing. Then he got pissed and walked out. Asshole."

"Me or the kid?"

"Both."

"Was it just sex or were you having an affair with Eberson?"

"And you're an out faggot."

"And with Peter?"

"With anybody I want."

There was an ego for you.

"Why are Eberson and Higden dead?"

"I didn't kill them."

"Who did?"

"I don't know."

The door began to open. A voice I didn't recognize called softly, "Mason?"

Spandrel swung the gun toward the door. The moonlight caught a metallic gleam in a hand that appeared in the opening.

I dove for the ground. Desks crashed and scattered out of my path. A volley of gunshots rang out. Shards of wood flew near me. I heard screams and grunts. I lifted my head up.

49

Spandrel's head rested on the top of my desk. Her eyes reflected the moonlight. She blinked several times and moaned. Blood pooled around her left arm. I saw a rivulet escape from the large mass, slowly work its way toward the end of the desk, then drip to the floor.

I heard a gasp behind me. I turned. One knee on the floor, one hand on the back of a student's desk, Amando Graniento seemed to be holding his breath. I began to get up. The gun in his hand moved wildly. He said, "It hurts." He gasped. The gun swung. It discharged. I hit the floor again. A window shattered.

From my spot on the floor, I could see Graniento's body draped over a student's desk. Moments later he slumped to the floor. The gun skittered away.

I know I gaped for a few moments, not quite sure which one I should go to. I'd banged my knee and my head. I felt a bit woozy. I began to pull myself up with one hand, and I reached for my cell phone with the other. I tried using a student's desk for leverage.

When I was halfway up, the desk began to skid away. I grabbed at it. My head swirled. I leaned over carefully. I heard a swishing noise, and then my head exploded in pain. Blackness.

50

When I awoke, I was staring into the jean-clad crotch of Steven Frecking. I was still on the floor. Blinding stabs of pain shot through my skull.

Kara Bochka's voice was saying, ". . . not to come here."

Frecking said, "I expected to find Mason alone." He looked down at me and said, "He's awake."

I got to my knees and heaved myself into a student's desk. My head throbbed.

Bochka stood next to Spandrel, who was taped to my teacher's chair. She had tears in her eyes. Blood caked the left side of her jacket and blouse.

Bochka paced. She directed her words to Spandrel. "You fucked everything up. We had Mason. He was a goner. The police were suspicious, but you screwed everything up." She swung a serrated-edge hunting knife back and forth in her right hand. "You did absolutely nothing right."

Spandrel spoke between gasps, "We planned together. I did everything you said. You can't kill me."

"I can. I have no choice. You know everything. You couldn't control that department. You couldn't even control this fag."

Spandrel said, "You can't kill everyone who knows. We were all in on it. Towne isn't here."

"I'll have to decide what to do about that idiot superintendent later. If I kill you, the police will put it down to whoever killed the first two." Bochka marched up and down the room. She swung the knife and raved about politics and changing the schools and how Spandrel had failed her with her incompetence. Asshole turning upon asshole. Bochka stopped next to the tied-up department head.

Mabel Spandrel certainly deserved to die. I certainly wanted to escape. I had to do something for myself, but I couldn't just stand there and let Bochka kill Spandrel. She was the most awful administrator in the history of the planet, little more than a Nazi in disguise. She bullied teachers. She would tell any lie to protect herself or just for the hell of it, but she couldn't just be killed in cold blood. Murder was not to be countenanced, but saving my ass was high on my priority list right then.

I willed my muscles to move. Nothing. I felt tears on my cheeks.

Bochka would swing her knife close to Spandrel's neck, then pace back and forth, return, threaten her with the knife again. Frecking's attention was riveted on the two of them. I almost gasped. I was sitting, and from my perspective, I could see his massive erection. Murder turned him on.

I was between him and the exit. Could I possibly make a rush to the door, get it locked with them inside, get away, and make a call? Not likely. Frecking had a gun. His own or Spandrel's? Graniento didn't move. I couldn't see him breathing. His gun was six inches away from his right hand. Maybe three feet from me. I could maybe get that gun. I could maybe raise and fire faster than Frecking could react. Maybe get to the door before he fired. Maybe. Maybe. Maybe. I had to try something.

Spandrel coughed and gagged for a few moments. Bochka brought the knife close to the department head's throat. Bochka said, "You are more trouble than you're worth. I should have stuck with my original opinion of you as stupid, useless fool. Ah, well, you were conveniently at hand, for a while."

I eased myself to the edge of the desk. Bochka raved. Spandrel and Frecking's eyes followed the knife. Less than an inch separated her from death.

I felt for my cell phone. Could I possibly punch in 911? Would whoever answered have the patience and the insight to figure out what was happening? I tried moving my arm. The movement caught Spandrel's eye. Bochka saw her gaze in my direction.

Bochka whirled toward me as I tried to rise. My head swam. I nearly made it to my feet.

Frecking said, "I wouldn't." He picked up the gun from the floor and pointed both of them at me. "There are two of us and one of you."

I said, "I got that part."

Bochka walked over to Graniento and peered down at his corpse. She said, "He was an officious dope. There are going to be a lot of corpses." She stood on tiptoe and looked at Spandrel at the far end of the room. "Why did you shoot him?"

Spandrel twisted in the chair, let out a gasp of pain. Through gritted teeth she said, "I was aiming for Mason. I missed."

Bochka frowned. Frecking laughed. I frantically tried to think of methods of escape.

Bochka began to pace again.

I couldn't tell how long I'd been unconscious. Moonlight still flooded the room. It couldn't have been that long. If anyone had heard the gunfire, they hadn't responded.

I asked, "Did you two just happen to be lurking around in the halls?"

Bochka said, "I was lurking. I called Steven on his cell phone when I saw Graniento leave the office. I believed he and Mabel might have had something cooked up for you or each other. I didn't know they were planning to shoot each other."

Spandrel said, "I didn't know who it was at the door. I thought it might be another one of his fucking spies. I told you. I was aiming for him. I saw the gun and didn't want to take a chance."

"This is all spontaneous?" I asked.

Bochka said, "Pretty much."

"You didn't plan the murders with them?" I asked.

Spandrel said, "I didn't."

Bochka said, "Dear me, I believe she's lying again. Their deaths are a bonus, but I didn't care if they lived or died."

I said, "I'm confused. Who killed who and why?"

Spandrel said, "Eberson and Higden were going to tell all about our conspiracies. They were going to break down and tell the truth. We couldn't have that."

"Eberson didn't sound like she was ready to abandon the cause when she was screaming at Jourdan last Thursday."

Spandrel said, "I'm sure she believed what she was saying, she just no longer wanted to be a part of what we were doing and all our plotting. Said she was tired of the lies and deceptions. Stupid cunt."

I said, "They'd have taken you all down in the scandal."

"Ah," Bochka said, "not quite true. I'm elected by the people. These administrators made their own decisions about their plotting and planning and what they were cheating on."

"But you knew about it," I said. "You planned with them."

"Yes, but they're dead, and there will be no proof. Frankly, it's good that Graniento is dead. One less person to worry about having a conscience."

"Towne will know."

"She'll realize what's good for her. She's in as deep as I am."

"Did she kill anyone?"

"No."

I said, "Frecking, you killed Gracie."

"It was great," he said. "It was maybe the most exciting moment of my life. My dick got hard as she flopped around. I was turned on as much by that as by that dope Benson."

"Why did you kill her?" I asked. "None of these scandals would have touched you. Even the grade scandal might have meant little more than a reprimand."

He snorted, then said, "I didn't have a lot of choice. Bochka had got wind of Benson's and my making out. This wasn't my first time at school. She'd set a trap and caught us once. She was blackmailing me."

"Were you blackmailing Benson?" I asked.

Bochka said, "He was cooperating without it. I was saving that to use it later. You don't want to give away everything if you don't have to."

Could I keep them talking? Scott would be negotiating traffic. Damn the Dan Ryan and reconstruction. He'd sit outside for a few minutes. Try to call me on my cell phone, get worried, and come looking. If he could get into the school. If he could get here fast enough.

"How'd you know Gracie would be there?"

"I didn't have to kill her that night," Frecking said. "It had to be soon, and I'd been checking on the opportunity for a few days. She happened to go to that room. It was perfect. That Benson would soon be there added to the thrill."

An insightful murderer, who would expect that in a PE teacher?

"What if he'd have walked in on what you were doing?"

"Then he'd have died, too. He wouldn't have told anyone where he was going. Of course, he'd never admit to having a tryst with me, especially in school. I'm much bigger and stronger than he is. I was having the best of both worlds— murder and sex."

My cell phone rang. Scott.

"Give it to me," Frecking ordered. Keeping the guns in one hand and out of my reach, with the other he grabbed my phone, then smashed it to the floor. The ringing stopped. Was Scott close?

I looked at Bochka. "But why did they have to die? Why not bribe them with something or threaten them? Something?"

Bochka said, "They wouldn't listen. As Mabel said, they were no longer willing to be part of the, as you would put it, suckup faction. They were planning to turn on us. Neither would submit to blackmail. Believe me, I tried."

"But why had they decided to turn on you?"

"It started with Gracie. Idiot Spandrel was winding down their affair. Then Peter was angry about that poker mess. He always wanted what was best for him, only him. Once they broke ranks, they had to die. Getting you accused of murder or fired for inappropriate behavior with boys would have been a bonus."

I said, "But Fred told the truth and ruined that part of the conspiracy."

"Yes, my idiot husband has corrupted that boy. He left me hysterical messages on my voice mail starting around 4:30."

I said, "You guys were either really daring, really stupid, or really desperate. How did you figure all this would be kept quiet?"

"All the conspiring we'd done had been concealed so far,"

Bochka said. "That's over two years since Mabel started. We figured it would keep working."

I said, "So Bochka plans and Frecking kills."

"Yes, that sums it up nicely," Bochka said. "Spandrel, Towne, and Graniento helped do the other dirty work."

I asked Frecking, "How'd you kill Peter?"

"I offered to give him head in his car last Thursday. We'd done that before. After Benson and I told our lies to the cops, I saw Peter. He was restless. So was I. It wasn't that odd. We went out and got in the back of his SUV. He left the car on to warm it up. After we finished—and it didn't take long—I got out first and ran around to the driver's seat. Higden thought I was playing some kind of joke, and he got out too. If I hadn't had to run him over a second time, he'd have died laughing. Putting his body next to your tires was a stroke of genius."

"Why didn't you come to me when she threatened you?"

"You fool, it wasn't because I'm gay that she was blackmailing me, it's because I was giving a guy a blow job in school. I was fucked."

Bochka said, "We've got to get this to look like Mason killed them both."

"Gonna be tough," I said. "I'll have to have powder burns from both guns." I hoped it was forensically provable—or at least I had to hope that they watched at least one of the CSI programs and believed it was forensically provable. "They fired separate guns at each other. You'll have to get the angles that they fired at accurate as well. I'd have had to fire at one from near the door, at the other from the desk. I can't have been two places at once. Are you going to slit Spandrel's throat? You'll have to get my fingerprints on the knife, and then it's got to be logical that I shot at her and then stabbed her. Why would I do that?"

"Maybe you're as poor at planning as she is."

"Why are you going to kill Spandrel?"

"She's expendable," Bochka said. "She's a loose cannon, and she's not too bright."

Spandrel swore.

Bochka laughed. "The conspiracy got out of hand. Too many people knew. I have to limit the number of people, especially now."

I turned to Frecking. "You think she'll let you live?"

Frecking said, "Mutual self-destruction. I know about her, she knows about me."

Bochka said, "As for making it look like you did it, easy as pie. You shot one of them from the door. When you got to the desk, the other one came in on you, so you shot him."

"How'd I change guns?"

"I'm working on it," Bochka said.

"It's all going to come out," I said. "You'll never keep this quiet."

Bochka said, "We'll work it out."

Scott said, "Not likely."

The three of us turned to the door. Scott and Frank Rohde stood there.

Rhode's gun was out. Seconds later, uniformed officers flooded the room. I knocked Frecking's guns away. Bochka's knife hung at her side.

51

I rushed to Scott's arms. He enfolded me in a fierce embrace. I felt dizzy and safe.

⸏ 52 ⸌

The state board of education took over the management of the school district. That happens once in a while in Illinois, although it's usually when a school district is in financial trouble.

Lots of bad things happened to bad people.

Grade fixing and statistic rigging: administrators and PE teachers and those who helped them were losing their jobs. Georgette went around with a permanent smile on her face. Double-dipping PE teachers were being reprimanded or fired.

The English department: kicking and screaming, I was put in charge. I insisted it be temporary. I insisted on having my own way. I stopped having departmental meetings. I figured, no meetings, no forums for acrimony. I told teachers that they could use the methodology they were comfortable with as long as the students performed up to expectations. This meant that they were to be judged on the progress the students made rather than on an arbitrary standard. You had the kids—you were responsible for them. I junked all the outdated textbooks. At a designated spot in the library I collected samples of all the textbooks and reading and English programs from all the companies that made them. I told the teachers to vote for their top three. Then I told them to vote for their top one. They could campaign for what they wanted. They chose a mixture of old and new programs, textbooks, novels, software. Good for them. Mrs. Faherty, the temporary head of the board of education, told the rest of the board they were going to "spend their goddamn money on kids." Nobody in the department got to impose their will on others.

Gambling: stopped. A few people got reprimands.

Schaven, Pinyon, Milovec, and Benson got fired. Benson's wife filed for divorce.

Towne tried to hang on, but she was fired that summer. Which might have had something to do with the suit for discrimination I filed against the school district and the administration and anybody else I could think of. My attorney expected them to settle for a hefty sum. I thought I'd donate any proceeds to the Point Foundation, a gay group dedicated to helping gay college kids pay for school.

Bochka, Frecking, and Spandrel were to be tried for conspiracy and murder. The States Attorney was confident of convictions, especially with each of them fighting to implicate the others.

Victoria Abbot agreed to testify against anybody she could. Later she found a job in a school district in California.

Spike settled on purple hair on a semipermanent basis. He and his motorcycle began attending junior college the next fall.

Fred rededicated himself to placing a verb in every sentence. The last bit of prose he handed in had been suffused with verbs, most of them used correctly. Mr. Zileski had full custody. Fred continued to distinguish himself on the football field. The team continued to lose more often than not. Without Graniento's warnings about booing and stomping, the kids had gotten bored. And as it was getting into November, fewer and fewer were showing up to cheer on their less than successful athletes. Fred did get a small scholarship to a Division II college for football. I wrote a letter of recommendation for him.

53

Much later Scott and I were having breakfast at his place. He was making banana pancakes from scratch.

After we were settled, he said, "You have triumphed."

"It doesn't feel quite like that."

"The suckup faction is out. The bad guys have been arrested. Some of the bad guys are even dead. How often does that happen?"

"For the moment, things are calm. I like calm."

"Why do all that lying about you, especially in this day and age?" Scott asked.

I said, "I think the key was that they perceived me as being in their way. Their homophobia fueled their hatred and their irrationality."

Scott said, "People keep saying they were sick or nuts. I'm not sure that sums it up. This was a pretty dysfunctional crowd."

"Despite progress for gay people, it still happens. You and I both know it. I think Bochka was the heart of it. Spandrel was kind of the new Nazi on the block. Their personalities meshed. They thought they could commit mayhem and get the gay guy. Unfortunately, such things happen to gay people. Still. Today. It's better than it was, but the world is not perfect. And remember, we're still the only country since the Nazi's in 1930's Germany where a major political party wants to legislate second-class citizenship for an entire group of people. That kind of thing enables those who hate."

Scott said, "It was a rough year."

"I'm going to be happy to not be head of the department."

He smiled. "Did they get used to no meetings?"

"Most of them.'

"How did those ninnies expect to get away with all this? The conspiracy was too big."

"Remember, they were amateurs, and a lot of the planning was relatively spontaneous. And their silence was monolithic for quite some time. The grade fixing was reasonably minor. Picking on teachers, unfortunately, was normal. Gambling limited to a few. Double dipping among the coaches barely affected the English department. Their social lives were complex but not necessarily felonious, but when things started to unravel, they got desperate."

"They were fools," Scott said.

"That too. And remember, only two of them knew who committed the murders: the planner, Bochka, and the killer, Frecking. Graniento's death wasn't planned. Spandrel might get off with a charge of manslaughter. The murders also offered a convenient chance to get me—it was sort of icing on the cake. Having to plan on the spur of the moment helped them screw it up."

Scott asked, "If Spandrel and Eberson were having a lesbian affair, how come they were so determined to discriminate against you?"

"I'm not sure I'd call them lesbians. I think it was more that they were having a good time with each other and Peter.

Remember, they were both married to men, and they had children. It might have been one of those 'I'm doing what I want and no one can stop me' moments. It felt good. They did it. They might have been having fun, but I don't think it means they were gay or any less prejudiced."

Scott said, "I still find it hard to believe Eberson and Higden were going to break ranks and tell."

"I'm not sure if they actually were," I said. "Bochka feared their threats as much as anything. She didn't trust them. She had a lot to lose. Or the web of lies and plots just got to be too much. Maybe one or both was getting a conscience. For Higden, it seems like he was angry at his poker buddies and once the dam was cracked, the rest of it was going to come out."

"As it kept getting more and more convoluted, why didn't they just stop?" Scott asked.

"Bochka and Frecking had murders to cover up. If Frecking hadn't been so worried about being outed, Bochka might never have been so bold." I quoted Sherlock Holmes: they "had not that supreme gift of the artist, the knowledge of when to stop."

Scott said, "Accusing them of any kind of artistic ability is a stretch. My concern is for you."

I leaned against the kitchen counter. I said, "I swing between lots of emotions. I'm still really angry. I'm ecstatic the good guys won and that the bad guys are going to pay." I hesitated. He waited. Those wonderful eyes gazed into mine. I whispered, "Sometimes I'm happy that some awful things happened to some awful homophobes."

He said, "A couple homophobic pigs died, others suffered."

I nodded. "I try not to do a dance of joy about that. It feels wrong. It's not seemly. But still, I'm glad awful things happened to them. I'm torn."

"That sounds really human to me. It's going to take time. They were as vicious as they could be to a gay person, and you survived."

"I'm not sure I could have done it without you."

He pulled me close and hugged me.

54

That night Scott and I were in front of his fifty-four-inch flat screen television. We cuddled together on the couch. His arm draped around me. I could feel his black cotton boxers against my briefs. We were watching the extended version of *The Return of the King* for the umpteenth time. The horns of Rohan were blowing, and the Rohirrim had begun their charge. I still get chills every time I watch that scene, and, frankly, I still get the same chills when I reread the scene in the book. Scott's hand caressed my arm casually. He leaned down and kissed me. When the battle had been won, I pressed pause.

I said, "I have something for you."

I'd sent away for it. I'd been planning on giving it to him for Christmas. He already had two pewter *Lord of the Rings* chess sets. Each set was completely different. I'd found a third set, again altogether different.

I brought in the box. I said, "I wanted to say thank you."

"You're welcome. You're safe. That's all I care about."